THE GROUSE MOOR
MURDER

THE GROUSE MOOR
MURDER

John Ferguson

COACHWHIP PUBLICATIONS

Greenville, Ohio

The Grouse Moor Murder, by John Ferguson
© 2017 Coachwhip Publications

Title published 1934
Simultaneous publication, NY/London.
No claims made on public domain material.
Front cover: Trees and fog © Guy Berresford Photography

CoachwhipBooks.com

ISBN 1-61646-407-0
ISBN-13 978-1-61646-407-3

CHAPTER I

MIST ON THE MOOR

Constable Munro lifted his eyes to the clock. He had cast many surreptitious glances at the clock in the last half-hour. The clock hung on the whitewashed wall, high above the sergeant's head. The sergeant's attention was concentrated on some report he was laboriously writing. For a time no sound broke the silence save the scratching of his pen and the ticking of the clock. Munro yawned so heartily that he seemed to be making a derisive face at the sergeant's back.

Time appeared to stand still on that hot summer evening. Even the ticking of the clock sounded sluggish and tired. Munro thought how good it would be when he heard it gather itself together to strike the six snappy strokes which would release him from duty. He had been out all day on his motor-cycle, and a mobile officer of the Inverness County Constabulary covers much ground in his day's duty. But Munro, who three months back at the end of his probation period had been reported by the inspector as a zealous and promising young officer, hated to look other than spick and span. And now the mirrorlike gloss was off his leather leggings, and much white road dust clung to the smartly cut, dragoon-like breeches. Young Munro was proud of his breeches. Those breeches were the distinctive touch which differentiated him from the other constables of his division. He loved walking about in them. He loved the beautiful outward curve they made above the slim, black leather leggings. He was conscious that he attracted the feminine eye as he walked about in his smart uniform. As for sitting with tunic unbuttoned at the neck, like the sergeant, he couldn't see himself doing it, even on a hot summer afternoon in the semi-privacy of the small divisional office. For all

5

that there was one costume detail on that unbuttoned tunic of the sergeant's which moved the young officer to a hopeless envy: just three little strips of particolored silk ribbon across the left breast. Munro had been at school when Sergeant Cameron was fighting in France; and those three glorious bits of colored ribbon on his superior's chest made the smart young constable feel himself to be like a flower that has never blossomed. Sergeant Cameron wrote on, the pen occasionally scratching. Munro knew he was entering up the conviction, and previous criminal history, of one Samuel Haggerty, who had that day received a sentence of six months for poaching on the lands of Arrochmore. A curious case that had been. Haggerty was alleged by the prosecution to have shot at the Arrochmore tenant, Mr. Willoughby, who, with the gamekeeper, had chased the poacher over the moor, till they lost sight of him when he dived into Keppoch Wood.

But Haggerty's gun had never been found, and the charge of shooting with intent could not be substantiated. That a shot had been fired, apparently from the wood, was proved by the evidence of Mr. Willoughby and the gamekeeper, Peter Murdoch, as well as by Haggerty himself. But while the keeper asserted the shot had been fired by Haggerty at Mr. Willoughby, the poacher asserted the shot had been aimed at himself by the keeper. And Mr. Willoughby was unable to offer any decisive evidence either way, for though he heard the shot, he being very blown, with his heart thumping and a drumming noise in his ears from the pursuit, could not say whether the shot had come from the wood ahead or from the moor behind.

What, however, stood beyond dispute, was that when a few minutes later they captured Haggerty in the wood, he, unlike the gamekeeper, had no gun. Nor did the most careful search by the police afterwards discover any gun. As a result, some people, who knew the trouble Murdoch had with poachers, were convinced that Murdoch—whose violent temper was well known—had fired the shot in order to get Haggerty brought up on a much more serious charge than poaching. This view of the affair was also that privately held by Sergeant Cameron and Munro, who had an hour or so after the arrest vainly searched Keppoch Wood for Haggerty's gun. It had told in the accused man's favor also that he admitted hearing a shot fired. But it was almost decisive evidence against the graver charge that when Haggerty was taken the game in the bag under his coat was found to be ground game which certainly had been snared, not shot. So the sentence of six months Haggerty received on account of being found in possession of the game appeared to satisfy everyone, except Murdoch and the prisoner's friends. Sergeant Cameron laid down his pen and applied the blotting paper to his ledger.

"Well," he remarked, "the road will be near finished before he's out again."

Munro knew to what he referred. Haggerty had been one of the hundreds of navvies employed on the construction of the new road between Kinlochleven and Inverness. That great road ran from sea to sea, skirting four lochs, running through pine forests and doubling the shoulders of mighty hills for nearly a hundred miles. It was not in human nature to keep from poaching in such a sporting country. And many of the men gathered from the cities who found work on that road learned how to poach when they came to those wilds. Herded together by fifties in wooden huts set at intervals along the road, there was little else to do when work ceased for the day except get drunk, and fight, or poach. And there had been enough of all three recreations to keep the law fully employed for the last two years.

"Ay," Munro agreed, "they'll all be out of our division, anyway."

He spoke half in regret at the prospect; for, as has been said, he was a very zealous young officer, and unlike his sergeant, who was all for peace and quietness, he had not yet had his fill of fighting.

But Cameron's nose was down again at his writing, and once more that somnolent silence pervaded the sleepy little office. Then just at the moment when Munro began to think with disgust of the reign of perfect peace and utter dullness which would follow the exit of the navvies, the telephone bell burst suddenly that silence like an explosion. Cameron moved to the instrument and put the receiver to his ear.

"Hullo!" he said. "Yes, this is the divisional office. "Who's speaking? . . . Oh! . . ."

While Cameron was listening the clock began to strike the hour. But Munro scarcely heard. The concern now visible on the sergeant's face arrested his attention. While he waited, Grant, the constable

who was to relieve him, entered the office. At a sign from the sergeant's back-swept hand Grant pulled up, waited a moment and then
tiptoed over beside Munro.

"Shot, did you say, sir? Where, exactly?" they heard Cameron ask.
He appeared to be getting rather detailed information, and Munro
judged it must be about the geographical locality rather than the
position of the wound. After listening for a breath or two longer
Cameron slewed his head round in their direction, his ear still at the
receiver. "Out with your bike, Munro, and fix on the combination.
You, Grant, get the stretcher. Quick now."

Munro and Grant hurried out and in the shed behind the office
quickly got to work on the job of fixing the side-car to the police motor-cycle. While Munro had his spanner on the last nut Grant was
belting the stretcher in between the side-car and the cycle. In another
two minutes Munro, mounted in position with his engine kicking like
a machine-gun, halted in front of the office just as Cameron, button-
ing the neck of his tunic, hurried out to step into his seat.

"Keppoch," he said. "As far as the hill foot. I'll tell you when to
stop."

Munro slewed his machine round in a curve and entering the
main street of the little town they set off in the direction of Keppoch
at a speed which appeared to satisfy the sergeant. Once the last of
the villas on the outskirts had been left behind, Cameron explained.
"One of the Arrochmore folk has been shot," he said. "That call was
from Dr. Macfarlane."

"Accident, is it?" Munro hazarded, as he opened out on the
straight after negotiating the right-angle turn at the bridge.

"So it would appear. Macfarlane rang us up for the ambulance.
Hadn't yet seen the man. One of the shooting party had just run from
the moor to call him. Macfarlane says he would leave this man to lead
us to the place. He's waiting on the roadside somewhere between the
forester's cottage and the lodge."

Then their speed was too fast for further talk. Munro, familiar
with all the roads, knew where their guide would be waiting. The
distance was not more than five miles along the great new highway,
and then about two miles up the narrow winding side road towards

Keppoch. It was a long pull up once they left the Inverness road behind; but, after topping the rise beyond Rigg Lodge, they saw a man obviously on the look-out for them. He stood by a car driven up close to the roadside, and came forward as Munro brought his over-heated engine to a halt behind the stationary car. The young man was rather short, had a chubby, fresh-colored face, and his mop of red hair was uncovered.

"Thank you," he said. "You've been pretty quick."

"Doctor's gone up?" the sergeant asked, getting busy unfastening the stretcher.

"Not ten minutes ahead of you. I've just been fixing up his car to make it easier for poor Brent." He nodded at the doctor's car, his hands busy with the straps at the other end of the stretcher.

"What happened?" Cameron asked.

"Put his foot in a rabbit hole, or tripped in the heather. Anyway, he lost hold on his gun, which discharged and hit him as it fell." He paused for a moment as if envisaging the sequence of events. "No one noticed at first. We were spread out, you know, in line, and there's a good deal of mist up there to-day."

Munro and the sergeant shouldered the stretcher. At first the going was easy enough to allow the young man to walk at Cameron's side.

"Rather a nasty business for all of us," he said a trifle nervously. "You see, before Mr. Willoughby went away this morning to give evidence against some poacher he'd caught, he remarked that, anyway, it wouldn't be a lost day since the mist up on the moor would be too thick to make shooting possible."

Cameron, after a minute, said: "Mr. Willoughby's been tenant here for years. He would know the conditions."

"Oh, yes, but of course we thought we knew better," the young man said in a tone of dejected self-disgust.

Munro looked up beyond the sergeant's peaked cap to the hills. The mountain top was still blotted out, but here and there a black section of its jutting shoulders pierced the white shroud. Lower down it seemed clearer. Around them as they climbed little wisps and puffs of mist floated across the green face of the ascent like thin blown smoke. It took them over half an hour to reach the moor level. There the mist was continuous, but diffused and more transparent, making bushes of gorse and broom seem ghostly and unreal.

"You never went shooting in this, surely," Cameron said, as he paused to shift the stretcher on to his left shoulder.

"Oh, it was nothing like this. Not when we came out," the young man said. "I assure you. Not really bad at all. What mist there was clung over the heights up there like a blanket. Could see nothing through it; but outside its lower edge everything was quite clear. Then, somehow, it seemed to break up and come down on us. About five that was." He spoke jerkily, as if blown by the rapid climb.

"The wind veered to the west about five," Cameron said. Munro knew this to be true. He had been on his cycle coming home just then.

"God! I wish we had stopped in time," the other burst out.

"Och, sir," Cameron said consolingly, "an accident like that might happen in any kind of weather."

Cameron forbore from any question as to the nature of the injuries. Perhaps he had no need to ask. Even Munro himself knew how deadly a wound almost invariably resulted from the discharge of a shot-gun at close quarters. But Munro's interest quickened when he began to observe the direction in which their guide was now leading them. He headed straight across the moor towards Keppoch Wood. Munro knew that as soon as they touched the slope which slid the grouse moor down into the gully dividing it from the steep side of the mountain. At the bottom of this little valley a burn ran with Keppoch Wood on its further side. That burn, in fact, formed the south boundary of the moor, and the slope down to it was dotted with whin and juniper bushes and clumps of small birch-trees.

Munro wondered what the sergeant was thinking; for both had spent hours together among those same bushes in their fruitless search for Sam Haggerty's gun. And he well remembered the spot on the slope where, presently, he discerned some men standing around another figure kneeling beside a man extended full length on the ground.

Nobody spoke as they came up. They laid down the stretcher and the sergeant went over to kneel beside the doctor. Munro saw the victim, a young man who, from his closed eyes and white, sharply cut features might be judged beyond help, but for the fact that the doctor was very busy with his implements and bandages. He gave an odd grunt of satisfaction when the sergeant went on his knees beside him. The jacket and shirt had been cut away from the man's left shoulder, and Dr. Macfarlane was engaged in some operation under his arm. Cameron, who appeared to know what was wanted, lifted the arm at the doctor's nod.

Munro, watching his sergeant's dexterity and envying him the knowledge his war experiences had brought him, was yet presently puzzled by the odd look that came over Cameron's face. Anxiously attentive, like the others who stood watching, he perhaps alone saw his superior officer's eyes dilate as if in surprise as he turned with what looked like a frown to stare at the doctor. But Macfarlane paid no attention to the unspoken question, unless indeed the momentary pursing of his lips conveyed something. Anyway, it seemed all the answer Sergeant Cameron required, for he gave no further sign, and, it appeared, needed no verbal directions as to what the doctor wanted him to do.

Munro, standing back, turned his inquiring eyes on the wounded man's companions. They were all young, every one of the five dressed in tweeds of the best sporting cut, though variation in taste was indicated by the differences in check and pattern. A common anxiety, however, was written on all their faces. The red-headed youth, whose brown Harris clothes seemed chosen to blend in with his hair, whispered a question as to whether the doctor had said anything in his absence. Munro noticed that the question passed unanswered. All eyes were on the prostrate man.

Macfarlane had now cut away both jacket and shirt, exposing the neck and chest, but without revealing further wounds. The sergeant seemed to know what Macfarlane wanted done. Standing astride the body, with one arm around the waist and the other behind the head, he gently lifted the man clear of the ground while Macfarlane dexterously wound bandages across the body and over the right shoulder to bind the left arm close to the side.

At a nod from the doctor Munro brought up his stretcher on which the wounded man was laid. Only then did Macfarlane break silence.

"Which was his coat?" he asked.

Someone picked up a white Burberry macintosh. But at the doctor's nod Sergeant Cameron put out his hand for it. After a quick look
he turned to Macfarlane.

"Something warmer would be better, doctor," he suggested.

From those offered he selected a light raincoat, and with this covered all but the face of the man on the stretcher. While Macfarlane
was packing his bag they began to question him.

"Is it—serious, doctor?" one asked, bending down to whisper.

Macfarlane, still busy, did not look round.

"You can never be sure with gun-shot wounds," he replied.

"I mean—will he—recover?" another breathed.

"Oh, yes, I think so—if no complications follow."

Macfarlane's encouraging tone brought an audible sigh of relief.
Instantly they passed to the next step to be taken. The tallest of the
five took control.

"Someone ought to go down to the house and prepare them—you,
Toplis."

The red-headed young man almost recoiled.

"No, no! You'd do it better, Harwood."

"But you can tell them it's not serious—the doctor says so. Come
on, now, buck up. We others will carry Brent by turns."

"Jolly sight harder that will be," another said with affected conviction.

Apparently they all shirked carrying back news of the accident,
and as if to force the duty on Toplis, they stepped towards the stretcher. But Sergeant Cameron, notebook in hand, intervened.

"One moment, gentlemen," he said. "As I have to report this accident I must get fuller particulars about it from you."

"Now?" one of them asked, lifting his eyebrows and looking
pointedly over at the stretcher.

Macfarlane, standing by the sergeant, replied:

"He's badly shocked. A little rest with his feet elevated, will do
him good, if you move out of earshot," he added.

"Maybe you could show me the exact place where he fell," Cameron
suggested. "It wasn't here, I think."

Munro saw that if they had been in line, and in sight of each other
at the time of the accident, it could not have been there, since a clump

of gorse and birch-trees would have hidden the wounded man from all of them. The spot on which they were standing was a small level place like a cut in the side of the ridge, three or four yards in extent with the shrubs and gorse growing on its upper edge. It looked the sort of spot where sheep and cattle might seek for shelter on a stormy night.

Cameron stood waiting for a reply from one or other of them. Munro noted that they exchanged a look as if each waited for some-one else to speak. Dr. Macfarlane, standing over the injured man, eyed them with interest. It was the tall fellow in check tweed, whom the redheaded youth had called Harwood, who eventually replied:

"No, we carried him here. But I think I can show you the spot."

They were all about to follow him when Cameron stopped them.

"Take your game-bags and these guns with you, please," he said. "I want to know exactly your different positions."

The bags and guns had been placed on a coat, and there were five bags, but only two guns. When each had picked up his own property, one gun and one game-bag remained unclaimed. The sergeant him-self took the remaining gun with him. Some twenty yards out on the ridge Harwood stopped.

"It was just here, wasn't it, Toplis?" he said.

The red-haired young man looked about him and agreed.

"As I told you, sergeant, we were shooting home and Brent was the last man on the extreme left."

Cameron handed Brent's gun to Munro and reproduced his note-book.

"Now, gentlemen, I'd like, if you don't mind, to set down your different positions in the line. Who was next to Mr. Brent?"

"I was," said Toplis.

"Full name?"

"Charles James Toplis."

"Thank you, sir. Sorry to bother you all like this, but you'll under-stand I have to send in a full report," the sergeant said. "Now, Mr. Toplis, just go and take up as nearly as possible the position you occupied when it first occurred to you that something had happened to Mr. Brent."

Toplis nodded assent.

"I can easily do that, for I dropped my gun at the spot," he said.

"You saw him lying here, then?" Cameron asked.

"No. But losing sight of him I came down to look and found him just here."

"After giving the others a shout to stop?"

"No. I didn't think of doing that till I found him."

"Well, sir," said Cameron encouragingly, "just go to the spot where you stopped when you thought something might have happened to Mr. Brent."

Munro was surprised to see the young man take a forward diagonal course which led him to a position above the clump of birches marking the nook to which the wounded man had afterwards been carried. But the sergeant showed no surprise; and Munro perceived that of course the party must have advanced some distance before Brent had been missed.

Presently Toplis, after several pauses to look around and about him, stopped at a point some forty yards off and put up his gun as a signal. Munro had to draw the sergeant's attention to the fact, for while Toplis had been scouting for his position the sergeant, as if to fill in time, had requested the others to show him exactly how they had found Mr. Brent lying when they arrived on the scene.

There was some slight disagreement over minor details, but when it was agreed that Brent had been lying with his head in the direction in which they were moving, Cameron himself extended his length on the ground and asked them to arrange him exactly as they had found Brent. Their first act was to turn the sergeant on his back. He seemed surprised. He let out a little "*Oh!*" as if he had been hurt. Harwood next placed the left hand against his side: it was about this the disagreement arose. But Harwood pointed out that Brent's wound was on the left side of his body and it was to this that his hand would naturally go as he fell.

"And the gun?" the sergeant suggested.

"I picked it up," Harwood said, "so I know just where it lay."

Munro surrendered the weapon and Harwood put it on the turf about two yards beyond the sergeant's feet with the muzzle pointing directly at him and the butt in a clump of heather. It was at this point that Munro drew attention to the fact that Toplis had found his spot.

At first Sergeant Cameron did not seem to hear.

"*Creag Dhu*," he said, staring up at Munro. "See where that gun is; he must have been looking behind him when he fell."

"Quite," Harwood agreed, "and that would explain why he tripped up."

"Stumbled, let's say," Cameron, still on his back, suggested, "there being nothing about his feet to trip on."

"The gentleman has found the spot, sergeant," Munro repeated.

Cameron rolled over on his side and looked towards the gesticulating Toplis.

"So he has," he said after a moment, "so he has."

As he lay staring, his slow deliberation appeared to annoy Harwood.

"Aren't we keeping the doctor waiting?" he inquired with obvious sarcasm.

Cameron got to his feet.

"If you knew him, sir," he said, "you would know he's not the one to be kept waiting longer than is necessary."

Harwood lifted his eyebrows.

"Necessary?" he echoed incredulously.

The sergeant, who had been sketching out a rough plan in his notebook, seemed not to hear.

"Who walked next to Mr. Toplis?" he asked, looking up.

"I did," said Harwood.

"Full name, please?"

The tone had something of a sergeant on the drill ground in it now.

"Gerald James Everard Harwood."

"Thank you, sir. Now, if you will go and take up as nearly as possible—" He waved his pencil, and Harwood set off at once. Cameron turned to the two who remained.

"Next?" he demanded crisply.

The slight, fair-headed man who had the second gun under his arm, stepped forward.

"Philip Herbert Cresswell," he said. "Must I really go up there again? It won't be so easy for me. You see, I'm the only one who didn't drop my gun. You won't see me from here, you know."

But the sergeant waved him away.

"Oh, I'll come on till I do," he said reassuringly, before turning to the last man. This was a stocky youth, plump in body and rather short in the legs.

"Ronald Henry Joliffe," he said. "But I was right at the top of the slope and didn't get down till they'd carried him to where he is now. So—"

"What brought you down, sir?" the sergeant asked.

"Well, I just missed Phil—Mr. Cresswell—you know, and, as it were, rolled down to see where he'd gone."

"You had been seeing him?"

"Oh, yes; it wasn't so thick as all that near the top. I could see Jerry, too, occasionally."

"Not continuously?"

"No, the mist lay thicker lower down the slope, and it had been growing more dense till he was blotted out."

"And Mr. Toplis?"

"Oh, him I hadn't seen for—well—the previous twenty minutes at least. Ever since the mist began to creep up the slope, that is. So you see when I lost sight of even Cresswell I began to feel it was time we chucked it. That's what I came down to suggest. We'd been shooting home, you know. And we'd have given it up sooner only we'd such a short distance to go till we reached the end of the moor."

While speaking, his eyes had been following the progress of Cresswell's climb, and hopefully he drew the sergeant's attention to him. "Look," he said. "You can't see Jerry now, much less Cresswell. Is it really essential for me to hoof it up there again?"

But the sergeant did not yield.

"Sorry, sir," he said, tapping his notebook with the pencil, "but it is essential for me to give an idea of the distances on the sketch plan my superiors expect from me in all such accidents."

Mr. Joliffe, with a deep sigh of resignation, but no further protest, set his short legs in motion for the climb. The young constable watched him go with contempt in his eyes.

"Lazy young beggars," he remarked. But before Joliffe had gone more than ten yards the sergeant called to him and the young man turned hopefully.

"Just one thing more," Cameron said. "Could you give me an idea how long you went on after you lost sight of Mr. Cresswell on your left?"

Joliffe removed one hand from a pocket to scratch his head thoughtfully. He seemed to welcome even a respite from his climb.

"Let me see," he drawled. "I didn't notice that particularly—not at first, I mean. Perhaps ten minutes. Maybe not so much. It would seem longer, wouldn't it, once I missed him and kept on trying to—er—pick him up again? Gave me rather a creepy feeling, you know, to find myself—well—alone on a wide, wide sea, as it were."

"There had been no shooting for some time, then?"

"No. Not, that is, till I heard one bang down below. That, of course, was when poor Brent tripped up and his gun went off. That's what put the feeling of being alone on the sea into my head perhaps. It sounded just like a rocket sent up in a fog."

"But surely you have an idea how long you went on after you lost touch with Mr. Cresswell?"

Joliffe shook his head.

"No. As I've said, it might be ten minutes, more or even less." He looked up suddenly. "But I do remember just where I lost sight of Mr. Cresswell. Is that any help?"

Cameron's forehead puckered.

"Might be," he admitted.

"Well, what I do recall, now, is that just after I couldn't see Mr. Cresswell any longer I came on the bare stem of a dead tree. White and barkless, you know, so that at first it looked rather like a ship's mast. I believe it was that that made the shot feel so like a rocket, when it did go off a little later."

Munro observed that this information brought satisfaction to his sergeant, and the feeling of bewilderment, which had been growing on him for some time, deepened. But when Mr. Joliffe, extracting a cigarette case, produced a mechanical lighter, he was stopped by Cameron.

"Now, sir, if you please. You're keeping them all waiting."

This was precisely what Munro considered the sergeant himself had been doing, and rather needlessly, for the last half-hour. All the same, the young fellow took it with resignation, departing almost meekly with no more than a shrug of protest. Munro put it all down to those bits of ribbon on the sergeant's breast.

When they were alone, Cameron turned to him.

"I wonder which of the four did it?" he said quietly.

Munro failed to grasp his meaning. He was bored too by having to remain so long inactive, accustomed as he was to high speed work on the road.

"Did what?" he asked casually.

Then the young officer, not having been to the war, received the shock of his life.

"Shot him, of course," said Cameron.

Munro jumped as if he had himself been shot. He nearly dropped Brent's gun.

"My God," he whispered, "what makes you suspect that?"

"I don't suspect, I know," said Cameron. He pointed to the gun in Munro's nerve-shaken hands. "You maybe have the proof of it there. Look here, no officer should be taken by surprise like that." Sergeant Cameron spoke sharply. Munro pulled himself together.

"Sergeant, I had no notion you were suspecting that."

"No? It never occurred to you to wonder why I am taking so much trouble, did it? Man, it's not because I suspect; it's because I *know*."

He pointed to the wounded man's gun which was in Munro's charge.

"Throw open the breech and see what you find inside." Munro had a grip of himself now. There was a click of the breech bolt. Cameron came close and their two heads bent together as they peered into the breech at the two round brass ends of the cartridges. Munro did not need to use the ejector to know that neither was empty. He knew that neither cartridge had been fired, for there was no trace of a hammer-mark on the copper nipples.

"Well?" the sergeant said, "what's your notion of it?"

"It was another gun that knocked him over," Munro declared.

"Clever lad!" Cameron patted him on the back. "And now we've got to find out whose gun it was."

Munro flushed at the sergeant's ironical praise while the sergeant was looking around, apparently puzzled and uncertain. It seemed as if Cameron had despatched the men to their former positions in the shooting line in order to find out something on the spot at which Brent had fallen.

"Andy," Cameron said at last, "you and me must not make a botch o' this affair."

"No," Munro replied, pleased to hear again the friendly form of address. "We'll have to get the man that did it."

Cameron stroked his chin thoughtfully.

"But did he know he did it?" he said, half to himself.

"Know he did it?"

"Ay. In this weather it might have been an accident. We can't be sure yet. There's just the one thing I'm sure of. One of them at least has been lying to me. Him that's nearest to us now, and was nearest when it happened."

"Toplis!" Munro's eyes went to where Mr. Toplis stood, a dim figure seen as through a blue veil.

"That's the man. He knows more than he's willing to tell, anyway. What I'm not sure of is whether the others know anything or not."

"Well, sergeant—" Munro hesitated.

"Well, what?"

"Well, I was just thinking they'll suspect something's wrong from the way you're keeping them up there now."

"Not them! If they know nothing they'll suspect nothing, or at least only what you were yourself suspecting just now."

Munro opened his eyes.

"What's that?" he asked.

"That I am only an over-offeecious country police sergeant mighty anxious to show his authority." Then cutting short Munro's stammering protest, he added, "You go back now to Macfarlane. You'll likely find the man's got over his shock well enough to be safely carried home. When I've paced out the distances I'll send the men down to you. You're to go with them, keeping your eyes open. When you get to Arrochmore you're to stay with the man till he recovers, if he does recover, to take a statement from him. Macfarlane will understand. Then when you're all gone I'll have a look round here."

CHAPTER II

SERGEANT CAMERON REPORTS

Superintendent Rintoul put out his hand, and, pushing the lamp on the table to one side, stared across at his sergeant. Rintoul had got back from Inverness half an hour ago. In fact he still wore the overcoat which he had forgotten to remove after the sergeant had stepped up to his car with his urgent news.

Rintoul, tall, but rather spare in body, looked his age of forty-five, his close-cut black hair being slightly shot with silver, though his equally close-cropped moustache retained its jet original hue. Out of his deep sunk eyes he stared across at the sergeant who was busy fingering over the pages of his notebook.

"You got no statement from the man?" he asked.

"No, sir. Dr. Macfarlane, when I called in at Arrochmore on my way back, said he was unfit to make one. But Munro is there to take a statement from him if he pulls round to-night."

"Dr. Macfarlane still there?" Rintoul asked.

"Yes. At least I take it he must be, for he undertook to call in here on his way home on the chance of seeing you."

Rintoul nodded.

"All right, sergeant. Go ahead with your story."

Cameron stated his case, Rintoul listening with but the briefest questions at rare intervals. And, as the sergeant was quick to observe, there was nothing in any of those questions to show how his story was being taken. That, of course, was all in keeping with Rintoul's character. Persons under examination by the divisional superintendent soon came to know those black inscrutable eyes set in the rather

21

sallow, mask-like face from which no sign or hint could be picked up as to whether they were being believed or not.

"Well, Cameron," he said, when the story was over, "it seems beyond dispute that the man did not shoot himself."

"That's a sure thing, sir," the sergeant nodded. "The gun was discharged at a distance of fifteen feet at least."

Rintoul shifted slightly in his chair.

"But that does not imply there was any deliberate attempt at murder. You see that, of course?"

Cameron put his notebook face down on the table.

"Certainly I do, sir. It's just within the bounds of what's possible that one of them may have lost his direction in that mist and shot the other by accident."

"And without knowing what he had done."

The sergeant rubbed his chin in slow deliberation. There were several comments he could make as to that.

"Come," Rintoul insisted. "They, unlike you, would never think of looking into the breech of his gun. They took it for granted, quite naturally, when they found him lying there, that he had tripped up and got hit by his own gun."

"But a gun discharged as close as that doesn't put a pellet or two into a man's biceps or collar bone; it either misses him altogether or blows his arm away."

Rintoul bent forward and rapped the table sharply with his knuckles.

"Yes, I know that. So do you. But how do you know that any of these young fools know anything about the extent and exact angle and range at which small shot begins to scatter?"

Cameron for a time regarded the polished surface of his chief's table through half-closed lids.

"I certainly cannot prove they did know that," he said. "When they let off a gun they may be such fools as to think the shot scatters from the muzzle like pepper from a pot."

"Well, don't you see that men who were fool enough not to know better than to go shooting on such a day might be fool enough not to know anything about such things?"

It was part of Rintoul's method to play devil's advocate in any serious case brought before him. His subordinates were quite familiar with this habit. They knew that he would act exactly as he anticipated any counsel for the defense would subsequently act if proceedings were instituted. It was probably owing to this cautious practice of visualizing and exhibiting all the weak points in a case that Rintoul hardly ever reported a case for the Chief Constable's consideration which did not bring from that authority an order to prosecute. In other words, Rintoul never sent up a case which was not safe to secure a conviction; and, of course, Sergeant Cameron, familiar with his methods, knew what he himself had to face in the present instance. He faced up to it now.

"Well, sir," he said boldly, "if *I* wanted to get rid of a man by shooting, I can't imagine a better day nor place for the job."

Rintoul's eyes flickered a moment.

"If—if—if," he said mockingly. "What evidence have you got of any murderous intent?"

The sergeant could not meet this challenge.

"Oh, I was only suggesting, sir, that to go shooting on such a day does not prove they were *all* of them fools about guns."

"No," Rintoul conceded, "not necessarily. But in this case what evidence of any intent to kill can you have? I may take it, I suppose, that you saw nothing but the deepest concern reflected on every face?"

Cameron flinched rather at this. It sounded so exactly like what he had heard in the witness box when under cross-examination. But he replied to the question differently this time.

"The more guilty a man is the more concern I'd expect to see on his face, sir."

"Oh, you would, would you?"

"Certainly," the sergeant declared. "As a blind he'd put it on as thick as he could."

"Thicker than the one among them who—let's say—was his dearest friend?"

Cameron, taken aback, almost gasped.

"Well—" he said, and was silent.

"Ah!" Rintoul nodded. "You see where this sort of stuff leads you. Let's get back to facts and stick to them, if you please." Then, as if to indicate that real business was about to begin, Rintoul, getting up, removed his coat and hung it on the peg behind the door. When he sat down again Cameron took up his notebook. He felt a little shaken. Although not unfamiliar with his chief's Socratic method, he had never before been himself led into absurd conclusions by such apparently innocent questions.

"Well, sir," he began, "there's one hard fact in this case I can't get over, and that is the lie one of them told me. A needless lie, sir, if everything had been what it seemed."

Rintoul, chin in cupped hands and elbows on the table, nodded.

"Go ahead, sergeant."

"I'd like you to follow it by the plan I drew out in my notebook," he said, reaching across the table and laying the book under the other's eyes. Rintoul narrowed his eyes over it and then looked up.

"Yes; you've made it all as plain as a pikestaff. There are the relative positions of the five men at the moment the shot was fired, I suppose. Now show me where the lie you speak of comes in."

"Not at the moment the shot was fired. If you remember, they went on for a while after that. The man on the right of the advance—Joliffe that was—said he heard the shot just before he came in sight of a dead tree that looked like a ship's mast, and the sound of that shot in the mist made him think of a rocket from a ship in distress.

"So his position on the plan represents the distance Joliffe advanced after hearing that shot?"

"Exactly. You'll notice he got farther than any of the others. Quite likely he did, since he was at the top of the slope, almost on the moor level, where the mist lay much less thick."

The superintendent, shutting his eyes, laid his cheek upon one supporting hand.

"That is to say, the farther down the slope you got the denser the mist became?"

"That's right, sir. When we reached the scene I noticed the burn at the bottom of the gully was quite invisible. In fact the mist lay down there like a snowdrift with just the tops of the pines on the other side of the burn rising about it. And it's there the lie comes into the story," he added.

"I'm listening," Rintoul said, as the sergeant paused.

"You'll maybe remember, sir, that according to Joliffe's tale it was not hearing the shot that brought him down to look for the others, but the fact that he had lost contact with the man Cresswell who was next him? Well," Cameron resumed after waiting for Rintoul's nod of assent, "that was exactly what Toplis said brought himself down to look for Brent. He too had lost sight of the man who should have been moving along on his left. In other words, both men told the same story."

"Why not—if both were true?"

But Cameron sat forward to tap the table.

"One at least was lying," he declared.

"Any idea which of them?"

"Yes. Toplis for a certainty."

"A certainty, eh?" Rintoul's eyes reappeared.

But the sergeant did not flinch.

"Toplis," he declared, "was certainly lying when he said he went down to look for Brent *because* he had lost sight of him. I know that, sir, because when I sent Toplis back to stand at the spot from which he had come down to look for Brent, I had no difficulty in seeing Toplis from the spot where he had found Brent. And the mist was thicker by that time, had, in fact, been getting thicker as the evening wore on. And Brent was actually wearing a white macintosh when he was shot."

Rintoul, with his eyes on the sketch plan, said nothing for quite a time.

"But if all that is true, this man Joliffe must also have agreed to lie about it. Since if you saw a distance of thirty yards down there where it was thicker, he must have seen Cresswell at a distance of only twenty yards up above where it was clearer."

"I don't think he was lying, sir," Cameron said. He spoke quietly, in a significant tone that made Rintoul throw up his head.

"Why not?" he demanded, reiterating the question sharply when the sergeant hesitated.

"Well, sir, to tell you the truth, I don't think Cresswell was there for him to see."

"You don't think—?"

"No, I don't think he was there simply because Joliffe *must* have seen him if he had been there."

Rintoul for the first time was really taken aback. He could have asked why Joliffe might not be lying as well as Toplis. It was indeed on the tip of his tongue to put the question. But he saw there must be more in it than that. It was, for one thing, a safer lie for Toplis to utter since Brent, unlike Cresswell, was in no condition to contradict him. Rintoul turned, impatient.

"Come," he commanded, "out with it, and all of it, at once. Are you bringing a charge of attempted murder against this man Toplis?"

"Oh, not against Toplis," the sergeant said quickly.

"Against whom, then?" Rintoul demanded.

Cameron for a breath or two fingered one of the bright buttons on his tunic.

"Well, sir, I was just wondering if it wouldn't be better for me to lay the facts before you, step by step that is, as I came on them, and let you form your own conclusions." Then, as Rintoul stared in perplexity, he added, looking over at his notebook, "it would be easier to follow what happened if we went over it step by step on my plan."

Thrusting out a hand, Rintoul pulled a chair close up to his own. Cameron came round the table to occupy it. Rintoul pushed the notebook forward, and then drew the lamp over to illuminate the drawing.

"First, sir," the sergeant began, "I'd like you to observe how straggling the advance became as soon as they got into the thicker belt of mist."

"Yes, it's evident enough from your plan. The young idiots, another fifty yards farther and they'll be firing at the backs of each other's necks."

Cameron's finger went to his drawing.

"I understand they could see each other until they crossed this burn that comes down the slope. You will remember that Joliffe lost sight of Cresswell just before he came on the dead tree."

Rintoul had his nose to the plan.

"That circle marks the tree's position?"

"Yes—a dead poplar."

Rintoul grunted scorn.

"A fool tree, too, to think it could live up there."

"Notice how they get separated after the burn is crossed. Joliffe tends to get closer to the top edge of the slope away from the others," Cameron went on.

Rintoul nodded.

"With some idea of getting out of range, no doubt. Seems to have hurried too, since he got so far ahead of the others."

"Yes, sir. His direction and speed should be remembered when we come to consider what happened to Brent at the other end of the line."

Rintoul's eyes travelled down the plan to the cross which marked the spot where Brent fell. Cameron continued:

"This plan shows the exact position of each man at the moment when Toplis found the body and shouted the alarm."

Rintoul looked up.

"The exact position? I can't imagine how you can be so sure of that," he said.

"It was very easy. When they heard Toplis shout for help—a scream is what Harwood called it—the first thing they did was to drop their guns so as to run better. With one exception these guns later on established the spot each had reached when Toplis shouted. The men simply went back and found their guns lying where they had dropped them."

"Which was the exception?"

"Cresswell. He had not left either gun or bag behind."

"So his position, at least, is more or less guesswork?"

"It is—from the time Joliffe lost sight of him after he himself crossed the burn. But my plan shows where he *said* he was."

Rintoul sat awhile staring hard before him. Sergeant Cameron sat silent too, as if afraid to intrude upon his superior officer's thoughts. After a time Rintoul laid his hand on the sergeant's arm.

"Get on with your process of elimination, sergeant. I begin to guess what you're driving at."

Cameron regarded the opposite wall with a set face.

"I look at it like this, sir," he said. "It's not to be denied that Brent was shot by a gun not his own. As Munro will testify, we found his gun still loaded. And it is certain the gun was fired from some position far enough off to allow the shot to scatter. These are facts there's no getting over. To tell the truth, as soon as I saw the way the man was hit I hadn't any doubt. And I saw Dr. Macfarlane knew it too. That's why I knew what Munro would find in Brent's gun when I told him to throw open the breech."

Rintoul here showed impatience.

"But look at your own plan, sergeant," he cried, jabbing a forefinger on the notebook; "it flatly contradicts you. How could Brent be shot on his *left* side by a man on his right?" Here the superintendent in his irritation again took on the part of a counsel cross-examining for the defense. "Are you suggesting that one of his friends had a gun which could shoot round a corner?" he asked.

Rintoul no doubt intended to give his sergeant a foretaste of what he might have to face in the witness-box. And put like that, the question did make the sergeant momentarily squirm on his seat. All the same, he refused to be treated as a hostile witness at that moment. "Wait a wee, sir," he pleaded. "I allow he was hit on his left side, and I allow it seems impossible that while he was advancing with men on his right he could have been hit by one of them. But it's not so miraculous as it appears. Suppose something made Brent turn and look behind him. The moment he did that his left side would be exposed to any one on his right, would it not?" Before Rintoul could reply he went on, "Further, sir, mark this: unless Brent merely turned his head for a moment's glance over his shoulder, he would have to *stand still* to turn round and look behind him. Then suppose one of them, for some reason yet unknown to us, wanted to get him, isn't that just the moment he would be watching for—when he was standing still, and when from the very fact that his left side was exposed, a wound there would suggest the shot had come from quite the opposite direction?"

"From someone farther down the slope, you mean, of course?" Rintoul said. "But why should not the shot actually have come from below? If that is a possibility you have no right to exclude it. It's the most natural explanation. Accept it and you needn't go on supposing one thing after another."

"Beyond supposing somebody was down there with a gun in his hands, sir," Cameron said mildly. "And we have no reason to believe there was."

The superintendent waved a hand half impatiently

"All right, let's leave that for the present and look at the men with the guns. You rule Joliffe out, I understand?"

"Yes, sir. The direction he took and his distance ahead of the others seem to me to clear him."

"And Toplis?"

"He told me a lie, of course. But I don't think he did more. Toplis and Harwood did not lose sight of each other. As I saw later each set down his gun within fifteen yards of one another."

"Then why the lie?"

Cameron's reply was prompt. He had evidently thought it all out.

"Probably because he thought one of his friends had shot Brent by accident. He may not have seen who did it, though he could have seen Brent fall. Something made him stop, whatever it was. Notice that the other man, Harwood, then got a few yards ahead—just about the distance a slow walk would take him—compared with the dash down Toplis made when he saw Brent fall."

Rintoul studied the plan once more.

"Yes, I see what you mean," he said, looking round. "So you rule them all out except Cresswell."

"Cresswell *could* have done it," the sergeant asserted, his eyes on his own plan. And Rintoul, seeing Cameron eyeing his plan with obvious pride and satisfaction, took the assertion as a challenge to himself. Cameron, he felt, was implying that with the facts now in his knowledge and with that plan of the ground under his eyes, he ought to be able to see for himself just how Cresswell shot Brent.

Rintoul, his elbows on the table, laid his cheek against his uplifted hands and thought hard. His eyes were shut; the sketch plan was by now engraved on his brain.

"When Toplis found Brent," Rintoul said, without opening his eyes, "he shouted to Harwood, expecting Harwood to call Cresswell. Did he call?"

"He said he did, but it was Joliffe who answered. You remember he said he heard a far-away sort of calling."

"What did Cresswell say?"

"Said he heard both Toplis and Harwood's shout and came down at once without waiting to throw off either gun or bag."

"Or even shout to Joliffe?"

"Says he was in too great a hurry and didn't think of anything except getting to the spot."

"A shout to Joliffe need not have delayed him," Rintoul mused. "Is it that he was possibly in some other position than that marked on your plan and dare not shout either a response to Harwood or a warning to Joliffe?"

"That's if he did not want them to know where he was," Cameron remarked.

"We're assuming that," Rintoul nodded. "Merely to see where it leads, of course. So, if he remained silent because he did not wish to show his position, he must have been at a considerable distance from where the others supposed him to be. I mean," Rintoul added, "in such a straggling line twenty or thirty yards one way or the other wouldn't matter."

Cameron agreed with alacrity: this point had not occurred to him.

"That's right, sir. See how far Joliffe had diverged. If the man kept quiet through not wanting the others to know where he was, he must have been—well—where they would not expect him to be."

"This is all theory, of course," Rintoul remarked.

"Of course, sir," Cameron agreed, expectantly.

"But it's fact, not theory, that Joliffe last saw Cresswell before he reached the dead poplar tree?"

"Just before they crossed the burn beside it."

"Yes, as you say, sergeant, just before they crossed the burn." Rintoul appeared to be contemplating the burn as it was imprinted in his memory, for though the plan lay before him he still kept his eyes closed.

"In your plan, sergeant, that burn has one defect. It shows the course it takes down the slope very clearly, but fails to show the depths of its channel."

Cameron's face lit up.

"Ah, sir, you're getting at it, I see," he said, adding with a mocking sort of sigh, "It's been running there a long while, that burn. Say a matter of two thousand years."

"But there's not much water in it now?"

"That's right, sir. It's only the winter floods that could have dug so deep a channel." Cameron nodded approvingly.

Rintoul laid his hand on the sleeve of Sergeant Cameron's tunic.

"Sergeant, was Brent by any chance found lying on his back when they reached him?"

Cameron bent forward and hit the table with his clenched fist.

"He was, sir, his head lying the way he'd been going, and with his gun at his feet, too, where it had dropped out of his hands when he turned right round as if to see something he'd heard behind him."

Rintoul looked up.

"I wonder if he saw what it was?"

"Maybe there's somebody else who's wondering that too, at this very moment."

Rintoul rose to take a turn about the room. Then he faced about.

"Mind you, Cameron," he said, "all this does no more than prove to us how Cresswell *could* have done the deed. When Joliffe lost sight of him it may have been that he dropped out of sight in the burn, and then stole down hidden by the banks till he got within range of Brent, where the burn takes that curve near the spot at which Brent was shot. Then he had time to creep back a hundred yards or so and come down openly after Toplis and Harwood had reached Brent. It could be done, but to fasten it on to him we shall need something very much stronger than a possibility."

While Rintoul stood, hands behind his back, lost in thought, Sergeant Cameron began to gather up his papers from the table. But when the sergeant picked up his notebook Rintoul came forward and took it from him to study the plan once more.

"To stage a murder as a shooting accident there are only two difficulties to be overcome," he said. "The first is that you must get close enough to your victim and then get away without being seen by others, and the second is the difficulty of shooting him with his own gun. Overcome these and you have the perfect murder."

"The burn and the misty weather gave him the chance to get close up," Cameron agreed.

"But not quite close enough. I must have a look at the place to-morrow. Perhaps the two sweeping curves that burn makes took him longer than he reckoned on, so that when he got there Brent had passed on just a shade too far. And—supposing this is murder, of course—I can't see how he meant to surmount the difficulty about the gun."

Cameron hesitated.

"Surely, sir, that would look the easiest part of it. He'd count on getting hold of Brent's gun while the others were busy with him, and slipping a spent cartridge from his own gun into Brent's."

"Ye-s," Rintoul said thoughtfully. "Yes. Yet after all, that trick didn't come off, sergeant. And if this is a case of attempted murder he must have been desperately anxious to get at Brent's gun. Just think, man! Nobody carries a dead cartridge in the breech of his gun, and one spent cartridge at least must be found in Brent's gun afterwards. It was simply vital for him to get that empty cartridge case into the other man's gun, and that too before any of the other men thought of looking into the gun."

Rintoul, in his perplexity, continued to stare at the green-shaded lamp with unseeing eyes. Characteristically his mind was concentrating on the weak points in the case against Cresswell. But the sergeant was satisfied. He knew his chief; it was a sure thing that the affair would now be probed to the bottom.

The fact that Cresswell had not been able to monkey with the gun did not trouble him at all. Several quite little, but unforeseen, accidents might have baulked the man. He might easily have dropped his spent cartridge, and it wouldn't be so easy to find another. For there had been no shooting since Joliffe had heard the fatal shot. And Cresswell, supposing he only discovered the loss of his essential empty cartridge at the critical moment when the others were bending over the wounded man, could hardly then fire off his own gun to provide himself with another. Anyhow, if that wasn't what had happened it was some other small mischance.

"I suppose, sir, you'll want to see some of these gentlemen yourself," he suggested, getting ready to leave the room.

Rintoul relaxed.

"Yes, of course," adding, after a glance at the clock, "the morning will do. By then we may have a statement from Mr. Brent."

"Very good, sir."

"Mr. Toplis first, I think. But you'd better get off home now. I can fix up the time with Munro, and can perhaps learn what chance there is of a statement from Brent." He took a step towards the table and picked up his 'phone receiver. Cameron intervened.

"Not like that, sir."

The tone arrested Rintoul. Sergeant Cameron was very much in earnest.

"For one thing, sir, Dr. Macfarlane gave him a sleeping draught so there will be no statement till he wakes in the morning. For another, a call will bring Munro downstairs to the 'phone, which is a long way from Mr. Brent's bedroom, and it's—it's very inadvisable he should leave that room for a single moment."

Rintoul, receiver in hand, stared at the sergeant.

After a moment he gently replaced the instrument.

"I see," he said. "I see. What a suspicious fellow you are, Cameron."

"Don't take any risks, sir," the sergeant pleaded.

"You aren't, if you're keeping poor Munro awake all night to take a statement from a man who won't wake till morning."

"I'm proposing to go up there myself now to relieve Munro, sir, if it's all right," Cameron replied.

"But, man, what are you afraid of?" Rintoul demanded.

Before answering Sergeant Cameron let the elastic band of his notebook go off with a snap.

"Just this, sir," he said. "I'm afraid, I'm very much afraid that Mr. Brent, when he turned, might have seen who was behind him before he was hit."

CHAPTER III

THE RED-HEADED YOUNG MAN

Sergeant Cameron left the police station after some further talk with his chief, and mounting his bicycle set off in the direction of Arrochmore. It was a clear, calm night, with the road along the loch now empty of traffic. For two miles he spun along with Loch Linnhe on one side, its dark waters merging into the black Ardgour hills beyond. Except for the lights of a small cargo steamer, evidently heading for Oban, he seemed to have the world to himself.

Strongly convinced as the sergeant was upon those points in the case about which his superior seemed doubtful, he was yet a little nervous as to whether sufficient evidence would ever be got to establish any one's guilt. Possibly this uneasy feeling may have been reinforced by the loneliness of the road. Had Cameron found Superintendent Rintoul rising more spontaneously to the facts placed before him, the sergeant would have felt more confidence. As it was, he felt for the moment as much alone in the case as he was on the road; and, if he did not admit it to himself, it is likely that this absence of a wholehearted backing by his superior left him somewhat nervous also of Mr. Willoughby.

The shooting tenant of Arrochmore was known well enough to him by sight. A masterful-looking man he was, to see sitting back at his ease in the lordly looking car as it swept through the streets of the little town. Once only, and that quite recently in the matter of Sam Haggerty's arrest, had Sergeant Cameron come into personal contact with Mr. Willoughby, and his experiences then did not belie the impression of masterfulness already received. On the whole, the sergeant felt that if it took Mr. Willoughby's fancy to stand between

35

the law and his guests, his own job was likely to be as tough as any he had known. At all costs he must avoid putting the big man's back up.

Approaching the lodge gates which opened the drive up to Arrochmore, Cameron saw the headlights of a car shining around the curve. Aware that in another moment the car would be passing through the rather narrow gateway, he hopped off his bicycle and stood aside to let it pass. Before its nose was through the gate he recognized its number as Dr. Macfarlane's. But Macfarlane did not recognize the sergeant in time to pull up till he had shot a dozen yards or so ahead. Cameron, setting his bicycle against the gate, went down the road towards the stationary car.

"Ah, Cameron!" the doctor greeted him, "thought it was you lurking there in the dark." He slewed round in his seat. "I often wonder why the police wear bright buttons that catch any sort of light."

Cameron smiled up at him. "Glad they caught you, anyhow, sir," he said, nodding back.

Dr. Macfarlane was a clean-shaven, middle-aged man, professional-looking too, although at the moment his bowler hat happened to be set rather far back on his head. He had an apparently recently lit pipe in his mouth, and sat relaxed in the attitude of a man who had just come off duty and was obviously satisfied with his work. Cameron easily read these symptoms.

"The superintendent would like to see you, sir," he said.

The doctor nodded. "That's all right. I was going to drop in as I passed."

"Patient doing well, sir?" Cameron asked.

"Oh, he's not going to die anyway, though he won't play the piano yet awhile. We've moved him over to the other house, where he'll be quieter." Macfarlane sniffed. "And leave the house party free to be as noisy as they wish."

"You mean to Duchray?" the sergeant said.

"Yes; he'll be all right there. But he won't be able to tell you anything about that accident till the morning."

"So I understand, sir." Cameron paused.

The doctor pulled his hat forward.

"I've taken care of that," he snapped.

"You—think he'll be able to tell us something then, sir?"

It was the doctor's turn to hesitate. After a puff or two he took his hands from the wheel and, removing his pipe, bent over the side of his car.

"I doubt," he said quietly, "if he'll be able to tell you much more than I can tell you now."

Cameron looked up alertly, stimulated by the doctor's confidential tone. "And what might that be, sir?" he inquired.

"Just this, sergeant—that young fellow didn't shoot himself."

Cameron did not seem to be as much surprised as the doctor expected.

"You don't think it was an accident then? You will say so to Superintendent Rintoul?"

"Of course it was an accident, but not one Brent himself made." He bent a little nearer. "I have no doubt it was one of his own pals who shot him without knowing what he had done. They all think Mr. Brent tripped in the heather and fell; but my belief is that is what one of the others did, only he's too ashamed to admit he was carrying a gun at full cock when he thinks that is what also Brent was doing. I can tell you more than that," Macfarlane went on. "I'm practically certain I know the man who did it."

In the darkness the doctor could not, of course, see the sergeant's mouth tighten.

"Indeed?" he encouraged quietly.

"Yes," said Macfarlane, "it must have been the man next below him."

"Next *below* him!" Cameron echoed incredulously.

"Oh, there's nothing very wonderful in knowing that, Cameron. They were shooting in line, of course, along the slope, and Brent was shot as you saw on the left side. If you were anything of a detective," he smiled, "you would know it for yourself—it must have been a man on his left. But *I*, as a medical man, have access to other evidence which proves the shot was fired by another man who must have been lower down the slope than Brent."

"Not lower, surely, sir?" Cameron protested.

"Certainly lower," Dr. Macfarlane reiterated. "The deepest shot I extracted this evening had travelled from the point of entry in an upward direction. And the upward course they took was clearly visible in most of the thirty shots that entered; which proves that the gun was discharged at a level considerably lower than that at which Mr. Brent stood when he was hit."

Cameron pondered this information while the doctor re-lit his pipe.

"Well, sir," he said, "there's no contradicting that."

Macfarlane, getting ready to go on, pushed back his hat. "Why in heaven's name should anyone want to contradict it?" he flung out, as he let in his clutch.

And Cameron, walking back to his bicycle, did not feel in the least any desire to do so. On the contrary, he saw that what the doctor had said about the course taken by the shot supported rather than contradicted his own convictions about the case. For, quite clearly, the shot could have been fired not only as the doctor assumed by a man lower down the slope, but also by a man hiding in the burn and aiming up at Brent with his gun thrust through the gorse bushes from ground level. Cameron had inspected just that point where the burn curved around to within fifteen feet of the spot where Brent fell. He had seen the bushes, and though he had inspected them carefully for any trace of broken twigs, just as he had searched the gravel bottom of the burn for footprints, without results. Yet he had no doubt that, if his suspicions had any basis whatever, that must have been the position from which the shot was fired.

Cameron's thoughts while wheeling his bicycle up the steep winding drive next turned to the possibility that Brent's statement might supply them with conclusive information. Not that he considered this more than a possibility. And the more he turned over in his mind the things he already knew or suspected, the less he felt inclined to build on it. In his imagination he pictured Cresswell selecting the scene and planning out the details for his deed. If those details had been as artfully fixed up as the scene of the crime had been perfectly chosen, there was little chance that Brent had seen anything.

Cameron did not like it. He saw the gun pushed through those bushes. He knew, as if he had seen them, the precautions Cresswell would have taken against being seen. Then a minute or two's wait till Brent came along. The sergeant had taken note of the grassy pathway that skirted the burn for a few yards; and he did not doubt that

Cresswell, noting it also, would count on Brent's keeping to it just as far as it led in the direction he was taking. And it did so long enough for his purpose. Then Cresswell did something—made some small noise perhaps which caused Brent to turn and thus expose his left side. The instant he did so the trigger was pressed. Did Brent have time to recognize any one? Cameron doubted it. His own failure after his almost microscopic search for any trace of Cresswell's presence at the spot left him nearly convinced that an equal precaution would have been taken against the chance of being seen. But at least it would be something to know for a certainty that the shot had come from just those bushes above the burn. The sergeant pushed his bicycle more quickly up the ascent.

Arrochmore stands about half a mile from the road, approached by a winding up-hill tree-bordered drive. At the top of the ascent one comes on an extensive plateau of open greensward on which are two tennis courts. At a point just before the house itself comes into view the road forks and divides; that branching to the right leads to Arrochmore itself, while the road on the left forms the approach to Duchray, a much smaller house used by the shooting tenant as a sort of annex when his house party happens to be too numerous to put up at the big house.

The approach was thus like the capital letter "Y," Arrochmore standing at the top of the right arm and Duchray at the left, the space between, about half a mile in extent, being open and well-kept turf. Both houses faced outwards. Over the tree tops each had an uninterrupted view of the Ardgour Mountains on the far side of Loch Linnhe, and glimpses of the loch could be here and there discerned through the foliage.

Behind both houses the hill rose steeply, like a wall almost, the lower slopes planted with beech, with, higher up, a great belt of the storm-resisting pine. Along the foot of the hill with the beeches on one side and the open space on the other, a footpath of crazy pavement served to connect both houses, thus avoiding any need to go down one arm of the fork and up the other.

Cameron halted when he reached the point where the road forked. The doctor's news about the removal of his patient to Duchray put him in a quandary. His superintendent had decreed that Toplis should be invited to police headquarters for an interview with himself next morning; and it was almost certain that Toplis would be at Arrochmore, while it was very certain that Munro would be with the patient at Duchray. The sergeant, however, did not hesitate more than a moment over his choice. As he took the road to the right a half sardonic smile of recollection made his mouth twitch. He knew exactly why Rintoul wished Toplis to receive the message that night. Out of past experience he knew the state of mind induced by such a message. Almost invariably, where the man had something to conceal, the invitation shook his nerve, and the interval between his reception of the message and his response to it was filled with doubts as to how much the police knew.

Rintoul evidently hoped to give Toplis a wakeful night in order to make him more squeezable in the morning. And Cameron, recalling what he believed to be that youth's fibbing exploit up on the moor, wasted no pity on him.

Coming within sight of the house he saw, late as the hour was, its lower windows luminous in the dark mass of its shadowy outline. He set his bicycle carefully against the wall and rang the bell. The man who answered his summons was too well trained to exhibit any outward surprise. Cameron, when the man departed in search of Mr. Toplis, had leisure to take note of his surroundings. The hall was large, square and lofty. Its chief decorations, apart from the mounted stags' heads usually found in Highland houses, were trophies collected by former owners of the estates. The portraits of the present impoverished owner's ancestors hung around the walls, and from the trophies surrounding each a good part of their biographies might have been written. There was, for instance, the Sir Ewan Mackintosh who fell at Culloden, below whose portrait hung his pistols and claymore. Farther along the line the boyish face of Ensign Alan Mackintosh, by Raeburn, from which no money had been able to tempt the present owner to part, looked as if it had been painted yesterday. Yet he had fallen at Waterloo.

Though the sergeant had been a soldier, had, in fact, served in the same regiment, and, a hundred years later, been wounded not so very far from where this young lad had been killed, it was another portrait on which his eye lingered. On the walls around it were no trophies of death, no Highland claymores or Indian tulwars, no tiger skins nor tusks of African ivory. Yet for all that the man with the proud, straight, thin-lipped mouth and hooded eyes touched the sergeant's imagination most at this moment. For he knew that this must be the famous Mackintosh who, as Lord Duchray, had been Lord Justice General. The scarlet and ermine robe told him as much, and sitting up there in the high-back chair he looked a judge from whom one could expect justice but little mercy. Yet somehow, while he stood in the hall cap in hand, the sight of that portrait put much more self-confidence into the waiting sergeant. He felt as if he had the stern old judge at his back in the business before him.

As Cameron followed the man into the small room along the corridor, his thought was that for all the signs of life about the place there was no need to remove Brent to Duchray. The only sounds he heard in passing a half-opened door were the murmur of low-pitched voices, and the click of a billiard ball.

Toplis appeared a little surprised as he entered, and after his nod of recognition gazed questioningly at his visitor.

"You wanted to see me?" he said.

The sergeant turned his cap in his hand. "Yes, sir. The superintendent has sent me with a message."

"To me?" the red-headed young man asked, his eyes dilating somewhat.

"To you certainly," Cameron said. "He would like to see you at the office to-morrow at ten, if that will be convenient to you."

"What about?" the other asked sharply.

Cameron slowly rotated his peaked cap in the reverse direction, hesitating.

"Well, sir," he said, looking up from his cap, "that must be a matter between you and the superintendent. Will the hour be convenient, sir?"

The red-headed youth considered for a moment, but whether his thought was on the hour of the interview or its nature, the sergeant could not guess.

"Oh, yes," he said, after a moment. "I suppose I'd better come."

Cameron was secretly delighted to see the young man's nervousness grow.

"I say," he burst out, "you don't think he supposes there's—there's anything wrong, do you?"

The sergeant might have allayed any foreboding by an offhand reference to routine, and to the fact that the police were bound to investigate the circumstances of all such accidents. Instead he began to brush an imaginary speck of dust from the shiny peak of his cap, while the young man regarded him with anxiety.

"Well—" he said, and stopped.

"Mr. Willoughby is angry enough about the business already, and I don't see why you pick me out for—what is it you call it—interrogation? Why does he want me?"

"That I can't tell, sir. But, since you ask me I'd say it's because you stood nearest, and the Chief will know you can tell us most about it."

"But I've nothing to tell."

The sergeant made a vague gesture with his cap.

"I've already told you all I know about it."

Cameron looked up to meet the other's eyes.

"We're not so sure of that, sir," he said. "Don't you be so sure. The Chief has a way of his own. His questions may bring out more than you would think you know—or saw," he added, pointedly.

Mr. Toplis followed the sergeant from the room.

Passing along the corridor, Cameron, on coming parallel to the staircase, heard a slight sound above his head. In the glance he shot up he saw a girl bending over the banisters. In one hasty glance he took in the impression of a sharp pair of dark eyes, a cloak of some dark material thrown over a white dress, and peeping through the banisters a pair of silver slippers. The brooding Mr. Toplis, however, did not seem to be conscious of her presence. Cameron heard a whisper behind him.

"Toppy," she breathed. "Toppy!"

Mr. Toplis pulled up. The sergeant slackened his pace towards the door.

"Hallo, Brenda," he heard the other reply.

"What—what's *he* doing here?"

If any reply was made the sergeant did not catch it.

But Toplis did not see him out. At the door the sergeant turned. The girl had come down and was standing on the lowest step, her face visible above Mr. Toplis's back. She was listening to something he was telling her. Then Mr. Toplis turned, made a gesture with his hand, and the sergeant bowed his leave-taking. Once outside he rode hard for the other house.

CHAPTER IV

NIGHT

Little Duchray, as it was called, was only a small house compared with Arrochmore. Built originally by Sir George Mackintosh who became Lord Justice General, it had been added to several times by his heirs, so that the small white cottage which Hanging George—as they nicknamed him—was said to have built as a place of refuge where he could be undisturbed when considering his judgments, no longer deserved its diminutive title.

The house was in darkness when Cameron approached. Stepping on to the lawn he noticed a window open at the bottom and went up to inspect it. Thrusting his head inside, he could see enough to tell him that this was some kind of sitting-room; but nothing to tell him whether the window had been left open by negligence or design.

Round the eastern end of the house he found what he sought: a lighted window on the second floor. Standing back, he sounded the bell of his cycle once or twice gently. And then, returning to the door, waited till it was opened by Constable Munro. The young officer seemed mightily glad to see him.

"How is he doing?" the sergeant asked.

Munro yawned heavily.

"Fine. Sound asleep. Just what I'd like to be myself."

Cameron leant his bicycle against the wall and, taking Munro's arm, led him along the lawn to the open window.

"See that?" he said.

Munro seemed surprised.

"Does it matter?" he asked. "It's a sort of study; there's nothing but books in there."

Cameron thought he was being oversuspicious.

"All right," he said. "Now tell me just who is in the house."

"There's only one that counts for much—the old lady."

"Who is she?" Cameron inquired.

"His mother. She's a sharp one. Can't walk, but she can talk. Wheels herself about in a chair."

"I see. And the others who don't count?"

"Well, there's the nurse, a little thing from the Cottage Hospital, you know; and there's Dr. Frossard, and a Mr. Bray who is tutor to young Master Willoughby, who—"

"One moment. Is this Dr. Frossard attending to Mr. Brent?"

"Oh, no, he's some other kind of a doctor. Beyond the maids that's all." Munro once more yawned heavily. "There were others, but they were all shifted to the big house to keep this place quiet."

Cameron nodded.

"All right. You can go home now. Take my bicycle."

But when Munro was about to mount, Cameron stopped him.

"That door," he said, with a backward throw of his thumb, "when you opened it just now I didn't hear you draw the bolts."

Munro, his foot on the step, looked back.

"I had to draw them both, though," he said, "and it was me who shot them back when Dr. Macfarlane left. The old lady told me to."

Sergeant Cameron, after watching Munro disappear, entered the house. He, too, in his turn, shot the two bolts behind the big door and then, slipping into the room on the right, shut down the open window and fastened the catch.

Returning to the hall, he mounted the stairs and was passing along a corridor towards what he judged to be Brent's room when a door on the right opened and he saw a wheeled chair turning out to come in his direction.

"What!" Mrs. Brent said, as soon as he approached. "Not another of you!"

Cameron explained he had only come to relieve his subordinate, and the old lady then waved him ahead, following him into the room at the end of the passage. As Cameron passed the half-opened door of the room from which she had emerged, he had a glimpse of the bed, and the wounded man's face, and a nurse in uniform seated beside the bed, watching.

"Sorry to bother you, madam," Cameron said, as soon as Mrs. Brent, having switched on the light as she passed, brought her chair to a standstill. "But we must know just how such accidents happen, and that is why we have to stand by like this."

"Well," she said, "that is why I am standing by myself like this."

"I hope you didn't find the officer in the way?" the sergeant suggested.

"Indeed, no. I thought he might be very useful," she replied heartily.

Cameron pricked up his ears, hearing this. Did she too anticipate danger that night?

"Be useful?" he repeated encouragingly.

"Why, yes," she replied. "My son is no light weight, and the nurse is small, and you see what I am. I can move very little except my hands, these days."

Cameron noticed, however, that her eyes kept moving from himself to the passage which was visible through the door she had left open.

Mrs. Brent seemed rather old to be the mother of the son Cameron remembered. But the marks of character were written very definitely on the mother's face, from the tight, thin-lipped mouth and the sharply cut nose to the alert eyes whose dark color and brightness made a marked contrast to the suggestion of age conveyed by the pallor and texture of her skin. There was decision too, as well as unexpected physical power in the way she propelled and controlled her chair.

"You see," she continued, "my boy, unlike some of those others, is expert in the handling of a gun. He's very clever with his hands; that comes of being a pianist, of course."

Something the doctor had said which at the time had puzzled Cameron, was now explained.

"Oh—he plays the piano then?" he said.

"Plays the piano! He's a genius," she said, with intense pride. "That fool of a nurse thought it was all right that he had escaped facial disfigurement. But I'll not be satisfied till I know his left arm hasn't been crippled permanently. Those young fools didn't think he could be a good shot and a fine pianist as well. But I know he's more likely to have been shot by them than to have shot himself."

Cameron's lifted eyebrows expressed incredulity.

"Really, madam," he protested, "that is a serious thing to say, unless you have some evidence to support it," he added hopefully.

She waved a hand.

"Don't be stupid, man," she cried imperiously. "I mean just what I say, that it would be easier to believe any one of those young fools mishandled a gun rather than Eric."

"A very careful young gentleman, is he?" the sergeant agreed, flustered by her tone.

"Careful? I hope so. I brought him up to be. Even as a child Eric never played with matches, or cut himself with a knife, or swallowed plum stones or anything that wasn't quite nice."

"Still," the sergeant ventured, "I suppose later on he—he had his little quarrels with other boys."

"Oh, he was no milksop, of course; he knew even at school how to stand up for himself."

The sergeant began to feel astute.

"And still does, I expect," he suggested knowingly. But she turned on him almost fiercely. Cameron could not tell whether he had touched a raw spot, or if she had suddenly repented this intimate discussion of her son with a mere sergeant of police.

"What can you know about him?" she said. "He has never talked to you."

Cameron sat back.

"Oh, no, indeed, madam; I've only heard what his friends had to say about him."

"His friends? What friends?" she demanded.

"Mr. Cresswell and the others. It was easy to see what they thought of him from their—well—sorrow over the accident—especially Mr. Cresswell," he added untruthfully. And the lie was rewarded when he saw the hard glitter that came to her eyes at the mention of Cresswell's name. He marked too the whitening of the knuckles of the hand nearest him, which gripped the side of her chair.

"Mr. Cresswell—sorrow?" she sneered, in tones of contemptuous incredulity. Then one vigorous pull brought the chair pirouetting round till she sat face to face with the sergeant. She appeared on the point of letting herself go on the subject of Mr. Cresswell's sorrow. But Cameron saw her put a check on her tongue, and instead, even as she stared at him, she laughed—a harsh, mirthless laugh which ended as abruptly as it began.

"After all, you are a brave man," she said.

The sergeant pricked up his ears again. Was she now about to tell him something?

"Brave?" he repeated.

She pointed to the ribbons on his tunic.

"You have served your country," she nodded. "I know what these ribbons stand for. That is why I am talking to you like this; because, after all, you are a man who served your country."

"Oh, madam, I hope I still do that," Cameron said pointedly. But if she understood the hint she did not respond to it. Whether she had been on the point of taking him into her confidence, he could not tell. He was not even sure she had anything to tell him. If she had, the impulse to speak it had now gone. She was eyeing him quizzically.

"The nurse was saying I ought to lie down for a little," she said. "But I couldn't trust her to keep awake. I wonder—" She paused.

"Yes?"

"Well, it would be merely serving me, not the nation, I suppose. Still, if you could keep an eye on her while I lie down—just step to the door from time to time, I mean, to make sure Eric isn't awake and she asleep—"

CHAPTER V
MORNING

But it was not Cameron who awakened the nurse: it was the nurse who awakened Cameron. Soon after six she had slipped into the room and, finding him asleep with his head perched on the back of his chair, had startled him with a touch on the shoulder and the whispered news that the young man had himself just awakened. The sergeant, who had cast an eye into the sickroom every half-hour since Mrs. Brent left him, had now been asleep for a matter of some minutes only. He leapt to life, feeling as guilty as any sentry caught napping at his post. But the girl was already hurrying off to call Mrs. Brent.

The young man's eyes were focused on the ceiling when Sergeant Cameron stooped over him.

"Feeling better?" he asked.

Brent fixedly examined the sergeant for quite a time. "Now who the hell are you?" he at last inquired in a tone of peevish perplexity. "Go away. I don't like you." Cameron took the hand that waved him away and felt the pulse. Even as he counted it came to his mind that the last time he had so held another hand was also early on a summer morning, kneeling behind that shattered wall outside La Boiselle. But there was much more "kick" in this pulse. Cameron replaced the hand on the coverlet as the nurse appeared at the other side of the bed.

"Feeling better?" she asked brightly, smiling down at him.

"My God, what's all this?" he sighed, and then shut his eyes as if to puzzle out the answer for himself.

The nurse glided over to prepare some sort of drink. While she was holding it to his lips Mrs. Brent entered in her chair. Brent finished off the drink with another deep sigh—this time of content.

51

Then the chair glided round the foot of the bed, and Mrs. Brent laid her hand on his right shoulder.

"Eric," she said gently. "Eric, it's me, your mother."

"You're pinching my arm," he said querulously.

She took away her hand.

"The other arm," he said.

"No, no. You're hurt, you know. Don't you remember? Up on the moor. You were shooting—all of you together."

Cameron saw the muscles of the man's face stiffen and something like light come to the eyes. His hand went to his pocket for his notebook. The nurse began to flutter, like a nervous, protective hen. Even Cameron, keen as he was for the facts, doubted whether Brent was yet in a fit condition to make a statement. But the mother appeared to be impelled by some force she could not resist.

"You were shooting—all of you together," she repeated. "What happened?"

Brent moved a little, then frowned and shook his head.

"I don't know," he said. "What did happen?"

Mrs. Brent leaned forward and whispered: "You were walking along—on the slope of the moor, with your gun; it was very misty."

The sergeant saw the young man's eyes open widely.

"Yes," he breathed. "Yes, I remember. I was walking along. Let me see. . . . Yes, I had just passed the burn. I'd been expecting to put up something from the bushes at its edge—" He stopped, his forehead again wrinkling into a frown in an effort to remember. "No, nothing got up. . . . So I put my gun on my arm again."

Brent closed his eyes and stopped as if he had reached the end of his story. The sergeant slipped round the bed and whispered something to the woman.

"Over the left arm, wasn't it, Eric?" she said softly.

"Yes, in the crook of my left arm, of course; that's where you carry it, then something hit it."

"Hit it? What hit it?" she asked.

He shook his head.

"Don't know. Something did. . . . At least I think it did."

Cameron bent down to her again to suggest a question.

"Something hit it when you turned round to look back at the bushes beside the burn."

After a moment he shook his head.

"No," he said.

"You did turn round, didn't you?" she persisted.

"Did I? I don't remember."

Cameron could endure the uncertainty no longer. Before he knew it he heard his own voice prompting Brent's mind.

"When you turned you saw somebody or something," he said.

The intrusion of the new voice, however, disturbed Brent and destroyed the sergeant's chance of hearing more. Brent, without opening his eyes, said:

"Don't know who you all are. Why can't you leave me alone?"

That brought the nurse to the front. She actually pulled Cameron away.

"Not any more till the doctor comes, please. I take no more responsibility."

"When's that?" Cameron asked.

"About ten," she replied, "unless he is sent for."

The sergeant seemed determined to send for the doctor at once, but the nurse pointed to her patient, and Cameron saw he was asleep already. So there was nothing for it but to wait. He slept himself, in the next room, till Macfarlane awakened him.

"They tell me," said the doctor, "you have been catechizing my patient."

"It was very important, sir."

"Oh, so I suspect, sergeant, but it is very important to me that he should not die on my hands. However, he's much better now." He nodded towards the other room. "You can try him again. I'll be there to stop you if necessary."

The sergeant found the young man in a distinctly better condition after his second sleep. He no longer looked dazed with the drug. Mrs. Brent sat by him in her wheel-chair.

"He's much better," she said. "Perhaps now he'll be able to tell us all about it."

Brent lay with his cheek on the pillow.

"That's what I want you to do," he said.

Cameron drew up a chair and took out his notebook. Remembering the doctor's warning, he went straight to the point.

"When you stopped and turned round, sir, did you see anybody or anything?"

"Turned round?" Brent repeated.

"Yes. You heard something, didn't you, that made you turn? What did you see?"

"But I didn't turn."

"Just after you had passed the bushes," Cameron said persuasively. Brent here revealed impatience.

"Who says I turned?" he cried. "I tell you I didn't stop or turn. I remember quite well passing those bushes." He began to breathe quickly.

"Gently," the doctor whispered, as the young man began to toss a bit, throwing up his free hand.

"Well," he cried again, "what the devil are you badgering me like this for? If that fellow knows what I did, why ask me?"

"It's very important for us to know, sir. And we have good reason to believe you did stop and turn," the sergeant said with extreme deference.

"Look here," said Brent in the cold tone of extreme anger, "I happen to remember very well. In fact, it's the very last thing I do remember. It disappointed me that I raised nothing from those bushes, and I was just thinking it was about the last chance of a shot that day, when through the mist ahead of me I saw a big clump of bushes. The very last thing I remember is walking straight towards them, and thinking there was still one chance left. That is all I've got to say."

"It seems conclusive enough," said the doctor. Cameron said nothing—nothing, that is, that was audible. But sitting still, notebook on his knee and unused pencil in his hand, he was breathing out curses of a type he had not heard since his army days. Dr. Macfarlane touched him on the shoulder.

When Sergeant Cameron got back to the police station about eleven o'clock Constable Grant informed him that Rintoul was at that moment engaged with three gentlemen, and that the chief had forbidden any interruption. If the sergeant had been less weary he might have whistled his surprise at hearing of three gentlemen where he had expected only Mr. Toplis. As it was, his curiosity did not remain long unsatisfied, for soon afterwards, looking through the window, he saw the three leave the buildings by Rintoul's private door. They were Mr. Willoughby, Cresswell and Toplis, and Cresswell was carrying a gun. Then the bell rang and Cameron entered his superior's room.

One glance at Rintoul's face was enough to show the sergeant there had been developments.

"Ah, Cameron, that you? Had a good night, I hope?" The tone was more baffling than the words. Looking up, he caught sight of two articles lying on the chief's table: a gun, and what looked like the white Burberry in which Brent had been shot.

"I got nothing satisfactory from him, sir."

"As against Mr. Cresswell, you mean?"

Cameron was quick to notice the significance in the prefix to Cresswell's name. Things must have been moving. As a potential criminal Mr. Cresswell had been merely Cresswell.

"The young man asserts that before he was shot he neither stopped nor turned."

Rintoul waved a hand.

"Quite right, he did not. We know that now. So," he added with a fleeting smile as he noticed his subordinate's face, "Mr. Cresswell is cleared."

"Cleared?" Cameron echoed incredulously.

"Absolutely," the chief nodded. "What Mr. Brent told you confirms all I have just heard. Your suspicions were entirely without foundation."

Cameron's eyes wandered back to the gun and the waterproof on the table.

"Yes," said Rintoul, observing his look. "I'll tell you about those presently. Before you came in I just began to wonder about yourself, Cameron."

"About me, sir?"

"Yes. Sit down. You look a bit tired."

The sergeant was tired, but when he allowed himself to subside into a chair while his superior still stood, he was feeling more surprise than fatigue.

"About me?" he repeated.

"Ye-s," Rintoul almost drawled. "I've been wondering what you've been reading lately."

"Reading, sir?" Cameron did not think he had heard aright.

"Yes—in your off-time."

Although astonished at such a question at such a moment, the sergeant was gratified by his chief's interest in his off-time hobbies.

"Well, sir, at the moment I'm about half-way through Boswell's *Life of Dr. Samuel Johnson.*"

"Really? Boswell's *Johnson*, eh? You surprise me."

"Why, sir?"

"Oh, nothing. I just thought you must have started reading detective stories. You've lately been developing such a fantastic imagination."

Sergeant Cameron visibly wilted under this accusation. While the chief toyed with his watch-chain, looking down at him, he stared with unseeing eyes at the gun and waterproof lying on the table between them.

"This means you think there's nothing in this case?" he said at length.

"Nothing against Mr. Cresswell or any of the Arrochmore people. Crime, in general, Cameron, is confined to no one class of society, but every class has its own type of crime. Take this youth, Toplis, as an example. He admitted he had lied. He did see, as you believed, Brent fall. More than that, he had caught a glimpse of Cresswell out of his position in the line a few minutes before the shot was fired. But he was quite sure if Cresswell fired that shot Cresswell was unaware of what he had done. You see? This young man is ready to conceal evidence which might involve a friend. That is to say, he makes himself an accessory after the fact. But a crime of violence is usually the work of the unintelligent or degraded who have not much to lose; and it is best in all such crimes to look first in that quarter for the perpetrators."

The sergeant pondered the lecture for a few moments.

"This man was not shot by his own gun," he asserted.

Rintoul, having delivered his lecture, took the chair at the opposite side of the table.

"I'm not saying he was shot by his own gun. I am only saying he was not shot by Mr. Cresswell's. We'd better make this quite clear before we go any further." Rintoul opened a drawer at his left hand and extracted an envelope which he handed to the sergeant. "These were extracted from Brent's wounds by Dr. Macfarlane," he said. "Tell me what you make of them."

Cameron emptied the leaden pellets into the palm of his hand and examined them.

"Number five, I should say, sir," he said, wondering if there was something else he ought to have had to say about them.

Rintoul nodded.

"What number were the Arrochmore party using yesterday?"

"I didn't open the cartridge to see," the sergeant admitted.

"If you had you would have found they were loaded with number six shot. I made certain of that this morning when I sent for the gamekeeper, Murdoch. The second fact now cleared up is still more conclusive: it relates to that gun."

Cameron stared at the gun again.

Rintoul observed the look.

"Yes. All the inferences you drew from the gun, sergeant, go for nothing. You see, the gun you took away and looked into was not Brent's, but Cresswell's."

Cameron stared, bewildered.

"Oh, it wasn't your mistake; no, sergeant, it was Cresswell's. He, as you know, was the only one of the party who carried his gun to the place where Brent fell. He put down his gun to help in carrying Brent. Someone else, Joliffe, it appears, took both guns to the spot to which Brent had been carried. Afterwards when you had arrived on the scene, Cresswell simply picked up the wrong gun. You merely assumed that the gun he left must be Brent's, and, quite naturally, on finding two unspent cartridges in the breech, you jumped to erroneous conclusions. Anyway, if you look at that weapon there you will find on the butt-plate the initials E. B."

Cameron stood up and lifted the gun. He was aware that the gun he had carried from the moor did not have any initials engraved anywhere on it. Nevertheless, he scrutinized this one carefully till he found what he sought. For there came to his mind something Brent had said early that morning, before the nurse had intervened to forbid further questioning. The young man had spoken then in a semi-conscious condition about something hitting his gun, though later on he appeared to have forgotten that anything did so. But Cameron soon discovered from his examination of the barrel that Brent's first statement was correct. Something had hit the gun; some twelve inches above the stock there were marks which certainly could have been made on the barrel by deflected pellets.

"You needn't waste time over that weapon, sergeant," Rintoul said dryly. "Both Mr. Willoughby and Mr. Toplis vouched for the facts."

"Well, sir, as far as that goes, this gun seems to corroborate what they say." The sergeant, taking the gun round to Rintoul, told him what Brent had said, and pointed out the slight indentations on the blue-black barrel. Rintoul, taking the weapon, placed it in the crook of his left arm, with his right hand holding the butt, that being the position in which Brent said he had been carrying the weapon. It then became obvious that any number five shot deflected at the points visible on the barrel, could have entered Brent's body in an upward direction just under the shoulder. Cameron pointed out the angle of deflection.

"Lucky for him," he said. "But for that, these shots would have reached his heart."

Rintoul nodded and laid down the gun.

"As they were meant to do," he said.

Cameron had now no doubt that he had been on the wrong track in regard to Mr. Cresswell. True, he had not seen into Cresswell's gun and could make no inference one way or the other from what he found in the young man's weapon. But, after all, the same held true of all the other members of the shooting party. Anyway, it seemed to be now established that they must look elsewhere. Still, Brent had been found lying on his back, though he himself denied that he had either stopped or turned. He put this difficulty to Rintoul.

"Yes," said Rintoul. "I spoke to Dr. Macfarlane about that when he came in last night to bring me the shot. He said a man hit like that, possibly at the moment when he was on one foot, might fall in any attitude or position."

Few better than Sergeant Cameron knew how right the doctor was in making that assertion; it was strange indeed that he could have forgotten. And then, while he was seeing as in a vision figures lying on the earth in a bewildering variety of attitudes, Rintoul drew him back to actuality by a tap on the table.

"You're asking yourself where we are to look now," he said. "That white Burberry there, it gives us the essential clue."

This brought the sergeant to his senses. "The waterproof?" he said, mystified.

"Exactly," said Rintoul. "It's a hint I derived just now from Mr. Willoughby himself. That waterproof, you see, is his. Brent borrowed it. Whoever fired at Brent yesterday thought he was aiming at Mr. Willoughby. Perhaps you have a notion who that would be," he concluded.

"Some of Sam Haggerty's friends?" the sergeant suggested.

Down came the clenched fist of the superintendent on the table.

"That's more like it," he cried. "Now, Sergeant Cameron, you've got a fair start. Get on with it."

CHAPTER VI
SERGEANT CAMERON ON THE TRAIL

Superintendent Rintoul, however, did his sergeant full justice on what was, after all, the important point in the case: he did not forget, then or afterwards, that but for Cameron this attempted murder might have been set down as an accident.

Cameron himself at once switched over his activities to the new group of suspects. He had no doubt whatever that the attempted murder was the work of Haggerty's friends; and he saw for the first time a motive behind the crime. These navvies, a very mixed lot drawn from all quarters and set down in strange surroundings, developed among themselves a feeling of kinship as strong as had ever been held by any of the clans through whose territory they were driving their road. And Haggerty's conviction and sentence aroused strong feeling, especially against Mr. Willoughby. Indeed, the country people themselves, as Cameron knew, sided much more with the poacher than with the rich tenant.

There were two points which now impressed the sergeant and made him feel certain that he was on the right trail. He had no doubt that the marks he had himself discovered on Brent's gun had been made by shots fired at him from somewhere below the point at which he fell. Cameron recalled how Brent, weak as he was, strenuously denied that he had stopped or turned round to look at anything. This could only mean, therefore, that he had been shot by someone lurking down by the burn, at the very bottom of the slope where the mist was thickest. The other point which Cameron found conclusive was that connected with the white waterproof; whoever fired that shot thought he was firing at Mr. Willoughby. For Cameron remembered a detail connected with the poaching case which he saw might be fruitful in immediate results.

Haggerty had been caught in Keppoch Wood by Mr. Willoughby himself. But for Mr. Willoughby, in fact, he would have got clear away. Murdoch, the gamekeeper, had been some distance behind Mr. Willoughby. There was that charge against Haggerty of shooting at him, and Mr. Willoughby had been unable to swear whether the shot came from the front or the rear. But Haggerty had no gun, and as the most careful search had failed to discover one, the Court had disallowed the charge of shooting with intent. Still, Haggerty might have had a gun, although it had not been found. If so, Cameron knew it must have been hidden in no ordinary place of concealment.

After some further hard thinking, and more talk with Munro, the sergeant perceived that a cunning rogue like Haggerty would contrive a cunning cache for his gun. Haggerty was not the man to be seen carrying a gun to and from the moor when he could plant it in a safe place, and after wandering about weaponless, pick it up when he knew the coast was clear. What followed was not hard to guess. Since his arrest Haggerty, of course, had been unable to get back to his weapon; but once sentence was pronounced on him he had been allowed to see such of his friends as were concerned in settling his affairs. He had told them where to find his gun, and they had prudently chosen that misty day on which to retrieve it. It was a day on which nobody would expect to find any shooters out. But probably at the moment when the man sent for the gun was bringing it away these five young fools were crossing the slope above. The man with the gun probably saw only the one nearest him at the end of the line, and mistaking him for Mr. Willoughby, the cause of all the trouble, crept near enough to have a shot at him, and afterwards slipped away safely enough in the thick mist.

Acting on this theory as to the course of events, Cameron that afternoon sent off Munro on his motor-cycle to interview the landlord of the inn at Keppoch. Munro carried precise instructions about the questions he was to put to Macdonald, the landlord. Cameron himself a little later left for Arrochmore. He had certain new questions he wished to put to Mr. Toplis, and he had no doubt that this time Mr. Toplis would be frank in his replies. At any rate, he himself, now that he had got a grip on the facts, would no longer be questioning him in the dark.

When Cameron reached the fork in the drive he saw the man he sought engrossed in a game of tennis on the court nearest him. It seemed an exciting single with Mr. Harwood, for the onlookers had deserted the doubles game on the farther court. At first nobody noticed the police officer standing on the road beside his bicycle. It was not, indeed, until the game had ended in Harwood's victory, and while Toplis was smoothing down his shock of red hair, that someone drew attention to Cameron's presence.

"Toppy, someone waiting for you," a girl called out, with a wave of her hand in Cameron's direction.

The titter which followed showed the sergeant that few of them were aware of the real seriousness of yesterday's happenings. And Toplis, turning round while mopping his overheated face, regarded the sergeant without surprise, just as he took Cameron's almost imperceptible nod without anxiety. As soon as another game got under way he joined Cameron on the road.

"I'm hoping you're going to help us now, sir," Cameron said.

"Instead of hindering, eh?" Toplis nodded.

"Well, sir," Cameron said, as they walked away, "it's always best to tell what you know—best for the innocent, I mean. You thought you were acting in Mr. Cresswell's interests. Actually you put him under suspicion. It's always best to trust the police."

"Yes, yes, of course," the red-head nodded. "I see that now."

"Good," said Cameron curtly. "Then you won't hold us up any more. Now we can get on with it. My first question is—just try to remember as well as you can—do you remember where you were looking when you heard the shot?"

"That's easy. I had been looking all round to see what the other fellows were going to do when we got into that mist, and I saw Mr. Brent at the very moment, saw him go down, in fact."

"Did you happen to notice which way he was looking?"

"Straight ahead towards those trees where we carried him afterwards."

"When had you seen Mr. Cresswell last?"

"A few minutes before the shot was fired. He had got out of position, you know; that's what made me keep looking around. I thought it high time we dropped it."

"I see."

There was a pause. The sergeant looked thoughtful and Mr. Toplis made a swing or two with his racquet at an imaginary ball.

"Mr. Toplis?"

"Yes?"

"What made you think it was Mr. Cresswell who fired the shot?"

The racquet arrested itself.

"Well, the—there wasn't anybody else there to do it. I knew it must be one of us; for I knew *I* hadn't fired, and I saw, of course, that Brent hadn't."

"Why not Mr. Harwood or even Mr. Joliffe?"

"Well, Harwood's too careful, and Joliffe was too far away; besides, I had just seen Phil rather out of position."

"You're quite sure it was Mr. Cresswell you saw?"

Mr. Toplis seemed amazed.

"Well, I made sure it was. There wasn't anyone else for it to be." He turned suddenly on Cameron. "There must have been someone else there, of course."

Cameron agreed to this.

"I was just wondering which of the two you saw," he said. "If this other man was out for a bit of poaching, at a time when he might very well believe he had the moor to himself, we want to get him, even though he shot Mr. Brent by accident."

Mr. Toplis almost jumped.

"You don't surely think he may have done it deliberately?" he cried.

"Oh, no, sir, nobody thinks he meant to kill Mr. Brent," Cameron said with entire conviction. It was just as well, the sergeant thought, to say nothing about the inference Rintoul had drawn from the white waterproof. Any talk in Arrochmore about an attempt on Mr. Willoughby's life would almost certainly be overheard by some of the staff, and from them could easily percolate, via some pub, down to some of Haggerty's friends.

"Now," Cameron resumed, "I was just wondering if it wasn't the other man you mistook for Mr. Cresswell."

Toplis shook his head.

"No, it was Cresswell right enough," he said. Then he looked up. "But Cresswell may have seen that other man."

"That's what I was thinking. Maybe you could get Mr. Cresswell to see me."

Toplis turned to regard the distant figures on the tennis lawn.

"Tell you what," he said. "You go over to that seat and I'll send him along as soon as he's free."

When Toplis had gone, Cameron crossed to the seat he had indicated with a sweep of his racquet. On this seat, which stood on the verge of the path backed by the beeches, Cameron waited for Cresswell. Cresswell let him wait for some time, but when the sergeant saw the young man coming along the path he guessed from his walk that the delay was not of his own making. A very taking fellow, he seemed, the flannels appearing to make his stride longer than it actually was.

"You want to see me, sergeant?" he said, with a purposeful nod as Cameron rose. He listened carefully while the sergeant explained. When he had finished Cresswell said, putting up a foot on the seat where he had been sitting:

"Well, as a matter of fact, I was behind Mr. Brent just before he was hit; but I'm afraid I can't help you. I didn't see any one else."

Cameron was disappointed.

"You couldn't perhaps say from what direction the shot came?" he suggested.

"No—at least not beyond being sure that it came from Brent's direction. You see," he added, "I had turned away up again as soon as I saw Brent, and assumed that he himself had fired the shot."

Cameron hesitated.

"Would you mind telling me, sir, why you had dropped behind?"

Cresswell in his turn hesitated.

"Well," he said, "to be quite candid, sergeant, when we walked into that mist I got rather panicky about Brent."

"Panicky?" Cameron echoed.

"Yes. I was frightened I might get in front of him; he's such a damned bad shot."

Cameron was startled.

"But," he said, "I'm told he was an expert with a gun."

Cresswell stared. "Who told you that?" he inquired incredulously. "His mother."

Cresswell relaxed into his former easy attitude.

"Oh, his mother!" he laughed. "I don't suppose she's ever shot alongside him."

Cresswell withdrew his foot from the seat and began gently slapping his leg with his racquet.

"Some poacher did it, I suppose," he said. "I wish I could help you to get him."

At that moment Cameron observed Mr. Willoughby with a girl at his side, coming along the path from the direction of the tennis courts. Cresswell, turning to go, also saw them.

"Mr. Willoughby's greatly upset about this," he said. "At first I fancy he thought one of us had shot his pet."

From this outburst Cameron divined that if Brent was a pet to Willoughby, he was something very different to Mr. Cresswell.

Cameron, in the act of wheeling his bicycle across the path, was stopped by a gesture from Mr. Willoughby who, leaving Cresswell and the girl in talk, came towards him.

"Want to have a word with you," he said, "about this unfortunate affair. I suppose you're getting on the track of it?"

"Well, sir, we still need all the help we can get," Cameron replied.

Mr. Willoughby sat down and pulled out his cigarette case.

"I might save you from getting on the wrong track," he remarked, applying a match to the gold-tipped cigarette while Cameron stood, attentive. "You, I understand, are inclined to believe that one of my young people is responsible for the accident." He held up the cigarette protestingly when Cameron was about to explain. "Oh, at first I thought so myself. But now I know the responsibility only extends to taking a young man like Mr. Brent out shooting on such a day in my absence."

Sergeant Cameron could not forbear one comment. "If he were such a bad shot, sir, surely the risk was theirs more than his."

"Quite. But, sergeant, I am concerned for the safety of all my guests; and you see what has come of it." He looked along the path to where Mr. Cresswell was parting from the girl. "My daughter is terribly upset." He said nothing more until the girl had paused opposite the seat.

"Shall I go on, father?" she said, hesitating.

"Yes, dear. I'll be with you before the doctor is due."

In passing on she shot a swift glance at Cameron. Miss Willoughby was not beautiful according to the sergeant's standards, but the face and the eyes especially touched his imagination. As he put it to himself, she looked like one who had just seen one ghost and was afraid she might see another.

"Very upset, poor dear!" Mr. Willoughby murmured, watching her go. "You see, she blames herself. The other night while Mr. Brent was playing to us, she had some childish dispute with Mr. Harwood. Oh, about nothing. She had laughed at Mr. Cresswell when it came out that he did not know the difference between a concerto and a symphony, or something like that. These young fellows are inclined to despise men who are musicians and artists. Think all that sort of thing proper for girls, but not for men, you know. Then, it appears, Mr. Cresswell had some words with Mr. Brent—I think it was Mr. Cresswell," he said thoughtfully. "Anyhow, she backed Mr. Brent to bring in as big a bag as any of them the next time they went to the moor. They had rather laughed too, you know, when they saw the gun his mother had bought him for his Arrochmore visit."

"Fair provoked him to go, sir?" Cameron commented.

Mr. Willoughby nodded as he threw away his cigarette.

"That's about it. Lord!" he said, rising, "and isn't it strange how things fall out?" He laid his hand on the sergeant's arm. "Just think, sergeant, if that poacher who took a pot-shot at Mr. Brent had only known of that quarrel between these young fellows, I'll bet he'd have risked creeping up much closer to make quite certain."

Sergeant Cameron permitted himself a grim little smile.

"If he had, sir—come up closer, I mean—he might have seen who he was shooting at."

"The wrong bird, eh?" said Mr. Willoughby. "Well, now you know all this, see that you go after the right man."

As Mr. Willoughby followed his daughter towards Duchray, Sergeant Cameron made off down the drive, quite certain that, at last, he

knew where to find his man. He was grateful for the confidence Mr.
Willoughby had made him. He was glad he had remembered to warn
him against going out in that white waterproof.

CHAPTER VII

THE TWO NO. 5 CARTRIDGES

Superintendent Rintoul was disappointed to learn on Cameron's return that he had been unable to get any description of the suspect from Mr. Toplis. But the fact that none of the shooters had got even so much as a glimpse of the man left him unshaken. The conviction that Brent had been shot by one of Haggerty's friends from some point near the burn at the bottom of the slope, was also shared by the sergeant himself. And when Constable Munro returned from Keppoch and laid before them the information obtained from the landlord of the inn there, this conclusion seemed inevitable.

Rintoul's face visibly brightened as Munro reeled off his story. Macdonald, the landlord of the inn, knew Haggerty as a regular frequenter of the bar. He and his friends had been coming to the inn for the past five months, in fact, ever since their hut had been shifted along the road to its present position about half a mile from the inn. Haggerty and his pals attracted notice because they seemed never to be without money for drink. Macdonald had overheard much of their wild talk when the place was quiet and they had the bar to themselves, which was practically every day of the week except pay-day.

"You've got their names?" Rintoul inquired.

Munro produced his notebook.

"Yes, sir. There are four. Joe Gallacher who, Macdonald says, speaks with a Glasgow accent; Ned Oakroyd, some sort of Englishman, place of origin not known to Macdonald."

"It's a Yorkshire name, anyway," Rintoul commented as Munro seemed to boggle and hesitate over the next name on his list.

"Hugh Cameron, a local man," he read out.

Rintoul looked up with a sudden grin.

"One of the clan, eh?" he said, looking at Cameron. "And the last?"

"A man they call Big Brodie, cook to hut No. 22, where they all live."

Rintoul laid down his pen.

"You were able, I suppose, to elicit something as to the nature of the wild talk of which Macdonald spoke?"

"Well, sir, little that I gathered seemed to have any connection with this case. They were all, Macdonald said, very great boasters. Brodie had been to sea as a ship's cook, Oakroyd is a discharged soldier, Gallacher had been in the Irish troubles like Haggerty himself. And they all boasted one against the other when in drink."

"Even Cameron!" Rintoul interjected. "Well, proceed. Did he hear any threats after Haggerty's arrest?"

"Not from them. There was a lot of wild talk among the others about what they would do if they got a chance. But Macdonald can't remember hearing any of the four say anything."

"That proves nothing. If they meant revenge they would hardly talk about it."

Munro looked up hopefully.

"Well, sir, Macdonald knew they had a gun. In fact, he put two and two together from what he overheard at different times, and he believes that it was through what the gun brought them in that they were so flush with money. They sold the game, he thinks, among the different huts."

"Did he know who owned the gun?" Rintoul asked.

"He gathered it belonged to them all—they had formed a sort of—"

"Syndicate," the superintendent suggested.

"They had all subscribed for it, anyway, and went equal shares in the proceeds."

"Did he gather who—er—operated with the weapon?" Rintoul inquired, his pen poised in his hand.

"They could all shoot except Brodie; at least they all boasted about what they could do with a gun."

"Even Cameron!"

Munro thought this was going too far. But Rintoul was a Lowlander; he would not understand how Sergeant Cameron would feel.

The sergeant found his voice. "I know about him," he said. "He used to be underkeeper up at Kinloch till he got into some kind of trouble, and took to work on the road."

Rintoul nodded appreciatively.

"An ex-gamekeeper, eh? Well, he'd make a useful member of such a syndicate. Yes," he nodded, after puckering his brow over the notes on the table before him. "I think you've done quite well, Munro. The next thing is to see if we can lay our hands on that gun, and ascertain where these four men were—let me see—between, say, four and six o'clock yesterday, when Mr. Brent was shot."

Half an hour later Sergeant Cameron mounted behind Munro, and with a search warrant in his pocket, was speeding along the new road towards Keppoch. Hut 22 stood picturesquely on a bank by the side of the road over-topped by pines, and backed by a dense under-growth of bushes. It was not yet five o'clock, and the men were still at work farther along the road. Munro wheeled his bicycle up to the door at the end of the hut. Cameron, after a formal tap, pushed the door open and entered. There was no one inside. Along each wall stood a row of beds, eleven on each side, and the sight evoked the memory of a certain clearing hospital behind Ypres, only things were tidier there, even amid the surrounding ruin and destruction. The unmade beds, however, did not hinder their search for the gun. While Munro took one side, the sergeant was busy on the other, turning up each mattress in turn, and examining the floor for any indication of a board that lifted.

Cameron had reached the second last bed when the floor at his feet was darkened by a shadow. Glancing up, he saw a huge face staring in at him through the window. The sergeant knew he had never seen the man before, for that huge white face with pendent jowls and small pig-like eyes, was not one that could be forgotten. As soon as he saw he was observed, the man angrily brandished a long wooden spoon which he held in one hand. Cameron went on with his work, and when he looked up again the man had disappeared. But just while he was helping Munro with the beds against the other wall the door flung violently open, and the man came up the room towards them, still grasping the long-handled spoon. Both the officers knew this must be Big Brodie. He certainly answered to the description, for under his huge bulk the floor boards creaked at every step.

"Very kind of you," he said. "Helpin' me to make the beds, I suppose."

Cameron produced his search warrant; but Brodie seemed not unfamiliar with such documents. He tapped at it with his spoon.

"That's foolin'," he said. "There's nothing here that paper will help you to get at."

Short of lifting every board, Cameron felt that was possibly the truth. The hut had no cupboards, and the lockers standing between the beds were too small to contain a gun. But the wood-shed, the kitchen and other offices still remained.

"I'll have a look outside, then," he said.

"It's something in my larder, I suppose," the cook sneered.

"Not unconnected with your larder," Cameron agreed. But he left Munro to continue his search of the hut's interior, and for a moment Brodie seemed undecided as to which man he had better watch. Cameron observed this hesitation with interest: the cook's decision as to which of them he had better keep his eye on could be taken as a pointer. He stepped round the corner of the hut and then heard Brodie hurrying after him. But as soon as he turned in behind the long building and saw the steaming cauldron standing over the burning logs, he thought it possible the cook might have been drawn there by a sense of his professional responsibilities.

Cameron went up to the cauldron and removed the lid.

"Good stuff that," he said as Brodie came up behind.

Brodie began to stir the contents with his wooden spoon.

"I don't ken what you're lookin' for," he said, "but I don't think you'll find it in this stew."

Cameron saw that no kind of game simmered among the steaming ingredients.

"Like a taste?" As Cameron bent over the pot Brodie suddenly thrust a spoonful of the stew within an inch of the sergeant's mouth.

The sergeant did not start back as the grinning cook expected.

"I like mine flavored with game," he said coolly.

"Game!" Brodie cried. "And how do you think poor working men like us could come by any game?"

"It's usually got with a gun, I believe," Cameron said in an explanatory tone.

"Do you tell me so!" mocked the cook, replacing the lid and wiping his hands on his apron. Then he looked up suddenly as if struck by a new idea. "You're no suspectin' us of havin' a gun, are you?"

"Oh, no," the sergeant said easily, "not suspecting you at all. I'm quite sure if you had a gun here there would be evidence of it in that pot."

Brodie seemed to be rather taken aback by this admission. As he watched the sergeant move towards the outhouses his face suggested that he was for the first time in doubt as to why the police were there.

Cameron hid the disappointment he experienced when he examined the contents of the stew; for he felt certain that had the gun been anywhere near at hand he would have found evidence of the fact where he had looked for it. This conviction, however, did not make his search any less thorough. He went through the store and the implement sheds, and looked among and under the piles of wood and empty barrels in a way that must have convinced the watchful Brodie that the search was for something much smaller than a gun.

Brodie, however, at the end of it all knew that, whatever the officer sought, he had failed to find it, unless indeed it was something he could put into the pocket of his tunic. Seeing him emerge empty-handed, the cook grinned.

"I doubt you've come to the wrong shop this time," he sniggered.

Cameron said nothing. Brodie, seeing him busy with his handkerchief, flicking his knees and coat sleeves, offered to find him a brush, if, meanwhile, he would keep an eye on the stew. Brodie, indeed, displayed much concern over the risk the sergeant's uniform had run, and moved round him two or three times to make a careful scrutiny. Although the mockery was quite apparent, Cameron could do nothing to resent it.

But just when Big Brodie was at the top of his triumph over the sergeant's discomfiture, Munro emerged from the hut. Cameron at once perceived he had got something. Brodie himself divined as much from Munro's alert advance, for the smile vanished as the two officers drew apart, leaving him with no more than a view of their backs.

"I got this in one of the coats hanging on the wall," Munro said, opening his hand to reveal a cartridge. Cameron picked it up, and turning it round, discovered with a thrill of satisfaction that it was stamped with the numeral 5, which proved it to be loaded with shot of the same size extracted from Brent's wounds.

"Do you know whose the coat is?" Cameron murmured.

"There was no name on it, but it was hanging above Hugh Cameron's locker," Munro said. "There were two cartridges. I left the other where it was."

"Quite right," the sergeant nodded. "We must get that coat identified."

Brodie, summoned to accompany them, followed into the hut doubtfully. About the coat he was non-committal. Unaware as to why information about it was wanted, he seemed unable to be positive about anything. How could he be expected to know all the coats in the hut? Did they think he was valet as well as cook? Yes, it was quite true the locker was Hugh Cameron's; but men were careless about where they hung their coats, and, if it come to that, not very particular about which bed they slept in. Not much could be made of Brodie. He would only admit what could not be denied, and in fact the only admission he made was that the locker had Hugh Cameron's name on it, which fact was evident to any one able to read.

Sergeant Cameron held the coat in his hands when the roadmen began to filter into the hut in twos and threes at the end of their day's work. The first comers betrayed much curiosity, but neither surprise nor hostility, on seeing the two officers. Heads went together as the men sat down on their beds to unlace their boots. The whispering was suddenly broken into by a young man who sat up on the corner bed.

"I know what they're after," he cried in the triumphant voice of one who has made a discovery. "All I wonder at is why they haven't been here before."

The men around lifted their heads.

"Not you!" a voice challenged.

"'Struth I do. So could you, Dandy, but for that cast in your eye. See how Cookie's all of a tremble." They all stared at Brodie, who scowled back.

"What's he been up to?" someone murmured.

"Poisoning us all with his filthy cooking, of course," the young fellow shouted.

Someone threw a boot at him which crashed against the wall. Then the door opened and three men entered. The sergeant guessed their identity, for he remembered one of them as his discreditable namesake, Hugh Cameron. Even had the sergeant not known who among all these men formed the gang with which he was then concerned, he would have divined it: the sudden silence following their entry was too significant to miss. The hut had suddenly filled with tension. Everybody waited expectant as the three advanced. When Hugh Cameron approached his bed the sergeant held up the coat.

"This is yours, I think," he said.

The other stared alternately at the coat and the man who held it.

"What about it?" he asked, as Gallacher and Oakroyd sidled up to Brodie.

"Just this," the sergeant said. "I hold a search warrant for this hut, and among other things I'm going to put my hand into the pockets of this coat."

This brought a number of the men off their beds, and a group formed round the sergeant, who stood in the middle rather like a conjuror about to perform some sleight-of-hand trick. Munro could see that while the mass of onlookers craning their necks were agape with curiosity, the members of the gang themselves were quite at ease. In fact, when the sergeant, thrusting his hand into an outside pocket, produced a cartridge, Oakroyd and Gallacher clapped their hands in ironical applause. "Ah!" said the sergeant, "perhaps you will tell me what this is for?"

Hugh Cameron glanced at his friends.

"Looks like summat they put in a gun to me," Oakroyd remarked.

"That's right," Gallacher nodded. "Sure, I've often put such a thing there myself."

It was easy to identify both men from their accents.

The sergeant looked at Gallacher.

"Done a bit of shooting in your time, I suppose," he said.

Gallacher stared truculently back.

"I have so," he said. "Quite a lot of us here have done a bit of shooting in our time, though we don't plaster three ribbons on our chest to make a boast of it."

A burst of laughter followed this sally. Young Munro, pale with rage, clenched his fists, and for a moment forgot he was a policeman. His sergeant, however, remained calm.

"No, I can believe that," he said mildly.

"Can you so?" Gallacher sneered.

"Yes, indeed I can!" the sergeant nodded. "Your kind of shooting is more likely to bring you three years than three ribbons." Then in the midst of the appreciative laughter this evoked, Cameron turned to his fellow clansman.

"What use have you for these cartridges?" he demanded, again exhibiting the one in his hand.

"He picked that un up on th' road," Oakroyd put in. "I was wi' him masel' when he did. Wasn't I, lad?" But when he turned for confirmation to Cameron the look he met showed him something had gone wrong.

"Just this one?" the sergeant asked.

"That's right," Oakroyd persisted weakly, feeling something had gone amiss somewhere.

Then the sergeant produced the other cartridge Munro had found.

"And this one?" he asked.

But Oakroyd was as silent as Gallacher himself now. Munro alone heard the soft curse that came from Big Brodie standing at his elbow. Then feet began to shuffle as the tension broke. The sergeant turned to Cameron.

"I'm going to take you to the station," he said, "so that you can explain to the superintendent for what purpose you carry ammunition."

CHAPTER VIII

MR. WILLOUGHBY LENDS A HAND

Superintendent Rintoul happened to be brooding over some difficulty not connected with this case when he heard Munro pull up. Glancing over the wire blind, he was surprised to see the sergeant on the pillion behind Munro, with what looked like a prisoner occupying the seat in the side-car. This was quick work indeed. He forgot the trouble on which he had been pondering, and waited almost with eagerness for the sound of the sergeant's step.

Cameron's story was soon told. Once Rintoul had opened the end of a cartridge to verify the size of the shot he felt that here, at last, they had got hold of something concrete. The possession of cartridges did not imply that they wanted this man on any graver charge than that of poaching. And from the sergeant's story Rintoul thought none of the others would suppose any graver charge hung over them. But the discovery that the shot found in this man's pocket was of the same calibre as that handed to him by Dr. Macfarlane, and now sealed up in his desk, did definitely bring the graver charge nearer.

"Still," he said, as Cameron waited for the order to bring the man in, "it is a pity you didn't get the gun."

"I'm almost sure they haven't got it, sir," Cameron said.

"You think it's still up on the moor?"

Cameron assented.

"I'm quite sure if they had a gun in their possession, with a man like this—this Cameron to use it, I'd have found proof of the fact. There was no trace of any game anywhere about the place."

Rintoul, stroking his chin, considered this.

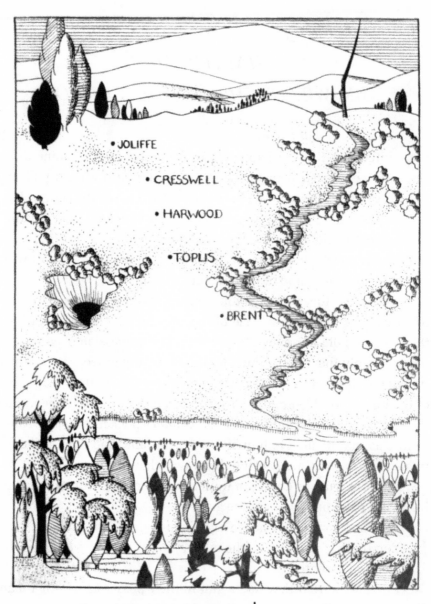

FROM SERGEANT CAMERON'S NOTE BOOK.

"Yes," he said. "The chances are that whoever fired at Brent would return the gun to its hiding-place. He would be too frightened, after yielding to his impulse, of being seen with it. He would be quite content to leave it in a place already proved to be so secure. He would know he could come back to retrieve it at a safer time."

"And that they haven't done as yet." The sergeant was very emphatic.

Rintoul was inclined to agree.

"All right," he said. "Now we'll have this man"—he avoided using the surname—"in, and ask him where he was between five and six yesterday."

If the honest Cameron thought he had cornered the other Cameron he was soon undeceived. Hugh Cameron, informed by the superintendent that a man not unlike himself was suspected of poaching between the hours mentioned, immediately produced an alibi. He had, he said, gone straight from his work over to Glendye.

"Glendye!" Rintoul exclaimed, for Glendye was five miles away on the Arkaig road. "What were you doing there?"

"My mother lives there. She washes my things for me, and I had gone to get them."

Rintoul looked at the sergeant. It hardly sounded like the alibi a man would fake; it could be so easily tested. There must be independent witnesses who would have seen the man either at Glendye or coming or going there. Asked to account for the cartridges found in his possession, Hugh Cameron explained they were two he had found in a coat at home on the previous Friday. He did not know they were there because he had not worn the coat since the time he lost his job as underkeeper at Kinloch. When it was pointed out to him that this did not tally with what Oakroyd had said, Cameron sullenly asserted that he was telling the truth and was not responsible for what Oakroyd said. Asked if he could name anyone who had seen him on the road between five and six o'clock, he said he had met several, none of whom he knew.

"None at all?" Rintoul inquired incredulously. "You, who belong to the district?"

"Except the shooting tenant of Arrochmore, that devil Willoughby who got Haggerty his six months." Cameron replied with a swift scowl of hate.

Rintoul attached no importance to this assertion as evidence for an alibi. It was an easy guess that Willoughby would be on the road about then, for they knew he was at Inverness in connection with Haggerty's trial, and, indeed, counted on his absence there when they sent one of their number to recover the gun. That Cameron asserted he had seen Mr. Willoughby on that road at that time went for nothing unless Mr. Willoughby could remember passing a navvy carrying a bundle.

Then Hugh Cameron sat up like a man who recalls something useful. He had seen the unbelief on the superintendent's face. So now with a gleam of triumph in his own eyes he said there was one man who could speak for him. He had asked a lift from a baker's van about a mile along the Glendye road. The name on the van, he remembered, was MacDougall.

Rintoul, at the mention of the name, exchanged a look with his sergeant. This would simplify matters. MacDougall's bakery was only about a hundred yards from the police station.

Sergeant Cameron was lucky enough to find the man who did the Glendye round as he was about to knock off work. He remembered a man with a bundle under his arm who had stopped him to ask for a lift when he was on his homeward run, about a quarter to six it would be. He did not know the man. He had refused his request. Yes, he might know him again, though he looked like a navvy, and one navvy looked very like another. He was quite sure of the time, because he was making for home and had done his last call.

While taking the vanman to the office, Cameron's thought was that if the identification was satisfactory his fellow clansman would certainly be cleared, for the position on the Glendye road where this man had spoken to him, was much too distant from the point up on Keppoch moor where the shot had been fired. And when the two men faced each other it was obvious both to Rintoul and to Cameron that the recognition was mutual.

"That's the fellow," said the vanman.

Hugh Cameron sniffed.

"I hardly thought he stopped long enough to remember me," he said.

Rintoul grunted his disgust.

"Lucky for you he did," he said.

Rintoul and his sergeant conferred together after Hugh Cameron had been sent back to Keppoch. The fact that he had been seen by the vanman going in the direction of Keppoch Moor at a quarter to six cleared him of the actual deed; but Gallacher, Oakroyd and even Big Brodie still remained.

Rintoul began to pace the floor.

"I thought we had a firm grip on it," he said; "but now it seems to be slipping."

The sergeant, after a moment, agreed.

"We seem to have put our hands on the wrong man," he said softly, remembering that man's name.

Rintoul kept pacing about.

"Munro had better go to Glendye to-morrow and verify further," he said at last. "We mustn't exclude the possibility of some sort of collusion between these two."

"Very good, sir," the sergeant said, thinking this as far-fetched as any suggestion he had made in regard to the young gentlemen from Arrochmore.

"We had better concentrate on finding that gun now," he sighed. "Any ideas, sergeant?"

"Well, sir, Munro and me hunted high and low for it up there. Do you think it wouldn't be better to set a watch on the hut from five o'clock on?"

"You mean follow any one who makes for Keppoch Moor from there?"

"Just that. He might lead us to the gun."

Rintoul shook his head doubtfully. "If they saw you watching, as they most likely would, they would never move. No," he continued. "You'll just have to search again—this time with a fine tooth comb in your hands."

And next day that is what Sergeant Cameron did with the assistance of Constable Grant. Grant, being new to the search, went about the business with great enthusiasm and energy, while the sergeant, if he did not cover the ground with the figurative small tooth comb,

hunted in places where such an implement could never have pene-
trated. He tapped the trunks of trees in Keppoch Wood for a possible unsuspected hollow interior, and even scrambled up among the
branches to make sure that in none of them a gun yet lay where it had
been hastily thrown. At the end of the day, Rintoul, on receiving the
report of failure, still stood determined to go for the gun.

"We know the gun must be there," he said. "Haggerty had his own
place for it. And I'm sure it's there now, though it has been used since
he used it. Otherwise, if it had been put in any ordinary place you
would have come on it already."

When Cameron assented to this, Rintoul's coolness left him.

"Look here," he said almost fiercely, "we've got to get that weapon." He came close up to the sergeant. "You see what it means? To be
fit for use that gun must have been kept in some absolutely dry place.
You can count on that. And that means it almost certainly has on it
not only Haggerty's fingerprints, but also those of the man who used
it last."

Rintoul waited only to see his sergeant's face brighten into agreement before he continued.

"My notion, sergeant, is to get Mr. Willoughby and Murdoch the
gamekeeper to give us a line. Show us, I mean, the line Haggerty
took when he ran from them. Mr. Willoughby had him in view almost
continually, and Haggerty must have planted his weapon somewhere
within a yard or two of the path he took."

Cameron could not comprehend why they had not thought of
that before. And those fingerprints of the man who had last used the
gun—they were what they needed; they would be as good evidence
for the identity of the man who shot Mr. Brent as the evidence of any
eye-witness.

Next morning, with Mr. Willoughby and Rintoul going on ahead,
Cameron, Munro, Grant and Peter Murdoch the gamekeeper once
more climbed to Keppoch Moor.

"Man, sergeant, I'd have had a shot at the fellow myself if Mr.
Willoughby hadn't been between us," Murdoch declared as they
reached the top.

Cameron shared the exasperation of the old gamekeeper, but was
not prepared to express it in the same way.

"Well!" he said, "I wish something had brought him down before he hid this infernal gun."

Murdoch grunted.

"Ay," he said, "ay. And thae damned fools in the court didna' believe he had a gun."

Munro looked round.

"They had to go by the evidence," he said. "And Mr. Willoughby, who was much nearer than you, could not swear he had one."

"Evidence!" Murdoch cried. "What about the shot? There's no smoke without fire, and I suppose there's no shot without a gun."

"And who had the gun?" Munro inquired. "Some folks think you had."

"Now, now," said the sergeant, "no more of this!"

There was no more of it till the party reached the point at which the pursuit of Haggerty started. At that point a long halt followed, for Murdoch and Mr. Willoughby were at variance as to the exact course Haggerty had taken. Whether or no the gamekeeper had been made cantankerous by Munro's innuendo, Cameron could not say, but he held to his opinion with all the stubbornness of his mulish nature. While the discussion was at its height Rintoul drew his sergeant aside for a word in his ear.

"I asked Mr. Willoughby just now about what Hugh Cameron said. He does remember meeting a navvy with a bundle just before he reached Glendye."

Cameron stared.

"*Meeting* him?" he said.

Rintoul nodded. "Ah, you noticed that?" he said. "So did I, but I made no remark on it. Odd, I thought, that two vehicles going in the same direction should both meet and overtake a man." Then as the sergeant was puzzling over this, Rintoul added, "I'm not so sure of that vanman. Some of these trades vans do a bit of business with the poachers up and down the road. We'll have to look more closely into this fellow's movements and associates."

There was no time for more as Mr. Willoughby beckoned the superintendent over.

"We are agreed on one point," he said with a smile. "Haggerty ran from here straight to those bushes at the edge of the slope." He indicated a clump of wind-blown shrubs which stood prominently up about two hundred yards across the heather. On reaching the bushes Rintoul looked back.

"When you reached here, Murdoch was well behind you, I understand," he said.

"He was about half way. I had a start of him, you know, for I saw the man first," Willoughby explained. As they stood at the top of the slope Cameron perceived that they were very close to the ground he had included in his sketch plan. Taking out his note book, he had merely to prolong the lines an inch or two to the west to include the position in which they now stood.

"You see," Mr. Willoughby was saying to Rintoul, "Murdoch here thinks he saw him going straight for that dip in the ground down there."

"And your view, sir?" Rintoul inquired.

Mr. Willoughby pointed to the right.

"By the time Murdoch arrived here," he said, "I was following him in that direction."

"Well," Rintoul remarked. "It certainly seems the more likely. He had ever so much more cover there."

Mr. Willoughby agreed.

"And I can tell you he used it too. It was amazing how he ducked and doubled and ran among those bushes at such speed. I had him in full view though till he was almost at the bottom of the slope, where I lost him again."

Rintoul removed the notebook from the sergeant's hands, and passing it to Mr. Willoughby together with his own pencil, asked him to touch in Haggerty's course. This Mr. Willoughby did, and then consulting with Murdoch, also touched in the gamekeeper's theory of the course taken.

"I stick to that," Murdoch declared.

"Well," Rintoul said, "if he was there at all you must have seen him, for there's nothing but the heather between here and the burn."

"It was doon by the burn I saw him."

Rintoul looked at the notebook in his hand and then turned sharply to the gamekeeper.

"You just assumed he followed this line, then?" He tapped the book almost angrily, and then turned from the man to his master.

"I think, sir, I see how it is," he said. "Haggerty, of course, made for the right, where there was so much cover. Then, near the bottom of the slope, he deliberately allowed you to see him before he turned away to the left, where you lost sight of him. He was trying to mislead you—to make you think he was heading straight on. Then he crossed the burn at a point invisible from where you had then reached, but not invisible from where Murdoch stood at the top of the slope."

"Does it really matter so much?" Mr. Willoughby asked, a little impatiently. "On one or other of these routes the man got rid of his gun, if he had a gun at all."

Rintoul turned again to the gamekeeper.

"You said you heard a shot fired, Murdoch. Where were you when you heard it?"

"Just before I reached here."

Rintoul looked down the slope almost ruefully.

"There's more to this than you might think, sir," he said to Willoughby, standing at his side. "That gun's going to be an ill thing to find. This slope has already been well hunted and also the wood beyond the burn."

Mr. Willoughby shrugged.

"Then it can't be here at all," he said.

"It most certainly is," Rintoul declared. "That gun is somewhere between this spot where we now stand, and the spot where you caught the man in that wood."

"Then somebody must have picked it up before your search began. For myself, I don't think the man had a gun at all."

Rintoul exchanged a look with his sergeant.

"We have good reason to believe he had," he said quietly. "We have also reason to believe it has not yet been removed by any of Haggerty's friends." As Mr. Willoughby moved impatiently, he added, "You forget the kind of men these are, sir. For them to carry a gun between this moor and their huts is out of the question. But it's a simple matter for them to keep it here. Remember their occupation. With one of their drilling tools a hole could be cut into the ground, the gun wrapped in a tarpaulin, thrust inside, and the opening covered with a tussock of grass no bigger than a man's hand."

"By George!—never thought of that," Mr. Willoughby cried. "No wonder you've worried so much about his line of flight."

Murdoch nodded to Munro and Grant. "Ay, they're sly devils. Shootin's too good for them. If I had my way—"

"We're not so sure you didn't try," Munro said, with a wink to Grant.

CHAPTER IX

FISHING ON A GROUSE MOOR

A really intensive search for the gun began on the afternoon of the following day. Heavy rain had fallen all through the night, but conditions improved sufficiently in the forenoon to allow the sergeant and his two officers to work over the ground an hour or two after the deluge ceased.

On reaching the slope Cameron saw that the water in the burn had risen. Fed by the many little streams which carried the rainfall off the mighty slopes of the mountains, it was a brown and creamy torrent almost worthy to be called a river. Apparently there were others of the same opinion. Munro, with a touch on his arm, drew the sergeant's attention to some men who seemed to be fishing in those waters.

Cameron, a trifle irritated with these intruders, who would probably watch the search and talk about it afterwards, went on ahead. His intention was to challenge their right to fish on Mr. Willoughby's land, if they did not decamp at sight of him. One of the men had no rod, and it was he who drew the others' attention to the sergeant's approach. Cameron resolved not to follow if they ran: he had more important business on hand. But they did not run, not even the boy who had the second rod. Then he saw that the man who had turned, rod in hand, was Mr. Harwood.

"Hallo!" he cried. "You up here again?"

"Fishing—like yourself, sir," Cameron said.

Harwood's mouth took on a grim little significant smile.

"Not quite for the same fish, though, eh?"

"I'd like to have a word with you about that, if you don't mind," Cameron rejoined, with a glance at the others.

"Oh, we're all fishers here," Harwood nodded. "Mr. Bray here is a fisher too—at least he's going to be. Not trout, you know, but souls."

The boy burst into a shriek of laughter, and Harwood, seeing Cameron standing mystified, explained.

"Going to be a parson, aren't you, Bray?"

"Such is my hope, certainly," the young man replied with naive earnestness.

"Been trying his 'prentice hand on Mr. Brent," Harwood said, as he made another cast.

Cameron divined that Mr. Bray was something of a butt for the other's wit.

"How is Mr. Brent?" he asked, watching Harwood's line float down the stream.

Harwood, the cast finished without a bite, thrust his rod into Mr. Bray's hands.

"Oh, he's all right," he said.

The boy turned his head.

"Pretty blue about his arm, though," he said.

"Richard, you mean disquieted," Bray protested.

Harwood laughed.

"Oh, the sergeant understood Dick all right," he said.

"Well, he is in a funk about his arm."

"Richard—*funk!*" Mr. Bray breathed reproachfully.

Harwood led the way along the bank.

"Now what are you after, sergeant?" he asked, when they were out of earshot. "You don't still suspect Cresswell of shooting Brent, do you?"

Cameron didn't like that. He liked it just as little as he had liked Harwood's jest at Bray's expense. Indeed, he rather disliked Harwood altogether. He remembered it was Harwood who showed such impatience on the evening Brent was shot.

"It's just this, sir," he said, ignoring the other's question. "We think we know now who shot Mr. Brent. We're up here to find the proofs. It would be well for us if you said nothing about seeing us here."

Harwood opened his eyes rather wide.

"Yes," he said, after a moment, "that will be all right. This means, of course, there's some clue on the spot which you know about but haven't as yet found." Cameron saw his eyes go up the slope to where Munro and Grant were already busy, poking about on the route Murdoch asserted Haggerty had taken. Cameron, however, had no intention of telling him what the thing was, but before more was said an excited shout came from the boy. He had hooked a fish, and Mr. Bray, dropping Harwood's rod, ran to his assistance. Cameron and Harwood got back in time to see a brown burn trout leap into the air.

"Hell!" cried Dick, as the gut snapped.

"Richard!" Mr. Bray expostulated.

The disappointed youth turned to Harwood.

"Think he was as big as the one you lost here last Tuesday?" he asked.

"Bigger," Harwood nodded.

Dick began to reel up his line.

"Well, fishing's a mug's game, anyway," he said.

"You struck too hard," Harwood said. "Like me, you were too heavy-handed with him, Dick."

"Oh, yes," the youth pouted. "Fishin's all right for piano-playing fellows like Brent." Then, as Harwood began to attach a new cast to the line, he added: "All the same, if you had taken me shooting last Wednesday you wouldn't have needed to stick me at the end of the line to save the other men from getting shot."

Harwood, his fingers busy, looked up with a wink at the sergeant. Dick Willoughby evidently nursed a grievance.

"Dick doesn't like lily-handed piano-playing chaps," he explained.

"Well, who does like him except Mary and dad?" Dick demanded.

"I like his playing extremely," Mr. Bray asserted, like one anxious to find the best in everybody. "Mr. Willoughby told me he had a great future as a pianist."

Dick sniffed.

"Oh, dad only said that because Mary's quite potty about him."

"Richard!" Mr. Bray exclaimed.

Sergeant Cameron glided away to rejoin his two officers busy on the slope. He felt sure Mr. Harwood would not talk about seeing him there, but his hope was that they might find the gun that afternoon. Then it would not matter who talked.

It was mighty laborious work probing the ground to find an opening that need not be more than six or seven inches in diameter. Munro and Grant each had a walking-stick, the end of which had been sharpened the more easily to penetrate the ground. But as the supposed hole might be covered by a tuft of heather as well as by a grass sod, the spiked walking-sticks were not so helpful as had been anticipated. Once Cameron's heart gave a leap in a fashion that revealed how eager he was when he heard a sudden shout of triumph from Munro. But it was a false alarm. Munro's stick had sunk not into the hoped-for cache, but merely into a rabbit-hole.

By this time the three searchers had worked down to within twenty yards of the burn, and then Cameron, looking up to ease the crick in his neck, saw without surprise that one or other of the anglers had caught his line on a rock. He did not think that even Mr. Harwood knew much about trout fishing: it was a day for bait, not flies. Munro and Grant, also with cricks in their necks, stood at ease for a moment to watch Mr. Harwood's frantic attempts to disentangle his line. Then Cameron recalled his subordinates to their duty by resuming work himself. He was pretty well hopeless now.

They had only a few yards to go. Keppoch Wood, in which Haggerty had been taken, stood on the other side of the swollen burn, and they were almost at the point where he must have crossed. It was unlikely that the gun would be hidden so close to the water. Even if it had, it was unlikely that the man who fired at Brent would come so far down the slope before getting rid of his weapon.

Looking up once more, he perceived that Mr. Harwood had not yet succeeded in freeing his tackle. Half impatiently, but acting on the impulse of the man who knows how a thing should be done, he thrust his stick into the ground to mark the point which he had reached, and then went over to assist the inexpert angler. Harwood was flushed with annoyance.

"The last bit of tackle I have too," he said. "Mr. Bray forgot this wasn't the Sea of Galilee and cast his fly on a rock."

But when Cameron took the rod in his hand he discovered that Mr. Bray had hooked something much less immovable than a rock. For though the rod bent almost double, there was a certain resilience at the end of the line, not unlike the resistance put up by a weighty, sulking salmon. Cameron was surprised that a fish of the size indicated could be in the burn at all, in flood though it was. Not wishing to disappoint the boy, he said nothing about his belief that a big fish had been hooked.

"It won't come away," he said to Harwood.

"That's an end to our fishing then," Harwood replied, with a nod of finality.

"Send Mr. Bray in," Dick suggested.

"He hasn't got his goloshes," Harwood said. "No, no; break it off, sergeant."

But Cameron had another try. He moved down stream to get not only a straight pull but also to take advantage of the downward rush of water. And then he felt the thing move. With great precaution he coaxed it on inch by inch, expecting each moment a vicious tug at the end of the line which would snap his gut asunder. A moment came when movement ceased. But there was no jerk on the line.

"It's coming away," Dick said.

"Ay, but it's caught again," Cameron replied.

Straightening himself, he looked towards where he had left his colleagues, and seeing them watching from a distance, beckoned to Munro. When both officers were at hand he told Munro to remove his boots.

"You have the best breeches for this work. Turn them up and wade in for it."

Munro looked first at his perfectly-fitting leggings, hesitated, and then, looking at his superior, read in his eyes something of the wild, undefined hope that had just burst into his mind. Without knowing what the look meant, he saw that the sergeant meant what he said.

"Oh, it's not worth a wetting," Harwood said, interposing himself between Munro and the water. But the sergeant was determined.

Munro certainly did get wet, for the water was soon swirling high above his rolled-up breeches. More than that, as he reached the point where the line disappeared under the surface, he stumbled on a hidden stone and went under altogether. But how well worth it the ducking was, became apparent, to Cameron and Grant at least, when he reappeared with a cry. For he stood upright with a gun in his hand. But it was a gun on which no fingerprints would be found.

CHAPTER X

TESTS FOR AN ALIBI

Superintendent Rintoul was not a man given to the display of his emotions; and so Cameron was not disappointed with the mere flicker of light in the eyes with which his superior received the recovered weapon.

"That settles it," he said, as soon as they were alone in his office. "No man throws his gun into water for a whim."

Cameron was so pleased that he could not forbear a jest.

"I've known a golfer throw his club into a burn after missing a shot," he said.

"Ay," Rintoul nodded, "but it wouldn't be dangerous for him to go and get it out again. He must have been hard pressed to throw this into the water." Rintoul was not so disappointed as the sergeant expected, that there was no possibility now of getting fingerprints from the gun. For one thing the gun almost certainly had been bought in Inverness. From what that inn-keeper at Keppoch told Munro they probably clubbed together to buy this gun, but it would be Hugh Cameron who chose it.

The sergeant agreed to this; the ex-keeper would be the only one who knew anything about sporting guns. Rintoul at once took the sergeant's suggestion that a visit to the Inverness gun-shops might be worthwhile.

"Probably the salesman who sold it will remember the man who bought it," he continued. "Then Munro can bring the man back, and we'll let him have a look at Cameron." Rintoul paused to look thoughtfully at the weapon on the table before him. "That prevarication about the cartridges you found in his pocket is likely to go hard with him."

"Of course his alibi still stands, sir," the sergeant reminded him.

"I doubt if it will when we probe a little deeper into it," Rintoul said with dry cheerfulness. "There's bound to be a hole in it somewhere. Where is Munro?"

When Cameron reminded him of the part played by the young constable in recovering the gun, Rintoul smiled.

"His breeches would be none the worse for a little shrinking. Anyway, it's too late now to send him to Inverness."

"And he's been over the nine hours on duty, sir," Cameron reminded him.

Rintoul did not appear to have heard.

"It's the alibi that bothers me now," he said. "You'd better go over to Glendye yourself, and see his mother. His story was that he goes each Wednesday to get his washing, isn't it? Well, I've left him time since we had him here to go back and put her up to what she is to say. We can't help that now. But if you find he has been home since Wednesday, that in itself will tell against him. And it ought to be easy for you to know whether she is lying or not."

Next morning Sergeant Cameron on his push-bike went to Glendye. The cottage he sought stood up on a bank above the road, and he found its owner surrounded by a varied collection of hens which she was feeding. The old woman seemed as startled as the hens themselves when the sergeant stepped round the end of the cottage.

"Has there been an accident?" she quavered.

Cameron reassured her.

"Och no, nothing like that," he said.

"Then he's been taken ill?" she said.

Cameron's eyes were on the basin in her shaking hands. He avoided looking at her face.

"He was all right when you saw him last, was he not?"

"Ay," she said, "but—"

"When was that?"

Now the sergeant was looking her straight in the eyes. He saw she was frightened.

"On Wednesday."

He waved a hand as if dismissing Wednesday.

"Oh, I know he comes to you on Wednesday. I meant since Wednesday."

She shook her head.

"He hasna' been here since then."

He saw she was speaking the truth. He saw more. He saw that there was no put-up alibi between this woman and her son. The son might be an ill-doer; the mother was not.

"Will you no' tell me what's wrong?" she pleaded. "He hasna' been fechtin', has he?"

"He's suspected of poaching," he blurted out.

Relief showed on her face instantly. Poaching was hardly considered a crime in that countryside.

"On Wednesday last," he added, "between five and six."

Cameron looked at her almost hopefully. After all, he would be glad to clear a fellow clansman. Besides, so far as poaching was concerned, his inherited instincts were always at war with his personal position as an officer of the law.

The woman laughed on hearing the time.

"You've come to the wrong house, then," she said, "for I met him myself between five and six."

"*Met* him?" Cameron cried. "Where did you meet him?"

"Along the road a mile or two. He—"

Cameron stopped her.

"Just where exactly was it you met him?"

"Well, it was a wee bit beyond the Fintry shepherd's cottage. If you think I'm no speaking the truth ye can go in and ask his wife as ye go back, for she saw us meet."

"He didn't come nearer here than that?"

"Not a step. Mrs. Macpherson can tell you that as well. He was in a great hurry to get back again, and Mrs. Macpherson came out— she's an old friend o' mine—and asked me to come in and have a cup o' tea and rest myself."

"Do you usually go to meet him?" Cameron next asked.

"No, but you see he was later than usual that day. I thought the poor lad would be tired with that work on the roads. That's why I took his things, and went to meet him, to save him coming so far. So," she laughed, "you'll have to go further yourself now."

Sergeant Cameron, however, was almost certain that he had no need to look further. This going to meet the man might make all the difference. They had concluded that if Hugh Cameron had been to his mother's cottage at all he could not have fired the shot at Brent. The distance between the place of shooting and the cottage in Glendye was much too great for him to go to the cottage after firing the shot and be seen returning from it by the baker's vanman at a quarter to six. But it was quite another matter if he had been met two miles along the road by his mother. This would shorten the distance he had to cover by four miles.

When Cameron got back to the office just before lunch he found Rintoul ready to agree with this opinion. The superintendent indicated how this new fact explained a detail which had puzzled him. Mr. Willoughby had remembered meeting a man with a bundle going towards Glendye, while the vanman said he had overtaken a man with a bundle coming away from Glendye at about a quarter to six. That was an odd thing which had perplexed him. But now the explanation was obvious: in between these two events Hugh Cameron had met his mother and exchanged the separate bundles of clothes, the bundle Mr. Willoughby had seen the man carrying being a different one from that which the vanman had seen. And the case against Hugh Cameron was advanced another step when Munro returned from Inverness with the gun. When they heard the detonation of his engine cease outside, both the superintendent and the sergeant knew he must have met with success to get back so early. Munro entered carrying the gun.

"It was at Macdougel and Smith's Cameron got it, sir," he said at once.

Rintoul with a gesture made him lay the weapon on the table.

"You found the man who sold it?" he asked. "Does he think he can identify the purchaser?"

"At first he could remember nothing about it," Munro said. "But as soon as he looked up his books it all came back. The gun was bought on the third of August last by Hugh Cameron on the license issued him while he was under-keeper at Kinloch."

Again Rintoul thought Munro was assuming more than the facts warranted.

"You mean, it was bought by a man who exhibited a gun license issued to Hugh Cameron, don't you?" he corrected.

"No, sir. Mr. Smith knows Cameron well by sight. All the gun-room stock at Kinloch is bought from his firm, and Cameron used to call for it regularly."

Rintoul looked over at the sergeant.

"They always do make some stupid blunder," he said. "I wonder why it is. Why didn't he use that license at a shop where no one knew him? Good Lord, if Mr. Brent had died the noose would be as good as round this man's neck already."

Rintoul's face fell, however, when he heard what Munro had to say in the matter of the alibi. Munro, who was familiar with all the roads, was more than doubtful whether the distance between Keppoch Moor and the shepherd's cottage at Fintry could be covered between the time at which the shooting took place and the time Cameron was seen by Mr. Willoughby. On the other hand, Cameron believed it could be done. But Rintoul was aware that his motor patrol officer knew the ground as well as any one. To settle the question Rintoul there and then dispatched them both to check up the time a man would take to go from the one point to the other.

Cameron sent Munro off with instructions not to start from the spot where Brent was hit till his watch showed a quarter past the hour. Then he himself returned on the cycle till he reached a position on the Inverness road where the burn from the moor passed under the road bridge. Dismounting there, he sat down on the parapet to wait. It was fairly certain that Hugh Cameron would have followed the course of the burn. If he had come round by the Keppoch road he could not possibly have been seen by Mr. Willoughby at Fintry about a quarter to six. He himself had taken not much less than that to do it on the cycle. The sergeant took out his pipe and filled it thoughtfully. A lot hung on this experiment. He noted the time on his wrist-watch at which Munro would have started. A little later he stood up, his eyes on the rising ground over which Munro would come into sight. Quickly the minutes passed. He knew he himself stood as nearly as possible half-way between the starting-point and the finish at Fintry; but half the time had gone and still there was no sign of Munro.

Cameron got a little flurried. He wished he had gone himself, and left Munro with the cycle. Possibly he was taking more care of his clothes than Hugh Cameron was likely to do at any time. Then with relief he remembered that the first half of the route was much harder going than the remainder. There were bushes to be avoided, and the banks of the burn made rough going, with a stiff climb here and there.

At last he caught sight of Munro's head bobbing among the whins, and then saw him descending the slope. By the time he was on the road he had a bare twelve minutes left in which to reach Fintry. Munro did not appear to be in the least blown. Perhaps he was not too anxious to prove himself mistaken.

"I did it just as I thought he would have done it," he announced.

The sergeant's nerves had been on edge too long.

"Just that. Stopping to pick a flower or two by the way, I suppose," he said.

He left him on the bridge with the cycle and himself set off down the road for Fintry. It took him seventeen minutes of very hard walking; but he returned satisfied. Munro, sitting on the bridge, cigarette in mouth, watched him come. For all his jaunty attitude and swinging legs, that young man seemed rather crestfallen.

"He could have done it," Cameron said, "even if he had loitered as much as yourself."

"It's shorter than I thought," Munro admitted; "but what do you mean when you say I loitered?"

Cameron laughed.

"You didn't hurry much anyway," he said. "There would have been more mud on your shoes and more thorns on your breeches if you had."

"Sherlock!" said Munro, springing off the parapet.

Soon after half-past three they got back to the office. Rintoul awaited them with eager expectancy. He was sitting at his table, his notes on the case spread before him.

"Well?" he demanded.

"He could have done it," Cameron said. "We did it in just three minutes over the time."

Rintoul's face looked rather blank at the mention of those three minutes, but Munro removed the doubt.

"I took it at a walk, sir," he said. "I thought it safer. If I ran I could do it in half the time."

Rintoul laughed.

The superintendent glanced at the clock, as if making a calculation in minutes. The sergeant followed his gaze and thus chanced to notice the time: the big hand was at the quarter to four.

"We'll make you do that to-morrow," Rintoul said, as the telephone at his elbow began to buzz, "in an older pair of breeches."

His ear went to the receiver.

"Yes," he said. . . . "Oh!—What's that?"

Cameron could just discern a voice, a feminine voice, he thought, coming through. But the change that came over the superintendent's face was startling.

"Door locked?" he said. . . . "You are quite sure it was a shot you heard? . . . All right, we'll be with you in a few minutes."

He replaced the receiver and stood up.

"That was from the housekeeper at Duchray," he said. "She's just heard a shot in the library. There's no one in the house but herself at the moment, except Mr. Brent. And the library door locked."

Munro's cycle with the combination attached was still at the door. In another minute they were on the road to Duchray.

CHAPTER XI

DEATH IN A LIBRARY

It was not usual to see the police dashing at breakneck speed through the town. It was seldom that Superintendent Rintoul occupied a seat in Munro's combination. People stopped to stare as the three swept on. Out on the open road, however, they were past before any walker had time to stare. Rintoul spoke no more till they reached the point where the Arrochmore policies border the main road. There just before Munro had to slow down in order to take the sharp turn through the gateway into the drive, they overtook Mr. Cresswell, striding along with a blue cardboard box tucked under his arm. They shot past before he could turn his head, but he gave them a hail, though whether to ask a lift or as a jesting protest at the dangerous speed, Cameron could not tell. Anyway a lift was out of the question. But Rintoul from his seat looked up at his sergeant perched behind Munro.

"Maybe there's nothing in it after all," he remarked hopefully.

Any comment from Cameron was prevented when Munro braked so sharply that the sergeant was flung forward onto the driver's back. In another instant all three went swinging over as Munro swerved his outfit round to enter the drive. But by the time they passed the fork and was heading up for Duchray, Rintoul appeared to have changed his mind and taken a more serious view of the housekeeper's call. For at this point he broke silence again, pointing to the pathway beyond the tennis lawns.

"You'll allow none of these people inside," he said. Cameron, looking across, saw several men running along the brick pathway towards Duchray. Presently, when the road converged a little nearer to the path, he recognized the men. Harwood was leading, followed by

Toplis and Joliffe with the boy Richard several yards behind. They were all running hard, but Munro soon left them behind. At the door two people awaited their arrival, one an elderly woman with grizzled hair and face working with emotion, was evidently the housekeeper. Beside her stood the tutor, Mr. Bray.

Rintoul entered the house with the woman at his heels. Cameron posted himself on the doorstep to execute his orders. He could hear the excited voice of the housekeeper explaining to Rintoul within. In another minute, one after another, the men they had passed coming up gathered round the tutor, questioning him.

"Well," Cameron overheard him say, "I really don't know. Richard and I were over at the edge of the wood there"—he indicated the belt of trees which ran along the edge of the hill parallel to the path connecting the two houses. "Richard was having a shot or two at the crows when Mrs. Murchison ran across to tell me Mr. Brent was in the library with the door locked and wouldn't answer her knocking. After trying the windows, I sent Richard for you fellows."

"But why send for the police?" Harwood said. "Did you see anything inside?"

"No," Bray replied. "We did that after we had—after Richard, I mean—had kicked at the door loudly enough to waken him if he had been only asleep."

Rintoul came outside again.

"There's no key in the lock," he said.

"Mrs. Murchison says she heard a shot," Bray announced.

Harwood looked at Rintoul.

"She must have heard several if Dick was shooting within fifty yards of the house," he said.

"Quite," said Joliffe. "He's probably only fainted."

Rintoul waved them back and turned to his sergeant.

"Go and have a look," he said. "I'll see what can be done with the windows."

Cameron put his nose to the keyhole; there was no smell of gunpowder. He could see the whole length of the room which, as he already knew, was lit by two windows in the front and one in the gable. The rows of books on the left wall were plainly visible as well as the arm-chairs fronting the fireplace. He could see the diagonal squares of sunlight from the two front windows which threw the variously colored book-bindings into bright relief. But the windows by which the sunlight entered were beyond the range of his vision. On that side of the room he could see no more than one-half of the writing-table which occupied the centre. When he saw Rintoul's figure at the gable window reaching up to examine the fastening, he went out to rejoin him. Munro was keeping the others well away from the windows.

"I can see the sole of a shoe behind the writing-table," the super-intendent whispered. "Bring me one of Munro's tire levers."

Rintoul pocketed the knife with which he had been vainly trying to push back the catch.

He inserted the level at the bottom of the window with a small stone as fulcrum.

"Funny there's no key in the door," he said, as he put his weight to it.

But the motor-cycle tire lever was too light for this work and made no impression on the window-sash. Rintoul, withdrawing the lever, put up his handkerchief close to the catch and with one sharp jab pushed the lever through the glass.

They got Brent lying behind the writing-table on his left side, one leg doubled under him and the other stretched full length. His right hand projected into the knee-hole of the writing-desk. His head had apparently hit the waste-paper basket when he fell, and the basket now lay on its side, making a sort of grotesque headgear for the dead man, whose face was half covered by its contents. It was this basket which had prevented Cameron from seeing more than he did through the keyhole. Rintoul touched Cameron's arm and indicated the writing-table. Lying on the maroon leather surface he saw a revolver and some blank sheets of notepaper.

"Ring up Macfarlane," Rintoul said. "This looks bad."

When Cameron returned, after getting the doctor on the 'phone, he found the superintendent on his knees beside the body, carefully removing the scraps of torn paper which had fallen about the head and face. Cameron could not then tell whether the man was dead or not. So far no wound was visible. Then, as Rintoul's deft fingers lifted away the torn scrap of a blue envelope from Brent's right ear, Cameron saw that the revolver had been used; on the temple between the eyebrow and the ear a round hole with discolored edges became visible. After that discovery there was little more to do until Macfarlane arrived. Rintoul, however, remained on his knees and Cameron went down beside him.

"Something fishy about it," Rintoul murmured, his eyes going everywhere.

"You mean about the key not being in the door, sir?" Cameron breathed back.

Rintoul did not seem to hear. He was gazing fixedly into the knee-hole of the desk.

"Look there," he said, pointing. Near the man's hand, on the floor there lay a pen.

Cameron heard Rintoul's breath coming and going rather like the breath of a man blown with running. The sergeant himself was struck by the juxtaposition of the pen on the floor, the revolver on the desk above it, and the dead man's hand between the two. Which had he been using last? The same tremendous question appeared to present itself to Rintoul. He stretched his hand over the body and picked up the pen by its top. Then, holding it carefully, Cameron saw him apply it to one of the scraps of paper on the floor: the ink on the pen was not yet dry. This somehow seemed a startling discovery. But the next moment the sergeant could not see anything this fact could prove. A broad-nibbed pen like that would remain moist for a long time. The significant thing to him was the absence of the door-key from the lock. It looked as if someone after shooting Brent had gone out by the door, locked it from the outside, pocketed the key and walked off. Whoever that assassin might be he certainly could not be Hugh Cameron, or any of his friends. Even if any of them could have come there, neither they nor anyone else could have shot Brent in mistake for Mr. Willoughby.

Cameron saw Rintoul step away thoughtfully till he reached the hearthrug. It was as if he too did not know what to make of this new turn the affair had taken, and wished to get far enough away from it to view it objectively.

As the superintendent stood leaning his forehead against his arms placed on the mantelpiece, a clamor of voices arose outside.

Through the gable window Cameron saw Munro's back and out-stretched hands. Beyond him Cresswell and Harwood were holding a young woman who was trying to break from them and enter the room. Cameron knew the wild-eyed girl to be Miss Willoughby. She ceased struggling as soon as she saw him emerge through the window.

"Is he dead?" she whispered.

"He is badly hurt," Cameron said. "We are waiting for the doctor."

"I must see him," she cried with sudden vehemence.

They all tried to keep the distraught girl quiet. But she listened to the sergeant when he told her it would be more helpful to Mr. Brent if she went with the housekeeper to get ready some room to which he would presently be carried.

When Cameron re-entered the library he found Rintoul waiting for him.

"It's not only the business of the key," Rintoul said, "there's the pen too."

"Yes, sir," Cameron said expectantly. He did not see that the pen said anything.

"The pen was wet with ink, yet as you see for yourself, sergeant, he wrote nothing."

The sergeant took the point: the sheets of notepaper lying on the desk had not been used.

"If he used the pen," Rintoul went on, "it looks as if someone has carried away whatever it was he wrote. On the other hand, if he wrote nothing why did he dip the pen in the ink?"

Cameron found no comment to make.

"It's curious too," Rintoul resumed, "that we should find the pen on the floor and the revolver on the desk—just the reverse of what you would expect their respective positions to be."

"I don't think he shot himself," Cameron said with conviction.

"Well, it's just possible the revolver could have fallen where we found it, supposing he'd been bending over the desk when he used it, and it's easy to suppose he flung the pen where we saw it lying, but where is what he wrote and where is the key of the door? No," Rintoul resumed, after staring for a time into vacancy, "it begins to look as if our original suspicions were well placed after all, sergeant."

Cameron did not remind his superior that those original suspicions had been scouted as far-fetched and fantastical.

"There's no getting over the fact that the key has been carried away, and possibly whatever this man wrote just before the shot was fired."

From outside they heard the throb of an engine, and the slight squeak of a brake as a car halted at the door.

"Macfarlane at last," Rintoul said, going towards the window which afforded the only entrance to the room.

It did not take the doctor long to see that Brent was beyond his help. Macfarlane evidently assumed that the wound was self-inflicted. As soon as he rose to his feet he turned to Rintoul.

"I wonder what the trouble was?" he said. "He did worry a lot over that arm. He was a fine pianist, I understand."

Rintoul looked down at the body.

"Never yet heard of a man shooting himself because he couldn't play the piano anymore," he said.

"Oh, I don't know," Macfarlane replied. "Some authorities will tell you every genius is half mad, peculiarly susceptible to fits of extreme depression, and of course musicians suffer most from egotism."

Rintoul assisted Munro to lift the body onto a couch. Cameron, at Rintoul's direction, was about to go through the pockets when both were attracted by a slight exclamation from the doctor. He had stooped to the floor and picked up a sheet of notepaper which had been lying under the body.

"Ah!" he said, handing the paper to the superintendent. "There you are."

Over Rintoul's shoulder, Cameron read:

"Darling—I am sick of all this. Why did yo—"

"Yes," Macfarlane commented, "poor young devil, he turned sick, it seems, even of writing before he got out what he was sick about."

Rintoul kept staring at the paper like a man who could hardly believe his eyes. Cameron felt that way himself. Macfarlane, of course, knew nothing of the locked door and the absent key. Suddenly

Rintoul stepped across to the couch and began to go through the dead man's pockets. Almost at once Cameron saw his hand stop.

"Ah," he said, "this explains it."

He drew out a key of a size which suggested it might be the missing door-key. Rintoul at once demonstrated this to be the fact by opening the door with it.

"You were right, doctor. Of course you've had opportunities of seeing his mental condition."

Macfarlane nodded. "He worried enough about that arm," he said. "And it was worse than I told him. He must have guessed what I didn't tell him."

Cameron covered the body up with a rug. The discovery of the key, and what was evidently going to be a letter of farewell to Miss Willoughby, had completely altered the case. Once more Hugh Cameron came into the affair. Not indeed as principal in Brent's death, but certainly as the ultimate cause of it, morally, though not legally, guilty.

Cameron drew Rintoul's attention to the presence of Mr. Willoughby, who had joined the group standing out on the lawn. He looked white and shaken. When the sergeant brought him inside, it was the poacher's responsibility for the tragedy that seemed to affect him most.

"That shot on the moor was meant for me, you know," he said. "I feel deeply about it. If I hadn't got that ruffian convicted poor Brent would be alive now."

Both Rintoul and the doctor attempted consolation.

"You only did your duty, sir," Rintoul said. "You couldn't foresee all that was to follow."

"I certainly never anticipated anything like this," Macfarlane added, "and I can assure you I kept a close watch on his mental reaction to his wound."

Mr. Willoughby sighed and shook his head.

"Perhaps I'm not quite so free of blame there as you think," he said. "Perhaps I ought to have warned you his father shot himself—"

Macfarlane threw up his head.

"Ah!" he cried, "that explains a lot."

"Too late to be of any good now," Mr. Willoughby said with remorse, "but, of course, I never anticipated anything like this," he added, appealing to Rintoul.

Rintoul sympathetically agreed.

"Of course you didn't, sir, and one naturally keeps quiet about such a fact when there is no occasion to mention it."

"Do you know if the young man was aware how his father died?" Macfarlane asked.

"I understood he did," Mr. Willoughby replied. "The case somehow did not get much publicity, but I heard the facts from Mr. Harwood. Mr. Brent was rather an odd old gentleman with a penchant for all sorts of inventions. He shot himself over the failure of some rather wild-cat invention on which he had spent a considerable sum."

Rintoul and Macfarlane exchanged a glance. The doctor waved a hand as if no more need be said. Rintoul, too, as he pocketed the revolver, considered that the tragedy now stood explained. Then something made him turn again to Mr. Willoughby.

"You said, sir, you heard the facts from Mr. Harwood. How did he come to know them if the case got little publicity?"

"Oh, that's quite simple," Mr. Willoughby promptly replied. "He had inside knowledge from his father, who was the senior partner of the firm of solicitors, Harwood and Cresswell, then acting for Mr. Brent."

Superintendent Rintoul, after assisting Cameron to seal up the room, left Duchray feeling that he had a perfectly straightforward case to put before the Procurator-Fiscal next morning. All the same, he was more than ever determined to get at Hugh Cameron for that attempt on Mr. Willoughby's life, which was, beyond doubt, the real cause of young Brent's death.

CHAPTER XII

MRS. BRENT SHOCKS THE FISCAL

Rintoul, on his return to the office, took up the case of Hugh Cameron at the point where consideration of it had been stopped by the telephone call from Duchray. But Brent's death made him keener than ever, since he now regarded Hugh Cameron as a murderer morally if not legally. The sergeant's investigations having destroyed Cameron's alibi, the next step was to establish his presence on the moor about the time of the shooting. Rintoul's idea was that the Sergeant and Munro might scout around Keppoch and find some shepherd, forester or road-man who had seen the man in the vicinity. It would be something if they could come on any person who had seen him— say—on the Keppoch road at all, since he had asserted that after leaving work he had taken the Arkaig road to his mother's house, and the Keppoch road to the moor went in exactly the opposite direction.

Cameron thought it not unlikely he would find someone who had seen the young man on the Keppoch road, for if he had been on it at all he had been on it at a time when road men and outdoor workers were usually making for their homes. After that his denial that he had been on that road to the moor, when taken together with the smashed alibi, his purchase of the gun in Inverness and his possession of the No. 5 cartridges, would leave him with a case to answer when Rintoul next confronted him with it.

So, at least, Rintoul was thinking when after a tap on his door Munro entered to say that Mr. Willoughby had brought down Mrs. Brent to see the superintendent. Mr. Willoughby, in fact, entered on Munro's heels.

"Sorry to bother you," he said apologetically, "but she insisted on coming, and in the circumstances—"

"Oh, I quite understand," Rintoul said as he rose. "I'll go and see her."

Mr. Willoughby stopped him.

"She insists on seeing you in private," he said. "I'm afraid we'll have to carry her in."

Cameron, gathering up his papers, was about to leave the room as Mr. Willoughby and Munro came back carrying the old lady seated in the office chair. But Mrs. Brent stopped him.

"No, no!" she said. "I want you. You seemed to understand that night."

At an imperceptible nod from his superior as the others left, Cameron shut the door and stood attentive till she ordered him to sit down.

Mrs. Brent's first words, however, might easily have made an officer of less self-control jump from his seat.

"I want Scotland Yard called in," she said.

This, at least, lifted Rintoul's eyebrows.

"Scotland Yard!" he repeated.

"Yes. This is a case for them."

Rintoul stretched out his hand on the table before which he sat.

"But, my dear lady," he said, "you forget you are in Scotland. Scotland Yard does not operate here."

"What!" she cried, a change coming over her features. "Ah, then they chose their place well," she said, with a nod of conviction. "Yes, this was the right place to do it."

Rintoul sat up.

"Oh, come, madam," he said half reproachfully, "we're not such fools as all that up here. If we were, you may be sure we would have had a Scotland Yard of our own. Come now, just speak to me as if I came from Scotland Yard."

"But you don't," she said. "You don't, and this is no time for play-acting."

Rintoul got rather nettled.

"Very well," he said. "I'm afraid I can't help you if that's your attitude."

Mrs. Brent nervously passed her hand across her overbright eyes.

"Then I shall have to keep what I had to say till the inquest," she said.

Rintoul looked over at Cameron.

"I'm sorry, Mrs. Brent," he said apologetically and half repenting of his previous sharpness, "but again I have to remind you we are in Scotland: there are no inquests here."

Mrs. Brent's amazement seemed to overcome her arthritis. She seemed about to rise in her chair.

"What!" she cried. "No inquest? What a country! Oh, but they chose well, they chose well!" she added brokenly, getting out her handkerchief.

Rintoul gave her a moment or two to recover.

"Now, Mrs. Brent," he said soothingly, "please let me reassure you. If we have no coroner we have an official which some consider rather more formidable—the Procurator-Fiscal—who is quite as thorough in his work, though he carries it through in private."

Cameron saw her head go up with almost a jerk.

"In private?" she repeated, her eyes glittering as she bent forward intently. "Do you mean none of the other witnesses know what has been said by anyone else?"

"Indeed they don't," Rintoul declared. "The Procurator-Fiscal takes precognitions from each in turn privately, and forms his own judgment on the evidence. And if he considers there is even a suspicion of crime he takes immediate action for a prosecution. He will be here to-morrow, you know."

There was a long pause.

"Very well," she said at length, "I'm glad you have an official like that. He sounds as if he is very suitable for what I have to say."

"Of course, if you would like to say anything to me—" Rintoul began.

She shook her head with decision.

"No, thank you. It will keep till to-morrow." Then looking round, she saw the sergeant. "There's just this one thing," she added. "This officer of yours, I know he suspected something that night when he stayed at Duchray after my boy was first shot on the moor. Will he tell to-morrow what it was he suspected then?"

Cameron shifted uneasily in his seat. Rintoul himself seemed to be hunting for an answer to this query. The sergeant could not imagine what his superintendent would say, for of course that far-fetched suspicion against Mr. Cresswell had been long since abandoned. Mrs. Brent got impatient.

"If I put it to him," she cried, "will he deny that he was there because he expected another attack to be made on my boy that night?"

"He will not," Rintoul said, sitting up alertly at the challenge; "but he will also tell the Procurator that his suspicion was a mistake."

In view, however, of what Mrs. Brent had said, Rintoul decided that Cameron must be present for possible questions by the Procurator-Fiscal next day. So Munro was sent off alone to scout for witnesses against Hugh Cameron.

The inquiry opened at ten next morning in the library at Duchray.

Mr. Murray, the Procurator-Fiscal, was a cold-eyed, tight-lipped man of about fifty, who brought much of the incisiveness of speech and curtness of manner acquired as a provost-marshal during the war into his postwar functions. Indeed, he looked quite formidable as he sat at the table with Superintendent Rintoul at one end and the sergeant taking notes at the other. Rintoul had passed him the word that there might be a little trouble with the deceased's mother. And this determined the Procurator as to the order in which the witnesses were called. He wanted to hear every one else before he heard Mrs. Brent.

The housekeeper, Mrs. Murchison, came first. It was, she said, half-past three when she heard the shot. She knew the time for she was about to make herself a cup of tea which she always did at that time. Except for Mr. Brent she was alone in the house. Mr. Willoughby, half an hour earlier, had called with his car to take Dr. Frossard and Mrs. Brent for a drive. While she went upstairs to help Mrs. Brent, Mr. Willoughby had gone into the library to persuade Dr. Frossard also to come. Yes, Mr. Brent was already at that time in the library too. She knew that because he had been using his mother's wheel-chair lately, and she saw the chair standing at the library door. She did not know if Mr. Brent had also been asked to go for a drive; but she did not think so. Asked why she did not think so, her reply was that if Mr. Brent went Dr. Frossard would have to stay, since with the chauffeur there would be no room for more in the car. It was Mr. Willoughby and Dr. Frossard who carried Mrs. Brent downstairs. After seeing them off she went upstairs and put Mrs. Brent's room to rights and then went to the kitchen and put on the kettle. She remembered it had just begun to boil when she heard the shot in the library.

At this point Cameron saw Rintoul scribble something on a scrap of paper and pass it to the Procurator. After reading it the Procurator put a question to Mrs. Murchison.

"Did you go at once to investigate?"

"Well, no, sir, not quite at once. You see, sir, I got so flustered I ran back upstairs to one of the maid's rooms, forgetting she had been sent for to Arrochmore, and that it was the other maid's afternoon off; but I did try the door as soon as I got downstairs again. Then when I ran outside I saw Mr. Bray, and after we had tried the door again and all the windows, he told me to ring up the police."

Mr. Murray looked over questioningly at Rintoul. Rintoul's nod brought an end to the housekeeper's ordeal.

"I'd like to see this Mr. Bray next," Mr. Murray said, while completing his notes.

Mr. Bray took up his position before the table with his hands behind his back, much as if he were about to face a *viva-voce* examination for deacon's orders. The Procurator, when he looked up, was quick to perceive the young man's nervousness, and as if in pity, put his questions with a suavity and gentleness worthy of any bishop's examining chaplain.

"Ah, Mr. Bray, you must have been alarmed to see the housekeeper run from the house," he began.

"Yes, I was," Mr. Bray agreed. "I thought the house had got on fire or something."

"You didn't hear the shot in the library?"

"Oh, no!"

"You heard no shot at all?"

"Oh, yes, I did—in the wood, of course."

The Procurator looked puzzled. Mr. Bray stood stiffly awaiting further questions.

"In the wood?" Mr. Murray repeated, his eyes narrowing. "Who was shooting in the wood?"

"Well, Richard was—Mr. Willoughby's son, who is my pupil. Thought him a bit reckless with his new gun. That's why I ordered him to leave the wood."

"Ah! Not your pupil in shooting then?" Mr. Murray permitted himself a smile. "Do you think a shot might have been fired in this room without your hearing it?"

Mr. Bray shifted about as if facing a poser from the bishop's chaplain.

"Yes," he said at length, "before I came out onto the lawn it might."

Again Rintoul pushed a scrap of paper along the table.

"Did you see any one leave the house as you came out of the wood?"

"Nobody but the housekeeper," Mr. Bray replied.

"And after hearing her story you examined the windows?"

"Yes. Then I sent Richard to Arrochmore for help."

Mr. Bray took his dismissal with a quite audible sigh of relief. He had answered all the questions.

When he had gone the Procurator and the superintendent put their heads together.

"The person who last saw him alive next, I think."

"Dr. Frossard." Rintoul nodded to Munro, who was acting as usher.

The doctor entered, as self-possessed as his predecessor had been nervous. He was a bulky man, so ponderous that his movements seemed lethargic. Indeed, everything about him, except his eyes, suggested he was only half awake. His voice was deep and sonorous and his slow utterances in marked contrast to the jerky replies of Mr. Bray. But he took quite as long to make his answers although the questions addressed to him seemed quite as simple.

"Mr. Brent was in the library with you, I believe, when Mr. Willoughby called?" the Procurator began.

"That is so."

"Did you have any talk together?"

Dr. Frossard stroked his chin several times before the reply came.

"No. I was reading by the open window when the young man entered and, as he did not look my way, I said nothing."

"You thought there was something peculiar about him?"

Dr. Frossard waved a hand.

"Not more than usual. We lived in two different worlds, he and I. I am interested in classic antiquities. We had nothing in common."

"So no word passed between you?"

Dr. Frossard shrugged in an almost foreign way.

"He did not even lift his head till Mr. Willoughby came in. When he heard Mr. Willoughby invite me to go out I saw him look up to see what I would say—that is all."

"Ah!" the Procurator nodded, "you think he was anxious that you should accept?"

"I think he was anxious to have the library to himself," Frossard replied more promptly. "He was quite cordial to Mr. Willoughby, and wished him a pleasant drive."

"Just one more question," the Procurator said. "Did you notice when you left the room whether the key was in the lock or not?"

Frossard appeared to be surprised at the question.

"I would not notice a thing like that," he declared, as if keys in doors were articles unworthy of notice by a student of classic antiquities. Then he looked up suddenly like a man who recalls something to the point.

"Yes?" Murray said, observing the symptom.

"It must have been in the lock though," Frossard said. "You see, after I got to my room I remembered some notes I had been making and thinking they might get scattered by the draught from the open window I went down again to bring them away. But I found Brent had locked the door." Frossard breathed heavily for a moment. "He—he gave no heed to my knocking." It was clear he had difficulty in suppressing the annoyance this remembrance brought back.

"What did you do then?" Murray asked.

"Went back to get ready for the drive, naturally."

"Let me see? You went down, I suppose, after Mr. Willoughby had left the room?"

"Yes. He had come upstairs himself, to help with Mrs. Brent. I heard him talking to her in her room as I went down."

The Procurator bowed.

"Thank you," he said; "that is all, I think."

Dr. Frossard lumbered out of the room.

Mr. Willoughby, who followed the doctor, proved to be more helpful. It was obvious as his answers proceeded that the Procurator foresaw an end to the case so far as he himself was concerned. Mr. Brent, said Mr. Willoughby, was a musician with genius, though as yet more full of promise than achievement. He was certainly, like all artists, liable to fits of depression. But he had certainly not revealed the extent of the depression caused by the wound to his arm. This unusual reticence deceived both the witness and his daughter, since the young man had no more capacity for hiding his feelings than most artists.

"Ah!" the Procurator nodded, "that artistic temperament again!"

Mr. Willoughby agreed, adding that he had carefully watched Mr. Brent's mental reactions to his injury, and misreading his condition, had not thought it necessary to inform his medical attendant of a certain fact in his family history.

The Procurator nodded sympathetically.

"I appreciate that," he said. "You mean—his father's death?"

"I blame myself for it," Mr. Willoughby admitted. "But, as I say, the poor young fellow gave no outward indication of the extent of his depression. Even when I left him in the library he quite cheerfully wished me a pleasant drive."

The Procurator took from his dispatch case the sheet of paper found under the body.

"Yet he wrote this note," he said musingly. "You have seen this? I suppose we can take it that it was addressed to your daughter?" Then he added, "I am anxious not to trouble Miss Willoughby, and I don't think we need, if you can tell me to what it refers."

"Obviously to the worry caused by his conviction that his career was ended," Mr. Willoughby replied. "That, of course, was very hard on my daughter, but you know that with artists their art comes first; and in any case he was not himself."

The Procurator sighed sympathetically.

"Yes," he said, "it seems a clear, straightforward case. Just one thing more, Mr. Willoughby, and there will be no need to detain you further. This revolver—did you know he had it?"

The question seemed to pain Mr. Willoughby. He shook his head sorrowfully.

"If I had known of that," he said, "I would have taken much greater precautions."

When the door closed the Procurator turned to the Superintendent of Police.

"I was wondering if we need trouble his mother," he said.

"I'm afraid she insists on being heard," Rintoul said. "In fact, I promised her a hearing." Then in response to Mr. Murray's lifted eyebrows he added, "Oh, the usual thing—the hen and her chicken, you know. When anything happens she suspects everything and everybody."

The Procurator nodded his understanding.

"Then we must certainly hear her," he said.

Mrs. Brent wheeled herself across to the table, rather startling the Procurator, who had forgotten her condition. Half in compunction he greeted her with great courtesy, and the old lady rather warmed to him, some of the hard determination melting from her face.

"You want to make a statement to me, Mrs. Brent?" he began.

"I want to tell you my son was shot by someone," she declared bluntly.

Mr. Murray bent forward over the table. His function as Procurator-Fiscal had brought him often enough face to face with wild charges, recklessly advanced by distraught relatives in these hours of shock and distress. He was not now so much taken by surprise as Mrs. Brent expected.

"Well," he said gently, "so far I've had no evidence that even hinted such a thing."

"That means you are going to do nothing—like the rest," she cried.

He put up his hand soothingly.

"If you have anything to go on, tell me. I don't ask for evidence from you, I'll act even on any reasonable suspicion."

Mrs. Brent lifted her clenched and trembling hand.

"My boy did not shoot himself," she declared. "I know him too well to believe that."

"Now, now, Mrs. Brent, let's be reasonable," Mr. Murray pleaded. "From the statements I have already taken I know your poor boy locked himself into this very room the moment he had it to himself. He was in a depressed condition of mind about his arm. Once you had gone away in the car for a drive with Mr. Willoughby and Dr. Frossard he was alone in the house except for Mrs. Murchison, the housekeeper. He had been waiting till he was alone. He was so determined not to be disturbed or interfered with that he not only locked the door and pocketed the key, but also shut and bolted the one window that was open when Dr. Frossard left the room. We know he did these things independently of all the statements made to me, for the police found the door locked and every window bolted when they arrived about fifteen minutes after the housekeeper summoned them."

Mrs. Brent shook her head with decision.

"All that makes no difference to me," she said. "I don't pretend to know how it was done, but done it was, by somebody."

The official patience seemed equal even to this.

"Suppose the impossible," he said. "Suppose it could be done in the circumstances I have stated, who was there to do it? Surely you don't suspect the housekeeper?"

"There were others," she declared.

"Not in the house. There was, in fact, no one near the house at the time except the young gentleman, Mr. Bray, who, I understand, is going to be a clergyman."

Mrs. Brent sniffed.

"Clergymen are not always what they ought to be," she said; "but I don't suspect him."

"Then whom do you suspect?" Murray demanded, with just an edge of sharpness in his voice. "No one else, I assure you, harbors any such suspicion."

The old lady fixed her glittering eyes on Cameron at the end of the table and then extended her hand at the sergeant.

"Ask him who he suspected," she cried. "Ask him who he suspected when he watched over Eric all the night after he was shot on the moor."

Rintoul intervened.

"We have good reason for believing there is no connection between that shooting and this tragic occurrence," he said firmly. "We believe we know who was responsible for the shooting on the moor,

Mrs. Brent. But the man who wounded your son on the moor shot at him mistaking him for another. The man, that is, shot at him because your son happened to be wearing Mr. Willoughby's coat."

"I know better. The man who shot at my son was well enough aware that he was wearing Mr. Willoughby's coat. There were four who had seen him put it on and who had been on the moor with him all day."

Quite a long pause followed this wild suggestion. Cameron began to wonder and doubt, once more, about his original suspicion of Cresswell. He had just decided against her that Cresswell at least was an impossible suspect when Mr. Murray, relaxing from his official attitude, again leaned over the table towards the grim figure in the wheel-chair.

"Mrs. Brent," he began gently, "I understand you do not approve of our Scottish procedure in a case like this. You would rather have a coroner than a Procurator-Fiscal. Let me show you one advantage we have over the coroner's court. We are here in private. You can tell me anything you know. Whatever you say, you say without the least fear of press publicity. You will find me ready to take action on something much less than evidence—even on suspicion."

Mrs. Brent seemed impressed.

"I'm not sure," she said in an altered tone, "just who did it; but I am sure it was one of the four young men."

"And the motive?"

"Mary Willoughby," Mrs. Brent replied promptly. "She's been coquetting with them all in turn, one after the other."

Murray and Rintoul stared at each other. Here at last was something new that might well have a direct bearing on the case, though in a direction quite different from that entertained by the young man's mother.

"A heartless little jade," Mrs. Brent interjected into their thoughts. "She wasn't above flirting even with that silly Mr. Bray."

Murray sat up.

"Yes," he said, "and am I to take it that your son was affected by her conduct?"

"Of course he was. He was practically engaged to her."

"He talked to you about it?"

"Never. He wasn't the sort to do that."

"Brooded over it?"

"He thought of nothing else. When he was lying there in bed I could see it in his eyes. She counted for much more to him after he had been wounded, you see. He thought she was all he had left."

The Procurator-Fiscal nodded wisely.

"Ah, Mrs. Brent, don't you now see what happened? It would have been better if he had talked about it. He brooded over it, and he brooded over the threatened end to his career so long that—well, he thought that an end had come to everything, and so he made an end to himself."

"No, no!" she cried, with sudden vehemence. "Never!"

"But yes," Murray persisted. "Why, look at this." He disclosed the revolver lying on the table. "That weapon, he died with it beside him in a locked room. There's no getting over that, you know."

She gazed with awe-struck eyes at the heavy six-chambered revolver.

"I never saw it before," she said. "It never belonged to him."

"He evidently had it without your knowledge," Murray said.

"Never!" she cried. "It's impossible. I've been too often through his things not to know what he has and hasn't got. Don't you believe that is his! When he was transferred here from Arrochmore I packed up all his things with my own hands, and I certainly did not bring that with me."

"But he could have got it afterwards without your knowing."

"How?" she demanded. "He has not been to Arrochmore since the attack on him. He has only been outside this house once or twice in my chair, and then only with someone to wheel him in it."

The Procurator-Fiscal for the first time betrayed a touch of uneasiness. He shifted about in his chair.

"You are quite sure of what you say?"

"Ask the nurse. Ask Mrs. Murchison. Both are quite familiar with everything he possessed. Ever since he got out of bed they've had to help him into his clothes. Mrs. Murchison has had to do it since the nurse left. Yesterday, as it happens, he changed his mind about what he would wear, and when the housekeeper got the flannel suit from the trunk in which it was packed, I took it on my knees and felt it all over to make sure it was not damp. You don't suppose I'd pass over a thing like that without knowing it was there."

The Procurator balanced the heavy revolver in his hand thoughtfully. Rintoul, who had been sitting with his chin cupped in both hands, looked up.

"Someone might have brought it to him, mightn't they?" he suggested.

Mrs. Brent's eyes flashed.

"Someone might," she said, "if they had had the chance. I took care they had not. Ever since he was shot on the moor and these people"—she waved her hand at Rintoul—"began to look elsewhere, I knew he had only me to watch over him." She bowed her head. "And someone got him the very first time I left him alone."

Mrs. Brent's intense conviction impressed the Procurator-Fiscal. He was fascinated, too, by the contrast between her deeply-furrowed and mask-like face and her glittering eyes. Incapable of moving much more than her arms and head, those dark, almost youthful eyes, set in the white, worn face, revealed the alertness of her mind.

"You surely see," she said, with sudden quietness, "that whoever shot him, simply had to leave that weapon behind for you to find?"

They left this unanswered, but an almost imperceptible sign from the Procurator drew the superintendent to his side. They conferred together in whispers, the old lady anxiously watching them. After a little the Procurator looked up.

"We're going to recall the housekeeper," he said. "You may remain on the condition that you say nothing."

They all sat in a queer, stiff sort of silence till Munro showed Mrs. Murchison in.

"Ah, Mrs. Murchison," Murray said, "sorry to bother you again, but we have just one more question to put. This weapon, do you think Mr. Brent could have had it without your knowing he had it?"

Mrs. Murchison, who had been gazing in horror at the ugly blue-black revolver, shook her head.

"Oh, no, sir," she said, "it isn't possible. With him so helpless like that. I know what he had and hadn't got as well as himself."

"You haven't seen it before then? I mean, don't you think it might have been lying somewhere about the house?"

"No, sir. I know what's in the house. Somebody must have brought it here and left it behind on the very day."

When Mrs. Murchison had gone another conference followed, this time behind the Procurator's chair, and this time the sergeant overheard something of what passed. The Procurator shook his head in response to something the superintendent had murmured almost in his ear.

"No," he said, "I don't like it. I don't like it at all."

"Why?" Rintoul's lips formed rather than uttered the question.

"I don't know. I just simply don't like the look of it."

Then he turned to Mrs. Brent who, if she had not overheard as much as Cameron, was quick enough to divine a divergence of opinion between the Procurator and the superintendent of police.

"This is a case for an expert," she said. "The police here have no experience of any crime worse than poaching. And it's my belief this crime was committed here because the police in a place like this are so unsuspicious and inexperienced."

Murray held up his hand protestingly.

"You are doing them an injustice," he said. "They are as anxious to see you satisfied as I am myself. Now look here, Mrs. Brent, I can show you an advantage our Scottish procedure has in such a case. I can recommend an expert to you who, if experience can do it, will set your mind at rest, one way or the other. It's true," he went on, "I do not know him personally, but I have heard good accounts of his work in London."

Mrs. Brent sat forward.

"Oh, London! That's talking," she cried. Murray continued as if he had not heard her:

"As a matter of fact I've just been hearing again about him from a doctor friend of mine with whom he happens to be fishing on Loch Laggan at the present moment. Now—of course this is between ourselves, isn't it?" He waited for her nod of assent. "Well, my suggestion is that he should come and see you. You needn't be told, I'm sure, that not another soul outside this room"—he glanced first at Cameron, the only other present except Rintoul—"must know who he is. He'd better come as your lawyer—most natural that you should have to consult your lawyer at this moment. If he consents I'll get him to send you a telegram. You will show this telegram to Mr. Willoughby, and I have no doubt that, in the circumstances, no one would think it unusual if you should ask for him to stay at Duchray for a day or two." Murray brought his eyes back to the figure in the chair.

"What do you think of that?" he concluded.

Mrs. Brent struck the arm of her chair.

"Think of it?" she cried. "It's exactly what I want. Now we'll see."

CHAPTER XIII
A ROOM IN LOCH LAGGAN HOTEL

That same night three men sat talking together in the little smoking-room of the Loch Laggan Hotel. Procurator-Fiscal Murray had
reached the hotel about six-thirty, and, hearing that Dr. Dunn and
his friend were not yet returned, but were certain to be back for
dinner at seven-thirty, seated himself on the wall with a pipe to watch
the loch for the returning boat. In the interval since morning his
mind was busy with the facts of the case he had been investigating,
and, until he heard the boat grate on the shingle below, he remained
doubtful as to whether, after all, he would call in this detective friend
of Dunn's. He had made the promise to Mrs. Brent on the impulse of
the moment, moved, too, by the knowledge that this Francis MacNab
of whom he had heard so much from Dunn, chanced to be on the
spot. Rintoul, on principle, had been against bringing him into the
case; but Rintoul later acknowledged that he himself had reached an
impasse. And, after all, the responsibility for reporting on the case
lay with the Procurator-Fiscal.

But as soon as Dunn performed the introduction Murray had
little doubt that here was a man whom he would trust. Indeed, it
amused him to see how neatly this MacNab would fit the part he had
suggested as a reason for his presence at Duchray. He looked rather
like a keen, shrewd lawyer, the junior partner in a firm of high repute
and long standing. Murray during dinner rather doubted whether the
trouble would not be to get him to take up the case at all. As it happened, however, luck was with him, for the pair had caught no fish
that day and, as it turned out, had little hope of doing any better so
long as the hot, bright weather lasted.

The cautious Murray, however, when an adjournment was made
to the smoke-room, began to state his case as a sort of after-dinner
story likely to interest MacNab. He told it, that is, in anecdotal fashion to illustrate the kind of duty occasionally put on an official in his
position. And Dunn, though interested in the medical details, obviously regarded it in the light in which it was presented. But out of the
corner of his eye Murray noticed before he had gone very far a change
come over MacNab's face. It was not that he altered his lazy attitude
in the big arm-chair, but just a certain tightening of the mouth which
followed a swift exchange of glances between himself and MacNab.
After that Murray knew that, though Dunn might still think his visit
was no more than a friendly call, the detective was under no such
misapprehension.

"You see," Murray went on, "this woman, Brent's mother, is convinced that he never shot himself."

Dunn nodded.

"That conviction of course has a psychological background," he
said. "As his mother, he was so precious to her, she is unwilling to
believe he could destroy himself."

"There's more in it than that," Murray said. "She's quite convinced
there's a connection between what happened on the moor and what
happened in the house. What happened in the house she believes to
be the completion of what was attempted on the moor. Well," he went
on, "of course when I heard from the doctor about the depression he
developed through fear that the injury to his arm would put a stop
to his career as a pianist, it seemed a straightforward case of suicide
in a moment of mental derangement. In fact, I was quite prepared to
be satisfied on the evidence advanced with that obvious conclusion
till I came up against one little fact." Murray looked over from Dunn,
who was nursing his knee, to the immobile figure lying in the big
arm-chair.

"And that was?" MacNab's voice came.

"We simply could not account for the weapon. Nobody had ever
seen it before. That began to interest me, and I can tell you I went
into it very microscopically indeed. Well, whatever lies were told me,
I made certain of this one fact at least: Brent neither owned such a
revolver nor had one in his possession, nor could have had access to
it since he got shot on the moor."

There was a silence for a time after Murray's last emphatic assertion, and through the open window from across the road there came the sound of lapping water, and the creak of an oar in rowlocks.

"Awkward fact that," came at last from the detective.

"I didn't like it at all, I can tell you," Murray nodded. "Neither did Superintendent Rintoul. We've both spent hours over that problem, but the fact stands. It's the one fact among a number of curious happenings for which no explanation could be found."

Murray began to fill a pipe with the air of a man who has reached the end of his story, and Dunn, taking this impression, went to touch the bell for drinks. MacNab put his clasped hands behind his head.

"Quite interesting," he said musingly, "to have so many odd things in one case."

Murray waited till his pipe was going.

"I know what you mean," Murray agreed, "but the odd things were odd at first sight only; they were all satisfactorily explained."

He was rather disappointed as he laid down the spent match, that he had not evoked more than this lazy impersonal interest from the supposedly great detective.

"I'd like to hear just one odd detail in the case together with the explanation offered," MacNab said unexpectedly.

"Well, there's this: The sergeant who went out to the scene of the accident on the moor came away certain that Brent had been deliberately shot. And it's worthwhile noticing as a warning what good grounds he had for that conviction. He saw at once that the shot must have been fired from a distance of some yards at least. That made him pick up the wounded man's gun, and he discovered both barrels still loaded. So he was sure Brent had been shot by one of his friends. He was almost sure he knew which of them it was, and even Rintoul himself was convinced he was right. But that was all dispelled when it was discovered that the friend suspected had carried off Brent's gun in mistake for his own, and that therefore it was this friend's gun in which the sergeant had found the two undischarged cartridges."

"But," Dunn put in, "he didn't shoot himself; the nature of the wounds would be proof of that."

Murray agreed.

"Oh, they soon knew that. You see, Brent had been wearing a white Burberry belonging to Mr. Willoughby, their host, and it is almost a certainty now that in the mist he was mistaken for Mr. Willoughby by the friends of a certain poacher who had got six months' on Mr. Willoughby's evidence. So you see Mrs. Brent's notion that what happened in the library was the completion of what was attempted on the moor could not stand."

No comment was made on this until the maid had set down the three glasses and departed.

"And the other curious happenings—they can be all as neatly explained?" MacNab asked.

"Every one of them," Murray said, "except that damned revolver."

MacNab sat up for a sip at his glass. Murray eyed him so hopefully that for the moment he forgot his own drink. The whisky apparently suggested a smoke to the detective, and he began to fill his pipe with leisurely thoughtfulness.

"Suppose this is murder," he said at length; "the revolver simply had to be left behind in order to suggest suicide."

Murray stirred impatiently.

"Of course," he agreed. "But you don't think it's murder, do you?"

"If the owner of this revolver cannot be traced," MacNab said, "it certainly doesn't look like suicide."

Murray's right fist fell with a thud on his right knee.

"Nobody knows anything about the weapon," he declared. "Nobody will own to having seen it before. It never was in Brent's possession; his mother, the nurse who must have known, never saw it. Mrs. Murchison, the housekeeper, denies that it could have been lying about the house without her knowledge. That revolver was brought into the house by someone other than Eric Brent."

Dr. Dunn sat up as if he now divined what Murray was after.

"By George, MacNab," he said, "it sounds rather like a case made to your hand."

MacNab gave one nod of unenthusiastic assent. "Well, it's very interesting. If I weren't here on a fishing holiday, and if someone in a position to do so called me in I certainly would have a try," he admitted between puffs at his pipe.

The two others exchanged a swift glance.

"Oh, come," Dunn said, "after all, the fishing is pretty poor."

"And if Mrs. Brent is right," Murray added, "there is a bigger fish to catch in this affair than ever came out of Loch Laggan."

"Deeper water, too," Dunn suggested.

"I said, if one in authority called into the case."

Dunn turned round.

"Well, Murray, what about that? You are a Procurator-Fiscal."

Murray smoothed his knee hopefully.

"Personally I'd be very glad of any help to get at the truth," he said. "Indeed, I'm bound by my office to do so. And I think Superintendent Rintoul would also welcome any efficient outside help, the case being, as he admits, at a standstill. But I happen to know a far greater authority than either of us is anxious for his assistance."

Murray's smile puzzled both the detective and the doctor, though Dunn alone gave any external sign of surprise. He sat forward eagerly.

"Who's that?" he inquired, inwardly thrilling to the guess that this far greater authority must be the Lord Advocate at least.

"His mother," Murray replied. "His mother, who had so little doubt about this being murder that she raised doubts in me when I'd begun to be sure it was nothing of the kind."

In the midst of Dunn's disappointment MacNab spoke.

"Very well," he said, "she can count on me."

CHAPTER XIV
DISCUSSION WITH RINTOUL

Next morning Dunn motored MacNab over for a consultation with Superintendent Rintoul. As they ran along the side of the loch there was nothing in the weather to deepen the regret MacNab now felt over the consent which had been wrung from him on the previous night. It was a glorious day, with no clouds to veil the sun, and the water lay clear and shining, every pine tree on the mountain opposite standing sharp and distinct. Not a hope for that kind of fish that day! But MacNab's anticipation of a cool reception from Superintendent Rintoul was not fulfilled. At first Rintoul was stiff enough in spite of the Procurator-Fiscal's preparation. And MacNab, quite understanding that Rintoul might resent receiving outside help called in by the Procurator-Fiscal, appreciated his attitude. But a chance remark of Rintoul's eased the tension almost at once.

"I used to know a man of your name in Perth," he said.

"In the constabulary?" MacNab asked, his eyes opening quickly.

"Yes. He was an inspector in the county constabulary," Rintoul replied.

"That was my father."

It was Rintoul's turn to open his eyes. He stared hard at his visitor.

"Yes," he said. "Yes. I was wondering who you reminded me of—in features, I mean."

MacNab laughed.

"Not in physique, of course. Ah, well!" he said with a half sigh, "I'd have been in the police myself if he hadn't married such a little woman."

Rintoul passed over his cigarette case, and from that moment the two men began to discuss the case with complete friendliness and candor. The detective had time for more than one cigarette while Rintoul traversed the various facts and aspects of the case as they appeared to him.

"So you see it would be all plain sailing but for that one thing."

"You mean the revolver?" MacNab said.

"Exactly. Not a soul knows anything about it. It clean beats us."

MacNab had had enough of this from Murray.

"I doubt," he said, "we'll learn nothing about that by any more direct questioning. If ever we establish ownership, it will only be by an indirect approach."

"Meaning?" Rintoul asked.

"We'll have to cast back further up the water, I think—to that shooting on the moor."

Rintoul looked almost pained.

"We're convinced there's no connection between the two," he declared.

"Well, you know," MacNab said, "having listened to all you've said, I'm not so sure the shooting in the library is not Chapter Two of the story which began with the shooting on the moor as Chapter One."

Rintoul laughed.

"If you think that," he said, "I doubt if there will be any Chapter Three to it."

The good humor established between the two men made this frankness possible. MacNab shook his head.

"Man, it's a longer story than that," he asserted, "and has more continuity in it. Just consider this one point. If this is murder staged as a suicide, what happened on the moor may well have been an attempt to stage murder as a shooting accident."

When Rintoul opened his lips to speak MacNab held up a silencing hand.

"Several things suggest a connection between the two events. What's your yearly average of murders in this district, Superintendent?" he asked.

Rintoul smiled.

"Can't call to mind any act of murder since Campbell of Glenure was shot in 1752," he said with a chuckle.

"Well," MacNab went on, "isn't it rather a startling coincidence that you should have not only two possible murders inside a week, but two *staged to look something other than they were*. Mind you," he added, "I'm only arguing that if they were murders this attempt to disguise them, as it were, seems to show the same mind at work behind both occurrences."

While Rintoul was thinking this out MacNab continued. "After all, it's not certain that Brent was first shot on the moor by the poacher. You found the gun in the water at the very point where Haggerty crossed to hide in the wood. I suggest he dropped it at the time he crossed, and that it has been there ever since. If so, neither this man Hugh Cameron nor anyone else could have used it to fire at Brent. You never found its supposed hiding-place on the moor, although I understand you searched every inch of ground. So I ask you to reconsider that shooting party. Admittedly there was lying to your sergeant about what happened that day. This young man Toplis, when your sergeant discovered the lie, explained it by saying he thought one of the party had accidentally and unknowingly hit Brent. But was that the real explanation? Psychologically, I find it difficult to believe. Isn't the impulse in such an accident to lash out at the perpetrator for his carelessness, not at the moment to hide it from him and everyone else?"

Rintoul, with head propped characteristically on his hand, considered the question.

"Well," he hesitated, "it seems unlikely he'd keep his mouth shut about it at the moment. Afterwards—yes; but not at the moment when the other men arrived on the scene."

"Quite," MacNab nodded. "Yet if this man Toplis had himself shot Brent he could not have shown more reticence."

"You're not saying you suspect him?" Rintoul said quickly.

MacNab looked down once more at the plan in the sergeant's note-book which lay before him on the table. "You forget," he said. "All we're considering at this time is whether there is a connection between what happened on the moor and what happened in the library. My suggestion was that they may well form two chapters in the same story—chiefly because the victim was the same, with the villain of our story showing the same type of cunning. To strengthen my theory we've been seeing who had a chance of doing the deed on both occasions."

Rintoul's mental processes were being pushed hard. To gain time he retrieved his cigarette case and struck a match.

"Look here," he said after a thoughtful puff, "you say the story has two chapters. So do we. Our first chapter brings in Sam Haggerty and his capture by Mr. Willoughby, and our theory is that Brent, wearing Mr. Willoughby's white coat, was shot in mistake for him on that misty day by one of Haggerty's friends, with revenge as the clear-cut motive. Brent's death we regard as but the epilogue to the story— self-inflicted in a moment of depression due to the belief that his career as a pianist was over."

"Well," MacNab admitted, "it makes quite a complete story, all neatly rounded off except for that one detail about the revolver. Do you really believe that nobody up at that house knows anything about that revolver?" As Rintoul hesitated MacNab continued. "Do once and for all consider this: Even if Brent ever possessed a revolver— which his mother denies—he at least had not got it with him on the moor. For after he was shot he was removed first to Arrochmore and then to Duchray in an unconscious condition, undressed and put to bed by those who must have found the weapon. He never was able afterwards to dress or undress himself. So if he owned a revolver at all it must all this time have been at Arrochmore. But as he never was again in Arrochmore, *someone*, unless we are to suppose that he himself before the incident on the moor happened foresaw every-thing, foresaw even that the doctor would order his removal to Duchray—unless, I say, he miraculously foresaw all this and plant-ed his weapon beforehand somewhere in the library for subsequent use—*someone else* took it to Duchray on the day he was shot dead in that same library."

Rintoul looked up.

"Someone who keeps *mum* about it," he said.

"Yes, but not, this time, because he thinks someone else put the revolver to his head and shot him accidentally and unknowingly."

"Yes," Rintoul conceded, "that does look like one up for your theory."

"Not my theory, Superintendent. Remember, it was your own theory at first. That sergeant of yours acted on the conviction that Brent was shot by one of the party."

"We had to drop that theory, however," the superintendent protested, "when Mr. Cresswell cleared himself in the matter of the two guns."

"But surely the fact that Mr. Cresswell was able to clear himself did not clear the other members of the shooting party."

"No. No one else chanced then to be under suspicion."

After Rintoul had sat for some time silently brooding over the various possibilities to which his mind had just been opened, MacNab rose and began to pace the room. He did not think the less of Rintoul for being so easily diverted from his original theory as to what had happened up on the moor. The superintendent, unlike himself, had no experience of this type of crime. The London detective smiled to himself as he recalled Rintoul's reply when asked the average annual rate of murder in his district. He had cited the Glenure murder of 1752! One murder was not much out of which to buy experience. And even that one was not only outside Rintoul's district, but also before his time! The more MacNab thought of it the more sure he felt that this was not a crime native to the district: it bore the stamp of the imported article.

MacNab had been amused also to hear of Sergeant Cameron's reluctance to believe in a fellow-clansman's guilt. But there were stronger grounds for rejecting the theory that Brent was shot on the moor by Hugh Cameron than clan feeling provided. Not the least of them was that though the Highland temperament is passionate and impulsive enough, it did not prompt men to nurse and cherish revengeful feelings, nor lead them to seek satisfaction in planned and cold-blooded murder.

MacNab took a turn to the window and looked out, smiling at himself as he remembered that the Glenure murder itself might have stood as the one known example of a planned, deliberate murder. Was it not more on account of the Glenure murder being carried out deliberately, on a prearranged plan, rather than on its being a murder that the whole country was ashamed of it to that day?

"We ought to have given more consideration to this man Toplis," Rintoul said.

MacNab turned and went back to his seat.

"Good," he said. "We'll consider him and the others as well. But first of all I'd like to clinch the conviction that those two events are connected. Observe that the pretense of a shooting accident fails. It was an excellent idea, and one that would be more frequently adopted, I have no doubt, if murderers had more chances of being included in a shooting party. There's no trouble, you see, in accounting for the wound or the weapon. And it was the first choice of the crafty mind behind this murder. It happened to fail, so the second method had to be contrived, a second shooting accident being out of the question. Unfortunately it was a second-best method, because a weapon—not the victim's own—had to be left behind.

"The irony of the thing is," MacNab continued, "that it would have taken us all in but for what this—this devil had himself already done. I mean it might well have passed for suicide if only Brent had not been rendered so dependent on others that we know he never could have had that weapon in his possession."

Rintoul waved a hand.

"You have enough excuse for laboring that point," he said, "but I see it now. What do you suggest as our next step?"

MacNab unfolded the plan of campaign evolved by the Procurator-Fiscal and himself in the hotel on the previous night. Rintoul, when he heard of the scheme for securing admission to the house in the guise of a family lawyer, looked askance at MacNab.

"The face is all right, but the clothes will surely hardly do," he said, glancing at the well-worn suit of brown homespun and the heavy brogues.

MacNab, however, explained that he had already wired for an outfit more suitable to his supposed character. There would be plenty of time, since three days at least had to be allowed for the exchange of letters between Mrs. Brent and the imaginary family lawyer.

"That will give me an opportunity for thinking over the various suspects," he added.

"Me, too," Rintoul said. "What do you want us to do?"

MacNab hesitated.

"Well," he said, "on the whole, it would be better if you did nothing except to go on as if you were still after this Hugh Cameron. Up at Arrochmore I suppose they know you are after him for the affair on the moor?"

"Of course they do. Mr. Willoughby is himself taking a great interest in that hunt. He rings up every morning for news."

"No wonder," MacNab said, "since he thinks it was himself Cameron meant to shoot."

CHAPTER XV
WHO WAS THE MAN

In the course of the next three days MacNab put in a lot of hard thinking over the Arrochmore murder. His friend, Dr. Dunn, must have found him rather a trial in the evenings. Out on the loch it was not so bad, for there was always the fishing, with the boatman ready to gossip at the least opportunity. And if the boatman wondered at the silent figure in the stern, at least the fishing was bad enough to give himself and the other gentleman full scope for cursing it.

On the evening of the third day, however, MacNab appeared to have reached the limit of his boring process of incubation. He became almost talkative. It was as if he now wished to use poor Dunn as a whetstone for his own wits. They had the little smoking-room to themselves.

"What I'd like to know," MacNab said abruptly, "is who suggested that he should wear that white Burberry."

Dunn, who had never remembered hearing anything about a white Burberry, betrayed no surprise. He knew his man. This sort of thing had happened in the Perigord case and several others.

"You would, would you?" he responded, as if he knew all about it.

"If it comes to that, I'd like to know who first suggested a shooting expedition on a mist-covered moor."

Dunn made a shot.

"Perhaps they were not two persons, but one," he suggested.

MacNab continued as if he had heard nothing.

"I'm quite certain the moor is the right place to begin on, and not the library," he announced. "His mother is quite right there."

Here Dunn found something on which he was not quite in the dark.

139

"I had the impression that Murray agreed in that, too," he said.

For the first time MacNab seemed to become aware of Dunn's presence. He sat forward, the light of abstraction gone from his eyes, and passed the sergeant's notebook over to Dunn.

"Let's look at each of them in turn," he said. "I'd like to get all this clear in my mind before ever I set eyes on any of them."

Dunn examined Cameron's plan with great interest.

"They began by suspecting Cresswell," he said.

"On motive?" Dunn inquired, noting the distance of Cresswell's position in the line from where Brent was hit.

MacNab explained the uncertainty as to where Cresswell had been when the shot was fired.

"The two things that clear him in the eyes of the police are, first that Brent was shot in the left side, and, second and far stronger evidence, is that Cresswell's gun, which the sergeant examined thinking he was examining Brent's, had two undischarged cartridges in it."

"Lucky mistake for him!" Dunn commented. "This man Joliffe is too far away, I suppose?"

"So it seems," MacNab agreed.

"Then there's this other man Harwood."

"The curious thing about Harwood is that no one has anything to say about him. You know," he went on, "if they were right in assuming that Brent was shot on his left side by someone firing below him down the slope on the left, I wouldn't put it past this Harwood. The funny thing about Harwood is that while the police were hunting the moor for Haggerty's gun, Harwood was fishing in the burn at the very spot where the gun was found. Oh!" he went on, seeing Dunn stare at the plan, "very likely it was merely a coincidence—only it's a point to remember."

"Well," Dunn commented, "it's not easy to see how Harwood could have done it—left his position in the line, I mean, got down below Brent and shot him from there. This fellow Toplis looks far the most likely of the lot, from the position he was in."

MacNab was ready enough to agree.

"No, it's not obvious how Harwood could have done it. But, on the other hand, I've yet to find a case in which the criminal desired to leave his method obvious. And that's just what's bothering me about

Toplis. It's so obvious he could have done it. He was on the spot; he was the only one who did not obviously need to get out of position; none of the others knew what had happened till he gave the shout at the moment it suited him to do so. Notice the position on the plan; it only marks the spot at which he laid down his gun and cried the alarm; he may have fired farther back, when much closer to Brent."

"Who was shot on his offside," Dunn reminded MacNab.

"But if that was the one bit of subtlety Toplis employed, it's easy to explain. He had merely to draw Brent's attention to something behind them. And observe this, Dunn: Toplis knew as well as anyone else that Brent was wounded in his left shoulder and arm. How then could he say he thought the shot had come from one of the others, who were all farther to the right than himself?"

Dr. Dunn made no answer to the question; he had another difficulty in his mind, one that weighed with him.

"But the track of the bullet through the wound proves that the shot was fired not only from the left but from below," he said.

MacNab sat up with a snort of disgust.

"Proves!" he cried. "Proves? Man, I wonder at you!"

"Well—tends to show," Dunn amended.

"Quite. Tends to show! His one bit of subtlety, that. But how easily it can be explained. Toplis had only to kneel down, pretending to tie a bootlace, say, draw Brent's attention to something behind, shoot him when he turned to look, get back to his approximate position in the line, while the others, as the plan shows, had meanwhile been walking on, drop his gun, give the shout of alarm and then run to Brent's assistance."

Dunn withdrew his pipe.

"Then you think Toplis is your man?"

"I don't say that. I've merely been saying he could have done it."

"But you do think one of them did it—after, I mean, getting him to turn round to suggest it was someone from below on the left."

"Yes, but he was got to turn for another reason than that, I fancy."

The doctor's pipe went back to his mouth. He was well aware he was expected to puzzle out this other reason for himself. After a time he shook his head. "Can't imagine what other reason there could be," he admitted.

MacNab laughed—his first laugh in two days.

"The heart is on the left side, doctor. He wanted to make *very* sure."

Dunn ignored the gibe. He had seen something for himself.

"Then," he cried, sitting forward, "he must have got the fright of his life when he discovered he hadn't made so very sure after all. Wouldn't Brent have known who hit him if it had all happened as you suggest?"

"Ay," MacNab admitted, "your finger's gone to the weak spot, Dunn. When we pass from the physical to the psychological, I mean. I went into that question very closely with Rintoul. He hadn't taken it up very minutely with the sergeant who went to the scene of the supposed shooting accident, so we had the sergeant in. I like the look of this Sergeant Cameron, not least because he was the one man who suspected foul play from the start. Well, even he would not agree that any of the party showed anything like fear or panic. In fact the closest questioning failed to yield one trace of anything but the concern and sorrow proper to such an accident. As it happened, he saw most of Toplis, for he was the young man who had gone down to guide them to the scene. And Cameron, who, of course, talked with him about the accident on the way up and thus had ample opportunity to observe his demeanor, said he was perfectly self-controlled. Though he did show a certain amount of dread, that was concerned with the fact that they had all gone out, without Mr. Willoughby's knowledge, on a day considered by their host unsuitable for shooting. As you can imagine, I pricked up my ears when I heard about the young man's dread, and questioned the sergeant closely about it; but the explanation seemed satisfactory, especially as he happens to be Mr. Willoughby's secretary. More than that, my doubts would have been dispelled on hearing about the young man's intense anxiety to get them as quickly as possible to the aid of his wounded friend. For it was Toplis also who had run to find the doctor."

Dunn stared at the sheets of foolscap lying on the table at his friend's elbow. They had filled the brown leather dispatch case lying at MacNab's feet. He knew them to be the signed precognitions taken by the Procurator-Fiscal at his inquiry four days earlier. Except when out in the boat, MacNab's nose had maintained contact with them more or less ever since. Dunn felt a pride in those papers. No other detective could have such assistance, nor any in Scotland in Mac-Nab's position had he not chanced to have a friend who knew the Procurator-Fiscal.

"And you've got no further than that?" he said, disappointed. "Didn't these papers tell you anything?"

"Not yet. I haven't examined them very thoroughly yet."

Dunn, remembering MacNab's three days' absorption in them, smiled.

"They just refer to what happened at Duchray," the detective explained. "I'll have to wait till I get there before thinking them out."

He picked up the dispatch case and began replacing the precognitions. Then, as if there had been no interruption, he ran on: "Of course Brent's statement shows us that the assassin had really nothing to fear. Brent did not see what fired—did not even know whether he had or had not turned. Yet two people suspected foul play."

"Yes. This Sergeant Cameron suspected Cresswell and Mrs. Brent some person unknown."

MacNab nodded.

"The police—wrong; the mother—right. I'm looking forward to seeing this Mrs. Brent," he added. "She's rather a character, I'm told."

Dunn knocked the ashes from his pipe. MacNab handed him the dispatch case.

"You might as well take this with you to-morrow, when you go for your stay with your friend the Procurator," he said.

"It's only three days," Dunn remarked; "then I hope we'll be back here to fish under better conditions."

MacNab rose.

"Yes," he reiterated. "I'm looking forward to meeting Mrs. Brent. Did I say she was rather a character? Well, she is. Rintoul has fixed it up for me. We're to have three days together, she and I. We can't pretend that this law business will take longer than that; but if I don't get on well at my own business she's to fall ill, and be unable to transact any business till she's better."

CHAPTER XVI
THE SOLICITOR FROM LONDON

When MacNab descended from the train at the station he perceived how perfectly Rintoul had carried through his part of the scheme. MacNab had joined the train two stations back, where Dunn set him down in the afternoon before going on to Inverness. Hardly had he stepped on to the platform before he was approached by a young man possessing the attributes of a well-trained man-servant, for he had evidently picked him out as the guest for whom the Rolls-Royce was waiting outside.

While his things were collected the detective stole a glance at himself, eyeing himself as it were from the footman's point of view. His outfit, from the bowler hat and the navy blue suit to the light grey spats, seemed to have the right professional air about them. He passed out content with himself.

He got a slight shock, however, on finding he was being taken not to Duchray but to Arrochmore. Till he came within sight of the great house he thought he must have got mixed up in grasping the description given him by Rintoul as to the respective position of the two houses. On the doorstep he suggested a mistake had been made.

"Oh, no, sir," the footman said. "You are expected here. Most of the house-party have gone away, sir, and Duchray has been shut up."

MacNab followed the man in, rather disconcerted. He found Mrs. Brent waiting for him in a small sitting-room on the second floor. She had apparently been seated in her wheel-chair at an open window with an outlook on Loch Linnhe and the Ardgour Mountains beyond.

MacNab hoped much from this old lady, studying her narrowly while he exchanged the commonplaces fitted to their supposed relationship. Her whole mind appeared to be preoccupied with thoughts of vengeance, even, so far as he could see, to the exclusion of sorrow for her loss. He discerned no trace of grief, though he did not know to what extent she had given way to grief before his arrival, and how much of her present self-possession was due to reaction from it. As she talked her eyes sparkled with lights, and though the face was worn and lined, these lines seemed to be the marks of distant rather than present troubles.

Abruptly her talk ceased.

"I think you'll do," she said with a nod of approval.

"I hope I look my part," he said, aware that if this little woman had done all the talking he himself had not done all the scrutinizing.

When she agreed that he did look the part, they fell at once into a consideration of the real business for which he had come.

"I was just wondering," he said, "if you had anything to add to the statement you made before the Procurator-Fiscal?"

"Nothing to add," she said, "except that I'm more than ever convinced that what I told him is true. I feel it in my very bones."

Although he did not think this was very much to go by, he thought that she probably knew more than she herself was aware of, the significance of which she did not then guess. A little deft questioning might bring more to light than she dreamed.

"You know," he said, "I'm inclined to share your view, as against the police here, that the shooting on the moor was an attempt on your son's life, and that—what happened afterwards tells us we must look to some member of the shooting party if we're to find the guilty man."

"Ah!" she cried, "I was right when I told that superintendent that what this case needed was a detective with London experience. If the police here had done their duty, none of them would have been allowed to leave this house."

MacNab reassured her.

"That will make little difference. If we find out who it is we'll soon get our hands on him."

From her he now learned that Harwood, Cresswell and Joliffe had gone. This was what he had expected. The secretary, Mr. Toplis, in whom he was at the moment chiefly interested, was still there. Of the others there remained only Mr. Bray, the tutor, and Miss Cresswell, who was staying on with Miss Willoughby.

MacNab went at once to the point on which his hopes at Arrochmore centred.

"On the question of motive, now, Mrs. Brent. If you could throw any light on that," he suggested. "For instance, had any of them any reason to—well, be hostile to your son?"

"Ah," she said, "I know what you mean! You're thinking of what I said to the Procurator about Mary Willoughby. Well, she made them all more or less jealous of him. My son was an artist. Mr. Willoughby at first didn't like to think of his daughter marrying an artist. He was very much against the engagement. He said artists always made bad husbands. He said an artist's wife had always to take second place to his art, whatever it was. Mr. Willoughby is a business man in a very large way." Her thin lips twisted into a distorted smile of derision. "As if money didn't come first with the business man," she scoffed. "But he gave way in the end and invited Eric here. Indeed he quite changed his views about my boy. The engagement was to have been announced this very week."

MacNab waited while she used her handkerchief.

"Well," she resumed, "after that the trouble began. I mean after we came here. Mary, of course, loved my boy; there's no doubt of that. I admit it. The fights she put up with her father over Eric were sufficient to prove it. But Mary isn't musical. She loved Eric for himself, and not for his genius. Of course he had to keep in constant practice. When the others went out he put in hours of work at the Steinway in the hall. She stayed there with him at first, and I think in time she got jealous of his music. I've gone into the hall—the wheels of this chair are quite silent, you know—and I have surprised her sitting beside him, stiff and rigid in a chair, with such a look in her eyes! Well, I think she got to feel that Eric was too sure of her. She started trying to make him jealous. Oh! and how these men played up to her. Not that it was play to them; they were ready enough to be serious. Harwood, I've seen him sitting on the back of the couch on which she was seated, and he looking down ogling, head askew, and she looking up, her eyes shining. Cresswell standing before her, legs astride, playing the strong man, she round-eyed with wonder and admiration at the tale he was telling of his doughty deeds. How she played one off against the other! Even that little Mr. Bray, the tutor—

she quite turned his head, too. I've seen him almost kneeling before her, all a-flutter and agape, like a little curate talking to a duchess at a church bazaar. She couldn't leave even Toplis the secretary to Brenda Cresswell."

MacNab interrupted the outburst with a comment.

"You said nothing of all this to the Procurator."

"I said enough. If I had said more the fools would have been still more certain that Eric shot himself through the depression all this caused him."

With this MacNab felt compelled to agree, and it left him astonished at the ease with which the true situation could have been misread. Then a crucial question rose up before his mind. "Mrs. Brent," he said, "do you think any one of these young men misunderstood, let us say, Miss Willoughby's eyes?"

"You mean took her flirting seriously. Well, as far as I could judge, they took it seriously enough to be madly jealous of each other, but if one showed it more than another it was that red-headed young man Toplis."

"And Miss Cresswell? I think you suggested there was something—something between Miss Cresswell and the secretary."

"Oh," she said, "I don't know how far that had gone, but one like myself who's apt to get overlooked can see a lot; and those two were certainly approaching an understanding till Mary took him up."

"Then I suppose strained relations followed between the two girls?"

"Till this happened. It is my belief that Brenda Cresswell—she's devoted to her brother, you know—hated Mary Willoughby quite as much for leading him on as for taking Toplis away."

For more than an hour MacNab discussed the various relations of the house party to each other without lighting on anything more likely to lead to a quick solution of his problem. Not yet, he felt, could it be safely narrowed down to a concentration on Toplis.

At seven MacNab had dinner with Mrs. Brent in her own sitting-room. Afterwards, when the old lady, who retired early, was taken to her room, he went downstairs for a look at his surroundings, and if possible at some of the people about whom he had heard so much. He was idling about the hall, looking at the portraits of Arrochmore's past owners, noting the position of the Steinway grand over in the far corner, and generally acting the part of a man interested in what he saw, when he was joined by Mr. Willoughby. Had he not known from Rintoul's casual description that this was his host he would have quickly gathered as much from the easy, proprietorial manner of his approach.

"Yes," Mr. Willoughby said after the preliminary exchanges, "it is a sad business that brings you here, Mr. MacNab, but I hope you will find your visit not without other interest."

MacNab, who could certainly share this hope, thanked him.

"But it's all so new to me, this part of the country," he said with a grave smile which did justice to the occasion, "that I must resist the temptation to prolong my visit unnecessarily."

Mr. Willoughby waved a hand in a manner suggesting that this was a temptation there was no need to resist. "You surprise me in saying it is all new to you," he remarked. "For though you have an English name, I seem to detect something of the Scot in your accent."

MacNab smiled again.

"You have a good ear, Mr. Willoughby. I owe that to my mother, who was a Scot."

Willoughby looked at the door.

"What about a saunter?" he suggested. "Or perhaps you are too tired after your long journey. A chair and a cigar in the smoking-room?"

When MacNab promptly agreed, Mr. Willoughby led the way along the corridor to a pleasant room that seemed full of easy arm-chairs. But MacNab was disappointed to find the arm-chairs unoccupied. While cutting his cigar his host indicated the table littered with a fairly complete array of current periodicals.

"You'll find this restful, I hope," he said, touching the bell.

When the man appeared MacNab expressed a preference for whisky, and Mr. Willoughby, when he had seen him served, hovered about for a time, moving and rearranging the papers on the table. To MacNab he appeared undecided whether to go or stay.

"Mrs. Brent seems to be bearing up wonderfully well," MacNab said, to fill up the silence.

"Wonderfully," the other agreed. "Of course, she isn't new to this sort of thing," he added.

"You mean his father," MacNab said. "Yes, I've heard about that. No more than a rumor, though. Our firm only took over Mrs. Brent's affairs later."

Willoughby came over and slipped into a seat facing MacNab.

"Yes," he said, "Harwood and Cresswell looked after the old man's business affairs in those days. That's why I know so much about it," he added.

MacNab looked up vaguely, like one who had missed something obvious.

"Oh, Harwood and Cresswell is my firm, too," his host explained; "in fact, their sons have been staying with us here up to a day or two ago. You've heard, of course, what led to the father's suicide?"

"Vaguely. Something about a patent, wasn't it?"

"Well, it followed a disappointment about a patent, certainly. Harwood and Cresswell didn't get the thing through quickly enough, and it appears someone else anticipated the patent. He blamed them for that, quite unjustly, I believe. An erratic old fellow by all accounts. Quite mad—so mad that if it hadn't been that patent it would have been something else."

As he concluded, MacNab happened to be in the act of sitting up to flick the ash from his cigar. He contrived to complete the operation without giving any outward evidence of the sudden, shattering possibility that had burst into his mind. Leaning back again and stretching out his legs, he took a breath or two as if to steady his voice.

"And, after all, I suppose the son was certain sooner or later to do the same thing," he said, looking at his host.

A queer little silence ensued. Mr. Willoughby looked like a man who was feeling he ought to say something, but was not quite sure what to say. Then in the midst of the silence the door behind Mac-Nab's chair opened, and a voice came hesitatingly:

"Oh, I hope I don't intrude."

Mr. Willoughby almost jumped from his seat, but not before Mac-Nab noted the relief on his face.

"Certainly not, my boy!" he cried heartily. "I was just going." He introduced Mr. Bray, patting him on the back as he did so. To judge by the young man's face, such heartiness from Mr. Willoughby was new to him. He rather gaped after his employer as he left the room. Then Mr. Bray collapsed into the chair just vacated.

"Have a cigar," MacNab suggested genially.

"No, thanks," said Mr. Bray, "but I'll have a pipe, if I may." From his pocket he produced a briar of large size.

Somehow MacNab could not associate Mr. Bray and a briar pipe. When the young man had filled and lit the pipe it seemed much too big for his face. It somehow gave the same effect as if he had worn a hat three sizes too large for him. He noticed MacNab staring, and removed the pipe.

"I'm only practicing with this, you know," he explained. "I take it as part of my training for Orders, you know." He took a few vigorous puffs to keep the thing going. "Nothing like a pipe together for establishing friendly relations with the men in a parish."

"Wouldn't a cigarette be easier for you?" MacNab asked. The question received no answer for a moment or two except an emphatic shake of the head.

"Cigarette no good for that. Has to be a pipe. Pipe the only manly thing, if you know what I mean."

"Quite. I agree with you," MacNab nodded.

"You are from London, aren't you?"

MacNab agreed, feeling that Mr. Bray was practicing at friendly relations with himself as well as with the pipe.

"You don't like London, of course?"

This brought the briar from the prospective curate's mouth in astonishment.

"Now, how on earth did you guess that?" he exclaimed. "Really! You'd make a good detective, I think, if you know what I mean."

MacNab shook his head as if the compliment were too high-pitched.

"You give me credit for too much," he said modestly. "You like being here, of course?"

"I do. I mean I did till—till—"

"Oh, quite. I understand. Very sad affair that."

"For the moment Miss Willoughby's quite broken, you know. We don't see her now. Takes all her meals upstairs in her room."

"Ah, yes, a terrible tragedy for her," MacNab said sympathetically.

"She'll get over it," Mr. Bray announced with an air of professional authority. "Sad as it is, this tragedy will turn out to be a blessing in disguise, if you know what I mean."

MacNab's eyes expressed astonishment. He began to be really interested in Bray.

"Well," he remarked in a tone of mild disagreement, "as yet the disguise is far more evident than the blessing."

Mr. Bray pondered this while pulling at his pipe. He sucked so strongly that moisture became visible at the corners of his mouth. Suddenly he withdrew the pipe and bent forward.

"You didn't know the man," he burst out. "He was a bad man. Talk about disguise! He was the one who wore it. He never let her see his real character. Had she married him he would have made her life a hell. Either that or brought her down to his own level. These were the only two possibilities. She was made for better things. Not one of the people here appeared to see that but myself. She told me once she was so glad I had come into her life, that I wasn't like any other men she had ever known. And of course after that it was my duty to do everything I could to help her."

"Of course," MacNab agreed. He was astonished. What he had heard was, he thought, almost equivalent to an unconscious confession. Had the foolish girl so bewitched this young man that she had turned him into a fanatic? It was easy to imagine her soulful eyes and internal laughter while she was telling him he wasn't like any other men she had ever met.

MacNab regarded the man lying back in his chair with half-shut eyes now, still shaken by his emotional outburst, and noting anew the small head, sharp nose and narrow face, thought it not altogether unlikely that he was sitting with the man responsible for Brent's death. Here was exactly that type of feeble intellect which, tipped off its precarious balance by a pretty girl's hand, could become convinced that evil was not really evil when done for a good purpose. It was not the first time MacNab had been in such a case; and he was well enough aware of the almost superhuman cunning developed by such fanaticism. Good as such a man believed his deed to be, it was a good he did by stealth, and had no more desire to find it fame than the ordinary criminal without his illusions.

A prolonged silence had followed the detective's murmured assent to Bray's last words. The young man reclining in the big red leather arm-chair seemed to be brooding over something. Over what? The thing it had been his duty to do if he was to help Mary Willoughby? MacNab broke the silence.

"I suppose you did, first of all, try to influence Brent?" he remarked.

Bray came back as from a long distance, fluttering his eyelids like one awakened from sheep. MacNab had to repeat his remark. The tutor shook his head.

"No good! I did try, though. He just treated me with amused contempt, if you know what I mean. He couldn't be serious about anything except music, which is a thing not worth being serious about, if you know what I mean."

"Don't you like music, then?" MacNab inquired.

"I like the organ; it's the only instrument with a moral purpose behind it." He thought for a moment.

"What I mean is that ordinary music merely rouses emotions without directing those emotions towards any worthy end."

MacNab thought the time had come when he could venture closer.

"Well, but aren't you wrong in saying Mr. Brent cared for nothing but his music?"

"What else?" the tutor demanded curtly.

"There was shooting, for instance."

Bray twisted impatiently in his chair.

"He liked killing things, if that's what you mean. He would have killed Miss Willoughby if he had lived—her soul, if you know what I mean."

MacNab placed the stump of his cigar in the ash-tray.

"I wonder just why he killed himself," he said gently.

Bray shrugged.

"Possibly it was in a moment of self-revelation," he suggested.

"Well," MacNab said, "I don't suppose you yourself think that. I happen to know some people don't think he killed himself at all."

As the detective brought his eyes round to the other's face he could see, although for some time past the dusk had been creeping into the room, that his words had startled Mr. Bray. A greenish pallor overspread his face, and he seemed to have gone suddenly limp. The pipe fell from his hand, hitting the fender with a noise that seemed to resound through the room in the silence.

"Feeling bad?" the detective inquired. "Have a drop of this?" he suggested, touching the whisky decanter.

The tutor pointed to the soda syphon.

"A little of that, if I may."

MacNab splashed the soda into the glass.

"Do you know," Bray said as he took the glass, "you quite made me forget myself while we were talking. I'm not really in training for this pipe yet, if you know what I mean. Smoked far too long," he added, between sips at the soda water.

MacNab stooped and retrieved the pipe.

"Perhaps a milder tobacco would suit you better," he suggested.

The tutor did not seem to hear the suggestion.

"You were saying something about some people thinking that Mr. Brent had not taken his own life," he said.

The detective nodded.

"Oh, yes. Some people have suggested it was an accident. He may have found the revolver somewhere about the room—hidden behind a book, let us say, which he had pulled out; started playing with the thing, not knowing it was loaded."

MacNab saw such color as the tutor's face possessed come slowly back.

"Oh, I see," he said. He finished off his drink and set down the glass. "Well, anyway, I think I'd better go to bed now."

After he had left MacNab stood for quite a time, his own unfinished glass in his hand, pondering the situation. But he had no feeling of triumph. There was a sense in which this young man was as much the victim as Brent himself. Innocently as she had no doubt acted, some responsibility for what had happened attached itself to Mary Willoughby. But it was to the tutor's responsibility alone that the law would look.

With something like a sigh, as if it were nasty medicine he was bound to swallow, MacNab finished off his whisky and went to bed.

CHAPTER XVII
TABLE TALK

Next morning MacNab awakened with a sensation of vague op-pression. Through the open window, which faced the terraced pine trees behind the house, the bright sunlight streamed in, and on the pine-scented air there floated the joyous piping and twittering of many birds. He lay still for a moment or two, trying to track down and account for his own sensation of sadness, which was at such vari-ance with his surroundings. Then he recalled the previous night, and the unconscious self-revelation of the young man Bray.

The Arrochmore murder was, then, a pathological case—a case that concerned the doctor even more than the detective. It would probably end not on the gallows, but in a mental home. Neverthe-less he recognized that he would still have to go on with the case. He wished he could drop it. He would like to be able to go to Mrs. Brent and explain as he saw it the pitiful situation. But he was not in this case on her account. He had taken it up because Dunn had put pres-sure on him on behalf of his friend, the Procurator-Fiscal, who was in difficulties over it. He had to carry on and establish Bray's respon-sibility, if only to free other innocent persons upon whom suspicion might fall, and to whom suspicion might cling for years to come.

That there was no evidence of Bray's presence on the moor on the day Brent was shot there did not trouble MacNab. He was not one of that class with whom a theory once formed becomes a conviction; in other words, he never tried to make facts bend to theory.

MacNab rose and dressed leisurely. He blamed Miss Willough-by more than Bray. Here was an earnest young man, quite without worldly experience, whose head had been so turned by this pretty girl that he was ready to do anything to save her from a supposed unworthy fate. Bray was, in short, the victim of his own ideals. Had his ideals been pitched less high he would never have done this deed. MacNab was curious to have a look at Mary Willoughby. As Mrs. Brent now breakfasted in her own room, he himself had to go down to breakfast with the others. But he doubted if Miss Willoughby would be there.

On entering the room, MacNab found its only occupant to be the boy Dick. From the stare he received after his greeting he saw that his presence in the house had not been explained to the boy.

"Early riser," MacNab nodded to him.

"Oh, you get used to it at school after they've soused you once or twice with a cold douche from your own water jug. Besides," he added as his attention went back to the sausages on his plate, "you get pretty peckish up here."

MacNab, under Dick's direction and advice, helped himself.

"Didn't know you were in the house. Suppose you came last night," the boy remarked.

MacNab explained himself as he took a seat opposite.

Dick nodded vigorously.

"Oh, *now* I understand. Yes, of course, that explains it. Having to do with dead people's wills, and that sort of thing, must make a chap feel pretty solemn."

MacNab could not restrain a laugh.

"Is that how I look, then?"

"Well, you did just now, rather. In fact," he added, confidentially, "you looked so glum, I half expected to hear you say grace."

Breakfast went on in silence for a time.

"Well," the man remarked, "even for you it isn't all fun up here. You are at work with a tutor, aren't you?"

Dick's face darkened. He appeared to take the remark as just the sort of unpleasant reminder one might expect from a gloomy lawyer like the man opposite.

"Bray is an ass," he said shortly; "not a funny ass, you know, but just what you'd call a—a nagging ass."

"Contentious, you mean."

Dick frowned thoughtfully.

"Doesn't that mean fighting?" he inquired.

"Well, yes."

"Then it's not the kind of ass I mean. Bray hasn't any fight in him. He's—he's just a nagger about things."

MacNab nodded.

"Conscientious—that's the word."

"That's it! Always preaching at a fellow. And he's such a funk." A sense of his own wrongs triumphed for the moment over his taste for bacon and eggs. He laid down knife and fork. "Look here, sir," he continued, "how could a fellow like me have any respect for a fellow who's more afraid of a gun than any girl?"

The stare of incredulity with which this was received was far from being assumed. MacNab believed he had well-founded reasons for believing Dick's assertion to be incorrect. The boy's face flushed up.

"You don't believe he's like that? I tell you he is, he is! If he'd only leave me alone when we've finished with that rotten arithmetic. But he won't. He's so infernally con-conscientious, he thinks he has to watch over me all the time. Even when I'm out with my gun. It's then he gives himself away. He will come with me; but he's so frightened, he always keeps well in the rear." Pausing for breath, Dick seemed to be seeking for a concrete instance with which to convince his listener. "Why yes, there was that day Brent shot himself, put us all into mourning, stopped all our fun and brought you here. Well, after lunch I took out my gun and went into the wood to have a pot at the rabbits. He insisted on going with me, and followed me all the time."

"Not *followed* you, surely!"

"I swear he did. Even when I'd stopped shooting as we came down on Duchray he kept behind. I had only a single cartridge left by then, but I'd got so fed up with him that I thought I'd use it to give him a fright. So as soon as I got into the open I turned round and fired back." Dick put his head up and laughed at the memory. "He cowered behind a trunk till I shouted to him and told him I hadn't another shot left. That was when Mrs. Murchison ran out squealing for someone to come and help her." Dick breathed heavily. "Would you believe me, she ran past me as if I hadn't been there to grab hold of that wretched funk Bray."

Dick was a poor reader of faces if he did not recognize how deeply he had impressed his listener. It was MacNab's turn to lay down his knife and fork. But he had still to make certain.

"And he had followed you about like that for the last hour?" he suggested.

"Ever since lunch, I said," Dick corrected. "The beggar hadn't once let me out of his sight for almost three hours." Dick nodded, resuming his work at the bacon and eggs, and leaving the other to ponder Bray's enormity.

If the boy had not now become so engrossed in the contents of his plate it might have given him a pleasant surprise to perceive how MacNab's face had brightened. It might have surprised Dick more if he had known he had just presented his tutor with an entirely satisfactory alibi in a charge for murder then hanging over him. For, to say no more, Brent had certainly been alive, had, in fact, talked to Dr. Frossard and Mr. Willoughby himself while those two inseparables— Dick and his tutor—were together on the hill behind the house.

So the whole case was in the melting pot again! He no sooner perceived this than the door opened and Miss Cresswell entered.

MacNab divined who she was from her explanation that Miss Willoughby was having her breakfast in her own room. He had little time to do more than exchange a few formalities with her before the door again opened, and he found himself bowing across the table to Mr. Toplis, the secretary. To judge by the way the redheaded young man bent over and attended to Miss Cresswell's wants, he must have returned to his old allegiance. MacNab was glad to notice he himself received no more attention from him than any lawyer's clerk whose presence had to be just tolerated.

Brenda Cresswell was a strongly-built, athletic type of girl, whose dark, closely-cut hair and clear brown eyes accorded well enough with an open-air life, even if her lips and her plucked eyebrows suggested something more exotic. Till Mr. Willoughby himself entered Dick did most of the talking.

After the usual kindly inquiries as to his guests' comfort, Mr. Willoughby turned to his letters while the secretary attended to his preferences at the sideboard. Once his father's eyes were on the letters, Dick slipped from the room. Nobody spoke while their host went through his letters. MacNab began to adjust his mind to the new situation created for him by the information just received from the boy.

With the tutor now as good as eliminated, he became interested in Mr. Toplis, studying the red-headed secretary meanwhile as covertly as he could. Once, looking away quickly, he surprised Miss Cresswell's eyes fixed on himself. When finally Mr. Willoughby pushed his correspondence away the act was taken as a signal that talk might be resumed. MacNab noted the almost abrupt and contemptuous push given to the pile of torn envelopes and crumpled sheets of paper. In its way, it was as revealing as the silence maintained by the others while he read. The iron hand in the velvet glove, the detective thought in himself. And it was the master who first broke the silence.

"Hullo!" he said, looking round. "Mr. Bray not down yet!"

Miss Cresswell and the secretary exchanged a questioning glance.

"I believe he's not feeling very well," Miss Cresswell said.

"That pipe again, I suppose." Mr. Willoughby smiled. "Quite heroic, the way he persists in it," he nodded to MacNab.

Mr. Toplis joined in with a laugh.

"He talks about *mastering* it, as if it were roller skating or a vicious horse."

"How about sending him up something?" Miss Cresswell suggested.

"Do," said Toplis; "a cup of tea, say, and a bath bun, if you know what I mean."

They all laughed. Mr. Willoughby shook his head.

"Too bad—too bad," he remonstrated, but laughing, too, all the same. Then, as if he judged that their merriment might seem a trifle heartless in view of the recent tragedy at Duchray, he looked over at MacNab deprecatingly. "Mr. Bray, my boy's tutor, is a very serious young fellow, who is going into the Church this autumn. I'm afraid these young people have made him rather a butt."

"None of us ever do it to his face, though, except—"

Miss Cresswell cut off the exception with a bite at her lip. MacNab guessed that the exception must be Brent, from the rather horrified glance she shot at himself. He relieved the awkwardness of the moment.

"Mr. Bray and I had a long talk last night," he said. "I quite understand."

After breakfast, when Mr. Willoughby and Mr. Toplis retired to deal with the morning's letters, and Miss Cresswell went up to see Miss Willoughby, MacNab lit his pipe and went for a stroll on the terrace. Mrs. Brent would not be visible till eleven. He had much to think about. Now that the tutor had apparently been placed beyond suspicion, he must cast about for someone else. Closer contact with Toplis left him where he was. His thoughts reverted to the break-fast-table talk which had more than once jarred on him. But if the red-headed young man had been flippant, and moreover flippant at such a time before a stranger who was only there because of the recent tragedy, the others had shared in that exhibition of doubtful taste. MacNab was not even sure if he ought not to be making al-lowances for the flippancy. It was possibly no more than a reaction against the restraint and solemnity imposed on the whole household by the tragedy at Duchray; and the absence from the breakfast table of both Mary Willoughby and Mrs. Brent would give free course to their reactions. No, from anything he had yet seen he might suspect Mr. Willoughby himself as well as Toplis.

But who else was there left open to suspicion? MacNab moved to the edge of the terrace to look over the tree-tops on the lower slopes to the world beyond. It seemed as empty of suggestion as the contents of his own mind. Gazing on the great stretch of the Loch Linnhe and the hills beyond, his lack-lustre eye took in nothing of what he saw. In his mind's eye he was looking into the little sitting-room in the Loch Laggan Hotel, seeing once more the Procurator-Fiscal urging him to take up this case. He remembered that official's face flushed with hope, the eyes bright and pleading. Murray's faith in him was, of course, based entirely on what he had heard from Peter Dunn.

And now, as the reverse of that picture, he conjured up another: a disappointed and disillusioned Procurator-Fiscal and a discredited friend. Horrid doubts began to assail him. What if there was no con-nection whatever between the shooting on the moor and the death in the library? What if Brent's death had been a case of suicide after all? There was that locked door, for instance, with the key in the dead man's pocket. And the shot overheard by the housekeeper with no one within call except Bray, who had certainly been cleared by the boy Dick.

But no! All that left the mystery of the revolver unanswered. Somebody either carrying that weapon, or knowing where to find it in the house, entered the library at some moment after the car containing Mr. Willoughby, Dr. Frossard and Mrs. Brent had left, and while the housekeeper was standing waiting for her kettle to boil, had found Brent in the library in the act of writing that letter, and shot him dead. As for the letter, the murderer certainly had not stopped to read it. MacNab was sure of that, not only because it had been found on the floor under the body, but chiefly because it was clear the man had to follow quickly on his preconceived plan, for he had provided himself with a duplicate key of the door, and so was able to place the other key in his victim's pocket. In other words, he had no time to spare.

MacNab had studied the plan of Duchray House provided by the police, and knew that close as the library door was to the main exit, the man ran a terrible risk of being seen before he was able to lock the door and turn round the corner of the house. But was the risk, after all, so great? If he knew the house well he would know that the housekeeper had a much longer way to come than he himself had to go. Yes, and even supposing he heard her scurrying footsteps behind him, and knew she had seen him, he had only to explain that, hearing a shot in the library as he came to the door, he had tried to enter, and finding the door locked, had been going out to try the windows. That explanation, especially as the key of the door was in the dead man's pocket, would serve, even had Mr. Bray and Dick appeared on the scene two minutes earlier.

Luck had certainly been on his side. How heavily the scales had been weighed in his favor this unknown must himself have recognized when the contents of Bray's letter came to be known.

MacNab turned away and, re-lighting his pipe, took a leisurely stroll along the pathway connecting the two houses. It was the first chance open to him for seeing the house of the tragedy. He had no excuse for seeking an entrance to the library then, but he intended to force an entry that night, and, of course, there was nothing to prevent his having a look at the exterior now.

He liked that path along the wood-side with its panoramic outlook on the Western seas and mountains. A good place for thought it must have been to Hanging George, the Lord Justice General, who had made it. He liked to think that so great a man had pondered criminal cases there; but he doubted if a detective before himself had ever done so. With a wry smile MacNab wondered how far the judge had to saunter along its half-mile length before coming to a decision.

He found himself in front of Duchray no nearer a decision than when he started.

CHAPTER XVIII
CHARACTER AND MOTIVE

He pulled up to stare at Duchray. Like most shut-up houses, it had something of a look of mystery about it, its drawn blinds suggesting concealment of some sort. Standing there in the bright sunlight Mac-Nab thought of the dark, empty rooms behind those blind windows, and the unbroken silence. Possibly he was importing into the external appearance of Duchray his knowledge of the crime perpetrated within. MacNab rather thought that must be what his imagination was doing as he stood gazing at the house. How numberless were the hotel bedrooms which had witnessed tragedies; yet the casual subsequent tenants of those same rooms slept none the less soundly in them so long as they knew nothing of what had happened there.

To the west side Duchray's grey stone gable, with what was no doubt part of the original cottage built by the judge extending beyond, showed him how far Mrs. Murchison had to go before reaching the library door. For the various additions had made it a higgledy-piggledy sort of place. It was quite certain that the man they wanted was one who not only must have been familiar with the ramifications entailed by the various additions, but more than that, he must have been familiar with the intentions and whereabouts of each guest at both houses on that fateful afternoon. At any rate, even though the murderer was someone prepared to take his chance when it came, he must be one who knew enough of what the others were doing that afternoon to see when his chance had come.

MacNab began to consider the crime from the point of view of character, mentally running over all the details and associated circumstances which bore on that point. It was, indeed, part of Francis

163

MacNab's method, when confronted with a complex case of this type in which there were many possible suspects, to study it as carefully from the character point of view as he did from that of motive. He considered this procedure to be far surer, if more slow, not only because character is a permanent possession while motive is variable, but also because he knew that even when a strong motive for the deed is clear as daylight, the question as to whether the man with the motive will yield to it is decided by his character.

MacNab, standing there looking at the house which had been the scene of the crime, could have kicked himself as he recalled how very nearly he had been betrayed into following exclusively the clue of motive in the case of Mr. Bray. Bray had as strong a motive for the murder of Brent as had moved Charlotte Corday to murder Marat. Indeed, of the two his motive was the stronger, for while the woman acted in the interests of a political party, Bray could have acted in the interests of a woman's soul. He certainly hated Brent as much as the French woman hated Marat. If the one acted and the other did not, it was not motive but character that in each case decided the issue.

Seeing no one about, he went over to have a closer look at the house. His intention was to get inside it that same night. Having no reasonable excuse for asking for the keys, and unwilling to risk awakening any suspicion as to his real business, he intended to force an entry, and for that reason wished to know in advance the type of window catch employed, and the safest window on which to operate. He discovered with satisfaction that all he needed to push the catch was a thin-bladed knife, but it was not easy to select the particular window. Finally he decided on the gable window of the library, for that window still bore the marks of Rintoul's efforts around the outer woodwork of the catch. MacNab believed in walking in another man's footprints wherever that was possible. Besides, with the blinds drawn as they were, it was not possible to see inside, and he could not tell whether the door of the library was locked or not.

Then as he stepped back from the window he had a shock. Miss Cresswell, hands behind her back, in thoughtful meditation, was coming straight towards him from the far end of the house. She hadn't seen him yet. But he judged it better to run no risk. He strolled towards her.

"I was just wondering," he remarked, "how long it takes for a house shut up like that to develop damp." At the sound of his voice the girl gave a start of surprise and a little cry.

"How you frightened me," she said, with a little breathless smile. "I thought I was alone."

After expressing his regret he pointed at the house. "It interests me as a lawyer, you know," he said. "I'm told it was built by a former great judge as a retreat in which he could consider his difficult cases."

"Part of it was," she corrected. "That long, low, white-washed section which now forms the kitchen offices."

They stood for a little on the grass, talking about the house and its former owner. MacNab felt drawn towards Miss Cresswell. Whether or not the presence of Willoughby had been a silencing influence at breakfast he could not tell, but now she was talkative and friendly. There were, it appeared, many surviving legends about Hanging George. As they walked back together she said:

"I'm interested in him, too, just because my own father was a lawyer. He made this path, too, you know."

When they reached the garden seat opposite the tennis courts MacNab stopped and, glancing at his watch, explained he had yet an hour to put in before Mrs. Brent would be ready for him.

"I think I'll pass it here with my pipe," he remarked.

She went off with a pretty gesture of her hand. She moved nicely. He watched her go with approval, and then, sitting down, took out his pipe.

He was conscious of being at close quarters with his problem. All that had gone before was no more than preliminary skirmishing. It was very quiet where he sat. Not a sign of life anywhere beyond the occasional crowing of a cock pheasant in the wood behind, and, except for the great white clouds deploying lazily among the mountain tops on the far side of the Loch Linnhe, not a sign of movement anywhere else.

For a long time his thoughts naturally circled among the hard facts in the case, like the clouds among those hard mountain peaks on the horizon. One after another the various persons possibly involved passed under review. From the nature of the murder, he knew the kind of character he was in search of. This was no impulsive deed of violence, but a predetermined and prearranged crime, the work of a subtle, calculating mind—a man who could wait patiently for his opportunity, and yet be swift to take it when it came. His first chance came on that misty day on the moor; his next on the very first occasion when his victim happened to be left alone. Yes, a man determined, patient, unscrupulous, masterful, alert—these were the qualities such a crime demanded, in addition, of course, to a perfect knowledge of the surroundings and the precise position of all the other persons likely to be about at the moment when the crime was committed.

And, having clarified his mind as to the character of the unknown man he was in search of, MacNab next passed under review the exact situation of every possible suspect at the moment when the crime was committed. From Rintoul he had learned that the housekeeper's call came through at a quarter to four. Allowing fifteen minutes for her investigations and for Bray's which followed, that fixed the murder within a minute or two of half-past three. Where, then, were all these people at that time? MacNab took out the note-book into which he had transcribed all the relevant facts obtained either from Rintoul's report, or the Procurator's precognitions.

Farthest away at the time, undoubtedly, were Mr. Willoughby, Dr. Frossard and Mrs. Brent, for they had left in a car almost half an hour before, and a car can move quickly. How quickly Mr. Willoughby's chauffeur moved his master's car that day MacNab perceived when he came to consider Cresswell. It was from Rintoul himself that the evidence came as to Cresswell's position, for Rintoul had overtaken Cresswell on the high road, returning with a box of tennis balls which the others, being short of balls, had persuaded him to go and buy in the town. And at the time the car passed, Cresswell, Toplis and Miss Cresswell were knocking a ball about on the tennis court, Joliffe and Harwood in deck chairs, looking on while waiting for Cresswell's return with the tennis balls. It appeared that the tennis courts not being netted, many balls got lost in the bushes or disappeared down the slope on the other side of the drive. Mary Willoughby, also to fill in time while waiting for the new balls, had gone to hurry up tea.

Nearest of any to the scene of the crime undoubtedly were Mr. Bray and the boy Dick. But, of course, MacNab considered Bray as free from suspicion as Willoughby and Frossard, who had moved away so fast that the returning Cresswell had not met them on the road. In fact Cresswell, the only one who had police evidence as to his exact position at the time of the murder, did not seem to MacNab to be more free from suspicion than the timid and guileless tutor.

But, as a matter of fact, so far as position went, MacNab could not conceive how it was possible for any one of them to have committed the crime. With rather a sinking heart he turned to the question of motive. For here motive as a clue seemed not only deceptive, but useless. Brent was unpopular with all the men. All the young men were in love with Mary Willoughby, and, for anything he knew, that might apply even to this Dr. Frossard. But, having allowed the question of motive to enter his mind, MacNab in his helplessness began to consider Mr. Willoughby himself. It was perhaps inevitable that he should. The thing had been hovering on the fringe of his mind all the morning. He recalled the queer shock he had received while talking with Willoughby the previous evening in the smoking-room. The shadow of suspicion then raised by something Willoughby said had been killed in his subsequent talk with Bray, who had drawn clouds of suspicion on himself. But since from the point of view of character Bray stood cleared, MacNab returned to Willoughby, who, at least, did possess some of the qualities of mind without which this murder could not have been carried through.

The moment MacNab let himself go on Willoughby he was amazed to see how strong a case could be made out against him. He was obviously a dominating, masterful type of man. MacNab remembered that gesture with which he had pushed aside his letters at the breakfast table, and, small detail as that was, he had little doubt the man had been accustomed to do the same with human beings. He recalled, too, the hush that followed his entrance, the look the others had cast on his face, as if to read his mood. Even the unobtrusive way in which his son had slipped from the room was not without significance. And then the relentless fashion in which he had pursued, caught, and got a conviction against the poacher, Haggerty, was in itself evidence of his determined character.

As for motive, that certainly was not far to seek. A man of much less strength of character than Willoughby might well object to see his daughter the wife of a man whose father had committed suicide. Willoughby had objected to the engagement at the start, on the score that artists made unsatisfactory husbands, but had later given way. Had he really or only pretended to give way? Had Brent been invited to Arrochmore simply because it was a place in which there would be excellent chances of making away with him under conditions least likely to awaken suspicion?

None of the other members of the house party liked Brent. Willoughby alone among the men was supposed to like him. Yet MacNab judged from all he had heard about the young man that he was not exactly a likeable person. True, Brent might very well have presented a very different side of his character to Mary Willoughby's father from that which he had shown to Dick's tutor. But Willoughby was far too shrewd to be taken in in such a matter. If, then, Brent at all merited the disfavor in which he was held by the others, it was a certainty that Willoughby's liking for him must be a mere pretense. But a pretense for what purpose? MacNab recognized that as host Mr. Willoughby had not the freedom of the others in showing their real feelings. He had a duty to his guest, and MacNab considered it probable, from the treatment he had himself received, that in this matter Willoughby would be rather punctilious. Still, that need only mean in Brent's case a little more effort and restraint than had to be exercised in playing the good host to the others. And it was precisely the clear evidence of the capacity for restraint in the Duchray murderer which had first taken MacNab's eye. That man was one who knew how to bide his time. He had waited for the favorable day on Keppoch Moor. When the single shot failed, he had waited for his next chance, and took it only when it seemed safe.

More than that, there was another item in the count which seemed not without significance. Brent's father had committed suicide. How easy to suggest that the son had merely followed his father's example! Was this the reason why Willoughby last night had been so ready to explain how and why the father took his own life?

MacNab had to steady his whirling head by trying to consider all that told against the theory of Willoughby's guilt. There was evidence that Willoughby had not been on the moor at the time of the shooting, and there was what looked like conclusive evidence that he had been far from Duchray at the time of the murder. There was, in a word, in each case that with which the man who plans a murder of deliberation is most anxious to provide for himself—an alibi. And it did not escape MacNab's notice that Willoughby was the one man among all the possible suspects who had an apparently complete alibi for both occasions. And each alibi, too, was one that, as it were, proclaimed itself. It was perfectly well known that Mr. Willoughby had gone to Inverness on the day of the Keppoch Moor affair, and there was even the murdered man's mother, who could testify to his absence at the time when her son was shot dead in the library. But, as many a criminal who thought himself safely sheltered under this cloak has discovered, an apparently perfect alibi is as likely to draw rather than avert suspicion on himself; and an alibi, if upset, has also the disadvantage of proving the crime to be one not of momentary passion, but of deliberation.

MacNab, glancing at his watch, rose to his feet. A certain sense of excitement came to him, something like what the hound must feel when he first scents the fox, or the angler when he sees the snout of a big fish break the water. He did not think much of the Keppoch Moor alibi, anyway. Willoughby might have been to Inverness, but he was not so far from the moor as that about the time of the shooting. Hugh Cameron, the navvy, had seen him on the road. In testing Hugh Cameron's alibi, the police had unconsciously been also testing Willoughby's. And in making it certain that Cameron could on foot have travelled from that spot on the moor to where he had been seen by Willoughby, they had made it evident that Willoughby in his car could have covered the distance much more easily.

Even the lie told by Toplis fitted better into a theory of his employer's guilt than anywhere else. When his untruth was discovered that young man had said he had acted as he did because he thought Brent had been unwittingly shot by one of the party. But if Toplis, who had been walking nearest to Brent, had seen something—Willoughby among the bushes possibly—it was at least as likely that he would lie for his master's protection as for any of the others. Well, Mr. Toplis must be put through it once more. MacNab reperused the statement Rintoul had given him which explained how his sergeant had come to discover the lie told him by the secretary on the moor.

No very expert liar, the red-headed youth could be, if he could be so readily found out as all that.

MacNab hurried along the path with a light step to his appointment with Mrs. Brent. True, Willoughby's second alibi seemed a much harder nut to crack. The time at which the shot in the library was fired had been established beyond any shadow of doubt, and it was equally certain that Willoughby was miles away at that moment. For all that MacNab went on, fortified with the conviction that if Willoughby were the guilty man there must be a discoverable hole somewhere, even in that alibi.

CHAPTER XIX

AN IMAGINARY GAME OF TENNIS

Mrs. Brent's lively little black eyes were on his face as soon as the door was opened.

"Well?" she demanded, her hand indicating a chair. She was too eager for news to wait until he had seated himself. "What progress? Who have you seen? What do you think?" she demanded again.

Inwardly MacNab marveled over her absorption in the one thing that had become the all-engrossing interest in her life—this thirst for revenge. Indeed, it was more than her chief interest—it was a passion that burned. He read as much in her burning eyes and in the tension of her hands on the chair. Possibly her helpless condition had something to do with it—as much, perhaps, as her naturally dominating will. Reduced to a state of physical inactivity, that strong will raged within her like some wild animal robbed of her cub while shut up herself in a cage. But MacNab had merely been waiting till the door was shut. He sat down beside her by the window.

"I had a nice breakfast," he said, adding quickly as he saw the frown come to her eyes, "It gave me much food for thought."

"Make anything of it?" she asked.

"Well," he admitted, "the process of digestion is not yet complete; but I'm fairly certain of one thing, and that is that the secretary, Mr. Toplis, knows more than he has ever told. More than that, I believe that complicity in the affair is narrowed down to one of two men, one of whom may well be Toplis himself."

"And the other?" she inquired.

But MacNab was not at this stage ready to mention Willoughby. Indeed, he thought it would be dangerous to bring in his name. He knew she believed Willoughby had grown to like his future son-in-law. She herself had told him how Willoughby used to listen in the evenings to his playing. It would take a great deal more, MacNab thought, than such grounds for suspicion as he yet had to convince her, or anyone else for that matter, that Willoughby might be the unknown criminal. He thought for a moment.

"I'm not prepared to say yet. Indeed, I'm not sure," he went on quickly, "till I find out a little more."

"From whom?" she inquired, obviously believing the answer would give her a clue to the unknown suspect's identity.

"Well, from you," he said. "There's this Dr. Frossard, now; I've been told very little about him."

Mrs. Brent flung up a wildly protesting hand.

"Oh," she cried, "you needn't suspect him; he's out of the question."

MacNab did not suspect Frossard. In bringing in his name he merely did so in order to obtain some information on a point concerning Willoughby without letting her perceive who the unnamed suspect was. Her disgust, however, at the notion of any one suspecting Frossard interested him.

"Still, I'd like to know about him," he said. "What sort of a man he is, for instance, and what he was doing here."

Mrs. Brent, like one yielding to an irrelevant curiosity, snapped off a description:

"A big, fat, lazy man, always half asleep. At least," she amended, "only awake to what had happened in prehistoric ages. He came here to rest, and looked as if he had never done anything else in his life." She pouted out her lips, either in contempt or in anger that a man with the full use of his legs could make so little use of them. "You needn't suspect him; he never had enough energy to take him up to the moor. As for what happened in the library, he hated noise too much ever to have used a firearm, even if he had known such weapons existed. Revolvers, you see, didn't belong to his period. A spear or a club, or a bow and arrow, maybe—but never that."

This brought MacNab close to his real question.

"You surprise me," he remarked. "I'd have thought a motor-car would be as much out of his period as firearms."

The twisted smile reappeared.

"You forget his laziness," she reminded him. "A seat in a Rolls-Royce is even more comfortable than any easy-chair in the library.

"Ah!" MacNab cried, like one who had received sudden light on a troublesome problem, "then it was he who suggested the drive in the car that afternoon."

Turning to look at her, he read in her eyes not only that he was mistaken in supposing such a thing, but also that he had risked his reputation in jumping to that conclusion.

"Of course he never did. For one thing, he wouldn't have enough initiative. For another, the car is not his but Mr. Willoughby's."

"Oh, of course, it was Mr. Willoughby who suggested the drive."

"Wrong again," she snapped. "It was Miss Willoughby."

This was a surprise indeed for MacNab. The stare with which he met it suggested incredulity.

"Are you quite sure of that?" he asked. "Forgive me, Mrs. Brent, but this may be more important than you imagine."

"It's quite true," she said. "Mary came over after lunch to see Eric; Toplis was with her, but didn't come in. She said the others would be playing tennis all the afternoon, and that if I liked to go for an airing in the car she would wheel Eric in my chair along to the tennis court, where he could be looked after and have tea with them later."

"But—Dr. Frossard?" MacNab reminded her.

"Oh," she explained, "his going was an afterthought. When Mr. Willoughby arrived in the car he found Dr. Frossard in the library and more or less forced him away from his book and his easy-chair. Of course he was unwilling. He grumbled to me about it afterwards in the car, saying there was quite enough fresh air coming in at the study window to satisfy him."

"I see," said MacNab.

"Afterwards Mr. Willoughby explained to me that he had invited Dr. Frossard because he saw that Eric wanted to have the library to himself. In fact he told me Eric had thanked him as soon as Dr. Frossard went upstairs to get his things."

MacNab bent forward.

"But, Mrs. Brent, wasn't your son going out to the tennis courts with Miss Willoughby?"

The question evoked a deep sigh.

"Ah, if only he had!" she said. "When they carried me downstairs, and I saw my wheel-chair had been removed from its place beside the library door, I thought he had already gone."

"So you never knew he had stayed on in the library till—till afterwards?"

"Of course not. Mary explained later that after she had seen me she went to him with the suggestion about coming in my chair to the tennis, telling him he could have the chair as I was going for a drive. But he refused to go—said he wanted to be alone." Mrs. Brent's voice caught at this memory, and there was a pause while she drew out her handkerchief. "The girl afterwards said she was sure Eric was angry because he saw Toplis outside waiting for her. But she didn't tell me about his refusal at the time, because she was afraid I wouldn't go for the drive, and she wanted me so much to go. Now," Mrs. Brent concluded, getting a grip of herself again, "perhaps you will tell me to what all this leads?"

MacNab prevaricated.

"Well," he said, "it more than ever forces me to believe that Mr. Toplis knows more than he has yet revealed."

"Then don't you think the time has come for telling Mr. Willoughby? He certainly could make the young man speak out."

MacNab almost jumped from his seat.

"No!" he said in a voice the old lady had not yet heard.

"But—" she began protestingly. He cut her short by rising from his chair.

"I throw up the case if you do," he declared. "I give it up now unless you undertake to say nothing under any circumstances to any person whatever."

His unexpected vehemence startled her. But she was not the kind of woman to be easily suppressed. Indeed, after a moment in which her eyes hardened and the muscles tightened about her mouth, it looked as if she might order MacNab from the house. Then she thought better of it. He saw her face relax. Probably she divined not only that he knew more than he had said, but also that it was something even she could not make him divulge. At any rate, from that moment Mrs. Brent had a deeper respect for him. Like most strong-minded women, she respected men who were at least as determined as herself.

"Very well," she said mildly after an interval. "With your experience one must suppose you know what you're doing."

Her capitulation relieved MacNab's mind, for he now recalled his undertaking to the Procurator-Fiscal, Murray, on whose behalf he was really acting.

"I must take the responsibility of handling this man Toplis myself. Mr. Willoughby might easily let out something which would put him on his guard," he said with decision—a decision born of his conviction that that was precisely what Willoughby would do if given the chance.

"Well," she said, "an idea came to me after I awoke this morning. If you suspect Toplis of sheltering any one, I think it's most likely to be young Joliffe."

"Joliffe? Why?" he cried in his surprise, for this was a name which so far had attracted little of his attention.

"Because Joliffe was his friend. He was invited here on that account. No one, I gather, knew anything about him except Toplis."

MacNab found the suggestion unwelcome. He didn't like this introduction of a new aspect at that stage. It made him feel like the tired traveler who turns a corner on his road and finds an unexpected extra mile still between him and his destination. Yet he felt bound to consider Joliffe, though he did so now only with the view to a quick elimination. But Joliffe, he found, bothered him at once. He had been within striking distance both on the moor and at Duchray. True, on the moor he occupied the position farthest away from Brent. But even from his own story, as given in the police report, he had lost touch with the others. That is to say, he had been out of their sight for quite a time, since he was the last to arrive on the scene after Brent fell.

The sergeant had suspected Cresswell mainly, it seemed, because Joliffe had said he lost sight of Cresswell at the burn. But that also meant that Cresswell lost sight of Joliffe at that important spot. So both men had identical chances of creeping down the burn to get within the necessary range of the victim. Of the two, Cresswell had drawn suspicion, because he was the only one who, after the shooting, came on out of the mist carrying his gun. Suspicion in his case was legitimate enough till the mistake about the two guns had been cleared up. But, after that, why had not Joliffe been considered?

The fact that he arrived on the scene without a gun proved nothing either way, for since he came in last he was the man who had most time to get back after shooting Brent, drop his gun in the forward position shown on the sergeant's note-book, and then come down again to look for the others, as he had said. Surely, of the two, Joliffe was the more suspect. To arrive on the scene without a gun was exactly what a guilty man would prefer to do. The fact that Cresswell alone came up with his gun told, if anything, in his favor, since, if not innocent and unsuspecting, he could so easily have dropped it as all the others had done.

It looked as if the police had blundered about more than Cresswell's gun. With apparently much astuteness this sergeant had picked up what he assumed to be Brent's gun, and on finding two unspent cartridges in the breech, concluded, rightly enough, that the man had been shot by another gun. But, not having made certain who the owner of the gun he examined was, he had drawn a totally erroneous inference from it. For since the gun examined happened to be Cresswell's he was more free from legitimate suspicion than any of them. Yet at the time he was the only one they suspected! This ought to stand as a classic example of the over-astute policeman. A simple, direct question as to ownership would have avoided this blunder, and might have put the officer on the right track from the start. But would that track have led to Joliffe?

Mrs. Brent's patience gave out.

"And what may that smile mean?" she inquired.

MacNab came back from his thoughts.

"Did I smile?" he asked.

"I'm not objecting; it's the first sign of life you've shown for the last ten minutes," she explained dryly.

"I was thinking of a policeman who was too clever by half," he said.

"As a warning to yourself, maybe," she suggested.

"Oh, I don't think I need that yet," MacNab protested.

"Well," she agreed, "you've shown no signs of being over-clever so far. I hope you'll not be so slow that I'll have to pretend indisposition, and take to my bed to give you more time here. I do not like lying in bed—nor waiting for things to happen," she added.

That afternoon MacNab did his best not to keep her waiting. While she was lying down he strolled along the pathway till he reached the seat opposite the tennis courts. The Joliffe possibility was still not cleared away from his mind. Almost certain that Toplis was sheltering someone, he now reckoned the chances to be equal as to whether that unknown person was his friend Joliffe or his employer Willoughby.

On the question of motive he recognized that the case against Willoughby was infinitely stronger, but, on the other hand, for all he knew Joliffe might have a motive that seemed strong enough to himself. Joliffe, in fact, was the dark horse in the case. He was simply the one man among them all who had been entirely overlooked. So, having decided that the new suspect could undoubtedly have shot Brent on the moor, MacNab sat fixedly regarding the empty tennis courts, peopling them with the figures who had played there on that fateful afternoon. He was trying to see how Joliffe could have got away to Duchray, shot Brent and returned without drawing any attention to his absence. The courts, it was true, were much nearer Duchray than Arrochmore; but even so it was impossible to see how the thing could be done. The figures he saw on the courts to start with numbered six—Joliffe, Miss Cresswell and her brother Harwood, Toplis and Miss Willoughby. Therefore, however they played, whether doubles or singles, if one went away there would be an odd one out. Now, with whatever absorption the others were playing, the one left out would assuredly notice Joliffe's disappearance.

But all six had not been on the courts all the time. He began to reconstruct the tennis party. Sometime later two had left. Cresswell had been sent into the town to buy a new set of tennis balls. In his absence Miss Willoughby had gone back to Arrochmore to hurry up tea. This was the crucial time. When the car passed there were but four on the courts—Miss Cresswell and Toplis playing, and Harwood and Joliffe looking on. But that situation left the difficulty still there. It was just as difficult to get away unmarked as before. Yet it had been done.

MacNab gazed along the pathway towards Duchray. It would be queer indeed if a figure conspicuous in white flannels against the dark green background of the trees would not draw attention to itself and provoke questions afterwards. No, if any of the players went to Duchray that afternoon it certainly was not along that pathway. And, of course, whoever went must have gone after the car with the older people in it had left for their drive.

In his mind's eye MacNab visualized the car as it glided down towards the junction where the two avenues met. As it could not pass the tennis courts without being seen and its occupants recognized, its departure would be like a signal to show the man his chance had come. But how had he got away unperceived? How had his absence remained unmarked? It was in obtaining answers to such questions as these that MacNab was handicapped by his supposed position in the house. All to the good as it was to be there unsuspected in the character of Mrs. Brent's family solicitor, he was precluded by that very fact from putting those questions which as a detective he most wished to have answered. He had to tread delicately. One question too many, or one too pointed, and the game was up.

He returned once more to consider the tennis courts. Overhead a wood pigeon began cooing a soft accompaniment to the current of his thoughts. Higher up the slope behind him the occasional staccato crow of a cock pheasant punctuated his difficulties. He soon heard neither. He did not overhear even when Mr. Toplis and Miss Cresswell, strolling along on the turf under the tree branches, paused at a yard or two's distance. But he did hear the secretary's chuckle.

"Pondering some knotty problem in law, I bet," Toplis nodded.

MacNab jumped to his feet.

"We came to ask you to have tea with us," the girl said with a bright smile.

MacNab expressed his pleasure. Toplis had his arm linked in Miss Cresswell's; they seemed on excellent terms with each other.

"What were you thinking about, really?" the young man asked, laughing.

MacNab smiled, too.

"Oh, I was only playing an imaginary game of tennis," he replied.

"But you looked so dashed serious."

"Well," MacNab rejoined, "and what is taken more seriously nowadays?"

"Oh, I don't know," Toplis said. "We don't, anyway."

They began to move back towards the house.

"Only when we lose the balls," Miss Cresswell amended.

"Lose the balls!" MacNab exclaimed. "Where? How?

As he paused and turned to regard the wide expanse of turf the others stopped, too.

"Oh, well, you've got to lose your temper, perhaps, and get as hot about it as Ronnie Joliffe before that happens. Mr. Toplis can tell you about that," she added with a smile.

"Can I?" Toplis inquired. "I've forgotten that I could, then."

"Oh, come!" said the girl. "Don't you remember that afternoon—" She stopped abruptly, and the smile went from her lips as she herself remembered that afternoon.

"Let's get on, I'm thirsty," Toplis cut in.

MacNab had to let the moment pass. Keenly aware though he was that something which might be highly significant lay behind Ronnie Joliffe's exhibition of bad temper on *that* afternoon, he dared not risk probing into it. He dared not seem too inquisitive about a man he had never met, especially when Toplis gave such evident signs that he wished to drop the subject. MacNab resolved to return to it when Mr. Toplis was not there, for he found himself deeply interested. He meant to find out what connection there was between Joliffe's loss of temper and the lost tennis balls.

CHAPTER XX
MISS CRESSWELL EXPLAINS

It was while they were at tea that MacNab for the first time saw Mary Willoughby. All the others, except Mr. Willoughby and Dick, who had gone off somewhere in the car, and of course Mrs. Brent, were there. Miss Cresswell was acting as hostess at the tea table when the door opened and Miss Willoughby came in. It was Miss Cresswell's exclamation that drew MacNab's attention to her appearance.

"Mary! How—how sweet of you!"

Evidently her reappearance among them had not been expected. When Mr. Toplis, to whom he had been talking, went to join the others who had crowded round the girl, MacNab was able to examine her at his leisure.

"Please don't fuss over me," she pleaded. "I just want . . . some tea." The pause and the break in her voice showed that the want she had first thought of was something else. Her voice, unlike the clear round voice of her friend Miss Cresswell, was soft and low in pitch. While Toplis placed a chair for her by the window, Mr. Bray almost rushed to the table to procure the tea. Before she moved her chair back out of the sunlight MacNab saw enough to comprehend how this girl might easily turn much stronger heads than Mr. Bray's. He had caught the questioning look she cast on him as soon as she perceived his presence. Her eyes were fine, though of a color he could not see at that distance, but probably seemed larger than they were because of the small, delicately pale face. She looked infinitely pathetic and appealing. There was a suggestion of—glamour was the only word he could think of—about her. All her movements had some sort of grace about them—natural, not studied, MacNab decided, since at such a time she would not be thinking of making any such effect.

Toplis pushed Miss Cresswell away in a fashion which revealed the good terms in which they stood to each other.

"No, no, Brenda," he said. "You've had chances Bray and I hadn't. You go away; it's our turn now, eh, Bray?"

Mr. Bray, who stood by with plates in each hand, and looking as if he would like to carry her another in his mouth, nodded a weak assent. Brenda Cresswell protested, but Toplis, who seemed to overlook nothing, drew her attention to MacNab, and she yielded instantly.

The Arrochmore drawing-room was large and lofty, a room which had in the old days—long before even the days of Hanging George— been the banqueting hall. Indeed, it was sufficiently spacious to have served as the gathering place for half the clan. At this moment, however, its great size served not only to dispense with the need for immediate introductions between Miss Willoughby and MacNab—it offered MacNab an excellent chance of talking to Miss Cresswell with no risk of being overheard. And she, with a little smile of apology for leaving him alone, led the way to a window seat still more remote, as if she intended to atone by keeping him to herself.

"Mary's hardly fit to meet—new people yet," she explained. MacNab liked the way she avoided calling him a stranger.

"Of course not," he agreed; "especially a stranger like myself, who is only here on account of what happened."

"Yes," she said, "there's that, of course. But what I feel is that the best thing now would be for her to see more people—of her own age, of course—and to give her something to do. I mean, take her out of herself."

"Seems a pity the others went," he said. "Mrs. Brent told me about them."

"Yes," the girl sighed. "We were so happy. Of course it seemed the right thing for them to go at the time. But now they could do so much good if they were here! We were all so happy," she repeated.

The moment did not seem suitable for a mention of Joliffe's ill temper. He switched over to the second matter he had on his mind.

"Happy till that fateful day on the moor, of course," he said, picking up his cup.

"Yes, that was the beginning of it. Do you know, I always say the wretch who fired at him there was the person really responsible for his death. Don't you agree with me—as a lawyer, I mean?"

"As a man I do most certainly. I only hope the scoundrel will be caught."

"Well, it's about that Mr. Willoughby is away seeing the police now. It appears they know the man—a road navvy—and they want Mr. Willoughby to have a look at him." She glanced round to make sure she was not overheard. "You know, of course, Mr. Brent was mistaken for Mr. Willoughby?"

MacNab nodded.

"Because of the white coat—yes, I've heard that. Tragic indeed to borrow a coat and get shot for it."

"Oh, it wasn't like that," Miss Cresswell corrected. "Mr. Willoughby wasn't there. That's the irony of it. He was in Inverness at the trial of a poacher he'd caught. He never expected them to go out, you know—not a good day for the moor. It was only later when it cleared up that Mr. Joliffe suggested the shoot, and Mr. Toplis in the end gave way. That's why he blamed himself afterwards for what happened."

Unaware of how much more time he would have with her, and fortified by the fact that he had been presented with an answer to one important question, MacNab thought he could safely risk just one direct attack. He did so, however, not without feeling half ashamed of himself. It was a feeling he had almost forgotten. But now this girl, apparently anxious merely to unburden her mind in a very human way, revived the old qualms he had once experienced when the interests of justice forced him to pump information from the unsuspecting.

"Ah," he said, "if only Mr. Joliffe had been content with tennis when it cleared up!" Then before any comment could come he added, "But no doubt he was better with a gun than a racquet."

Brenda Cresswell stared at him blankly, almost stupidly, for what seemed a full minute.

"You did not know him," she said. "How can you know that?"

MacNab smiled.

"Oh, no, I don't know him. But I think I heard you say something about his losing his temper at tennis."

Her responsive smile came quickly.

"Oh, yes, I see; but that only happened that afternoon."

"Something annoyed him?"

"Yes. I think it was because—well—because Mary went away after my brother had gone to get the new balls. He began to knock the few we had left out of the court." She smiled reminiscently. "Soon there weren't enough balls left for more than two of us to play with."

"How extraordinary. Couldn't you get them back?"

A light had begun to dawn upon his understanding. Remembering the surroundings of the tennis courts, he knew her answer before she made it.

"Not those that get stuck up in the trees," she said, "nor those he banged down the slope among the bushes. Let me give you another cup of tea."

MacNab thanked her—in his heart for much more than the tea. Yes, he thought to himself while she was pouring it out, this riddle seems more than half solved. It was not impossible, now, to understand how Joliffe had got away from the others without his absence being remarked. With a sense of exhilaration he offered her a cigarette in exchange for the tea.

"But I suppose the poor young man was penitent afterwards," he said, feeling quite certain his guess was correct.

She looked up while he was holding the match, like one who did not comprehend.

"Oh, yes," she said, "I see. Mr. Joliffe, you mean?"

She blew out a cloud of smoke. "Indeed he was, and showed it, too, by going off to retrieve the lost balls."

"Climbing the trees, eh?"

She laughed outright, and then suddenly checked herself, glancing towards the other end of the room to see if she had been overheard.

"Oh, no. He didn't climb the trees; but he did go hunting after those that had run away down the slope among the bushes."

Whether or no Brenda Cresswell's laugh had been overheard, an end to their talk came at this point. Mary Willoughby disappeared through the door by which she had entered, and Toplis and Bray came along to join them.

Afterwards MacNab once more took a saunter along the pathway. Having reached a position at which Arrochmore was out of sight, he crossed the tennis courts, and, coming out on the Duchray section of the drive, stood there awhile in some thought. It was certainly very easy to knock a ball from the tennis court on to the road. A ball hitting the hard road surface would certainly bound over it and conceivably roll down the slope quite a long way. Among those trees and bushes it was easy to understand that a man might search for a long time without much success—even long enough, once he was out of sight, to get round to Duchray and shoot a man dead before he reappeared.

MacNab went back to resume his legal deliberations with Mrs. Brent, well satisfied with the way things were going.

CHAPTER XXI

THE SCINTILLA ASPERA

He found, however, when he reached Mrs. Brent's room, that she had much more important news for him than he had for her. At least, so the thing seemed to Mrs. Brent, and MacNab, having listened to her, was not disposed to disagree.

"Are you quite sure?" he asked, after hearing her tale.

She was in a highly excited state.

"I have no proof, if that is what you mean," she said, "but I'm morally certain it is as I say. Someone has been in this room while I was taking my usual siesta this afternoon, and whoever it was went through all these papers."

She pointed to the pile of letters and documents lying on her small table by the window. He sat down, wondering if some suspicion of his real profession had been aroused. Was this an attempt to find out whether any work connected with Mrs. Brent's legal interests was actually being done by him? He had had the foresight to have a nice black japanned deed-box sent on from London with his clothes; but he had not thought it necessary to provide himself with legal documents to fill it. So far from that, he had divested himself of all papers or letters which could give a hint of his identity; and all those papers he left behind with his other baggage at the Loch Laggan Hotel.

Still, he had with him the various precognitions taken by Murray and the plan of the section of Keppoch Moor removed from the sergeant's note-book. All these papers were in the locked deed-box which he had left with Mrs. Brent to supply a silent witness, if such were necessary, to his supposed business with her. MacNab unlocked the box and had a look at its contents. He did not think it had been opened. It was highly unlikely, too, that anyone could have come into that room and, seeing the box for the first time, find himself by chance the happy possessor of a key that fitted the lock. And it was a certainty that if the papers had been read it was by someone much more methodical than the person who had rummaged through Mrs. Brent's letters. No, he was nearly certain no one had handled the papers in his deed-box. But that did not save him from further anxiety.

He looked down at her pile of letters.

"It was some servant," he said, "some curious prying maid. They are often like that."

She nodded assent after a moment.

"That's quite true, as I know from experience," she said with a breath of obvious relief. "I've caught them before now with their noses in my letters, so taken up with what they read that they never heard my wheels."

But he wished he could be more certain.

"I suppose," he said, "there wasn't much in any of these letters that would be—well—compromising. You hadn't, I mean, made any references to me in any letter to a friend?"

"Certainly not," she retorted almost acidly; "and even if I'd been such a fool, there's been no time for anyone to refer to it in her reply. These letters on my table, as you might know without being told, are letters of sympathy to which I was trying to reply."

So far, so good, MacNab thought to himself. But if no hint as to the suspicions they held had been gleaned from her correspondence, the fact still remained that the room contained no papers bearing on the complicated legal business for which he was supposed to be there. He thought over the situation for a few minutes. If the prying eyes were merely those of a servant, no attempt would be made on the deed-box. On the other hand, if this had been the work of someone else who had far more at stake, he did not doubt the box would receive further attention. And he had as little doubt that next time their visitor would come much better equipped for opening it. The man who had provided himself with a duplicate key to the library door at Duchray so that he would be able to place the other key in the murdered man's pocket, was not likely to be beaten by the lock of a small deed-box.

When he had explained the situation to Mrs. Brent, they spent, at her suggestion, a couple of hours in fabricating on sheets of foolscap a variety of documents in the wording of which all the legal jargon known to either of them was embodied. MacNab, who had an idea of his own on how to handle the trouble, yielded to the old lady's whim, thinking that it had just a chance of allaying suspicion if the documents had to be hastily examined.

From time to time, however, as he wrote, he kept puzzling as to what had roused suspicion of his *bona fides*. What had he said, and to whom had he said it? Finding no answer, he tried to argue himself into the belief that it could only be some prying, nosey-parker of a maid servant, although he hadn't really believed that when he suggested it to Mrs. Brent. Of course, if it wasn't a servant the position was serious, even if the document he was concocting served its purpose, since suspicion, once aroused, would be very easily reawakened. And it was very certain that after this there would be little scope for putting questions to any member of the household.

"And the said property as heretofore specified," Mrs. Brent dictated.

"And the said property as heretofore specified," MacNab wrote.

"Shall be held in trust for—"

"Shall be held in trust for—" MacNab repeated.

"And on behalf of," she continued.

MacNab laid down the pen.

"I've got it!" he whispered. "I've got it!"

"You mean—?"

He drew his chair closer.

"Notice this, Mrs. Brent. We have good reason to suppose that the person wanted is no longer in this house. I could give you my reasons for that belief. In fact, I came here prepared to tell you, since it was yourself who put me on his track. The point, however, now is that *if* your room was visited this afternoon while you were resting, and if it was because suspicion of why I am here had been somehow awakened—you follow me?"

"Quite. Go on," she responded impatiently, recognizing he had something new up his sleeve.

"Well, that means there's someone now in this house who is acting in the interests of the man who has left. Well, if you are right about this tampering with your letters, we have as good as got both of them."

The gleam of expectancy died out of her eyes.

"I don't follow you now," she said. "The man here—Toplis, of course—" she interjected confidently, "will simply warn his friend Joliffe."

"That's just the point," MacNab said; "he'll warn him, and we'll get our hands on the warning." He stopped her when she was about to interrupt again. And perceiving from his eagerness and confident tone that he felt sure of his facts, she kept silent. "Mrs. Brent, you don't know how we manage these things, of course; but it's quite a simple matter to get hold of all the letters which leave this house. I have merely to convince the Procurator-Fiscal that information vital to the case is likely to be found in a certain letter which will leave this house to-morrow morning, and he will see the postmaster and arrange that before dispatch that letter will first be read by Superintendent Rintoul. Then the man is as good as lost."

Watching her, he saw the wicked gleam return to her eyes.

"You are right," she cried, smiting the arm of her chair. "We've as good as won already."

That wasn't how he had put it; but he understood her point of view well enough. Her extreme bitterness could only be judged by one in her own condition who had suffered the same loss. The next breath her wits, sharpened by hate, pounced on what appeared to be a flaw in his strategy.

"The letter may have already gone by this evening's mail."

But he was able to reassure her. Nothing decisive, either way, could have been gathered from the search among her letters. And though the person in the house might have dispatched a letter that evening, he could do no more than communicate his suspicions. That he was unlikely to do until he had verified them—if he had a cool head, that was. In any event there would be further letters. More than that, the Police Superintendent would stop not only the outgoing but also the incoming mail as well.

"What do you think of that?" he demanded as he finished.

She yielded her objection, her tense face muscles relaxing.

"I see that after all you know your business," she said, sitting back contentedly. And then her gaze went away through the open window, over the tops of the tree-clad slopes, over the loch and up to the high hills beyond. MacNab divined she considered the case to be practically over, and her immediate thirst for revenge being satisfied, she was now contemplating through the open window not the glories of the sunset, whose scarlet streaks had paled down to amethyst, nor the purple of the Ardgour Mountains, nor the darkening waters of Loch Linnhe, but life, her own life in the future, fixed in that wheel chair, without her son, and robbed of the glories which his fame would have reflected on herself. He broke into her thoughts with a question.

"Mrs. Brent, you can tell me where the telephone is placed at Duchray?"

"Yes," she said, "it's not easy to find unless you know. There's a small cloak-room behind the stairs; it's there, against the wall at the right of the door."

She appeared to know why he wanted this information, and her eyes went back towards the hills. He stood behind watching her for a minute or two. It was yet too early to think of entering Duchray without risk of being seen. And as he watched something came fluttering and dancing in at the open window. He put out his hand.

"Hullo!" he said, "a *scintilla aspera!*"

"A what?" she said, turning her head.

"A *scintilla aspera!* Look," he whispered, pointing.

"One of the rarest of British moths. I really must get him. Do you mind if I shut the window?"

Before she could reply he had the window down and went after the moth. He knew she thought him childish. But she wheeled round her chair to watch the hunt. He caught it at last as it nosed its way up the wall, and brought it to her imprisoned in both hands. In between his fingers she caught a glimpse of the light-grey wings, tipped with red.

"It's a sort of counterpart to the Red Admiral butterfly," he explained; "just as he flies quite a bit at night, so this little fellow's got the habit of roistering about in daylight before his enemies have gone to bed. That's why he's so rare." He looked round for something in which to put him. "Open the deed-box," he said, "he'll do very well there."

She wheeled her chair up to the table and at his request took out all the papers. Deftly, while she watched, half contemptuously, he got his hands inside the box, turned them down, and while holding the insect with one hand, whisked the other away and had the lid down before the *scintilla aspera* knew what had happened. That done, he locked the box and pocketed the key and the papers it had contained.

"Well, that's that," he said with an air of great contentment.

Suddenly she threw a swift glance at his satisfied countenance and then burst into a queer grating laugh.

"I see the idea," she said. "Yes, I believe I do."

"You do?" He was very pleased with himself.

She nodded, more pleased with him than even he was with himself.

"But there's one thing I don't believe."

"What?"

"I don't believe that moth is so rare as you said."

He smiled.

"Well, anyhow, Mrs. Brent, you must admit it came in here at the right moment."

A little later, when darkness had fallen, he got away from the house unobserved by any one, so far as he could tell, and made for Duchray.

The window gave him little trouble. He entered, shutting it behind him, pushing the catch home. Carefully holding his torch low to avoid throwing any of its radiance on the window blinds, he made his way along the room and out into the hall towards the telephone. Much as he would have liked a look round the library, he was well enough aware that even if there had been interior shutters for him to close, this was not the moment for the sort of examination he would like to make. As a matter of fact, MacNab now believed the time for bothering about what the library might reveal had passed.

He found the telephone at once—an old type of instrument with a bell and handle to turn. It was only when he began to whirr this handle that a sense of the eeriness of the old empty house closed in upon him. It wasn't that he felt the presence of any of its former tenants, not even of Hanging George himself; yet all the same he wanted to make as little noise as might be. Why there should be this desire in just the place noise did not matter he could not tell; but he turned the handle as warily as if it were something fragile, and when the answering bell went off in the dark at his ear it sounded like an unexpected scream echoing through the empty house. He knew he could hardly be in a safer place from which to get into touch with Rintoul. Yet for all that the eeriness of the tenantless house touched his imagination sufficiently to make him grope for the door and shut it gently.

On getting the police station, he was told the superintendent had gone home. However, on giving the assurance that his business was of sufficient importance, he was put through to Rintoul. Rintoul's acceptance of the call suggested he had been interrupted at some interesting moment in his domestic life.

"Yes, Superintendent Rintoul," he gruffly agreed.

"MacNab speaking. I want your help."

"Yes, what is it?" The question came sharply, charged not with impatience, but anticipation. "Where are you speaking from?"

"The cloak-room of an empty house. I've lost something you alone can recover for me. Can you see me about it?"

"Important?"

"And urgent. Matter of life and death."

A few minutes later MacNab was threading his way down the slope towards the arranged meeting with Rintoul. A meeting between them could not be avoided, since it might have been unsafe to have spoken with the police over the telephone about the interception of letters from a house like Arrochmore. MacNab did not know what the opportunities for telephonic interception were; but he was well enough aware how rapidly gossip spreads in country districts, and therefore took no risks. He had not even named the house from which he spoke, and of course Rintoul did not need to be told. When MacNab said he would meet him at the point where the boundary wall touched the road, Rintoul knew what grounds the wall bounded.

He found the descent easier than he had anticipated. The slope of the ground from Duchray down to the high road was thick set with trees and laurel shrubs, and in the dark he had expected to find the going difficult. But he discovered there was a rough foot track which ran down parallel to the wall, obviously formed by estate workers and the Duchray staff as a shorter cut than the winding drive farther to the west.

In ten minutes he was leaning over the low wall fronting the main road, waiting for Rintoul. He knew he would have to wait some time. From across the broad road, faintly white for a long distance on either side with its new surface, came the ripple and sigh of the tide flowing up Loch Linnhe. Overhead a half-hearted wind, which was uncertainly trying itself out now and then, fluttered the leaves off the trees. Across the velvet blackness of the loch a single pin-head of golden light from a cottage window alone marked the position of the farther shore. Occasionally a car swept past, its headlights laying two snowy pyramids on the road, and then going on to rake the trees as it swept round the curve on his left.

Rintoul might have arrived sooner had he not parked his car half a mile down the road. MacNab had drawn back when the footsteps came close, as he had done once or twice already. But when the steps ceased and he took a peep over the wall, he recognized Rintoul in the dim figure looking up from the roadway. Rintoul, as soon as he saw MacNab, slipped up the bank and over the wall like a shadow.

"Got hold of something?" he suggested.

"We think so," MacNab replied.

"We?" the superintendent repeated.

"Mrs. Brent is the other. In fact, if there's any credit going, it should be to her."

"Tell me what it is and I'll judge," Rintoul retorted.

MacNab did not make a long story of it, and Rintoul soon had a complete understanding of the position to which the case had been advanced. At the end he seemed a little disappointed.

"It boils down to this," he said: "if the person who interfered with Mrs. Brent's papers was not an inquisitive domestic, you think it must have been some person who suspects you to be interested in, let us say, what happened to Brent."

"And to-morrow we may know on whose behalf he became interested in her papers," MacNab said. Rintoul shook his head doubtfully.

"It's such a slender possibility, I'd hardly be justified in arranging to have the letters stopped," he said. "The plain fact is, we have still nothing tangible to suggest murder, except that revolver, and even it might have a perfectly natural explanation, if we only knew it, like Mr. Cresswell's gun," he added.

MacNab himself was only too conscious of the truth of what Rintoul said. They knew nothing against any one as established fact; however strong suspicion might be, it is one thing to suspect and another to know, and even to know may be a long remove from being able to prove. Rintoul, MacNab admitted, was quite right about that. He was aware that the number of what are called the unsolved mysteries of crime is far less than the public suppose. In most cases of murder at least the police usually know who the man is, but cannot prosecute because they have not sufficient evidence to secure a conviction.

"You see," Rintoul broke in, "we're already in Willoughby's bad books. He came to see me this afternoon. Cannot comprehend, he says, why we have failed to connect up someone with the affair on the moor." Rintoul sighed gently. "I don't know whether he's nervous that a man who is supposed to have shot at himself is still at large, but he was very unpleasant about it all. What he'd say if we stopped his letters to no purpose, and he got word of it—"

Though MacNab appreciated Rintoul's difficulty, it was of tremendous importance to him that next morning's letters from Arrochmore should be examined. To miss next morning's mail might be to miss getting the all-essential proof.

"Oh, well," he said wearily after they had debated to little effect for some time, "by to-morrow morning I'll *know* who the man in the house is. Unfortunately for me you won't act till you know yourself, and by that time the letter which might easily bring you a conviction will have passed beyond your reach."

That touched Rintoul up. As if to get away from MacNab's influence on him, he took a few steps along the side of the wall. MacNab watched him, a dim shadowy figure leaning with his arms folded on the top of the low wall. He watched in doubt as to the result. Had he known that already in this case the superintendent, after playing the

part of counsel for the defense, had yielded to his sergeant's arguments, only to discover later that those arguments had no foundation
in fact, he would have understood Rintoul's reluctance now. The superintendent, as he leaned on the wall, saw not the loch before him, but
that interview with Sergeant Cameron in his office. Cameron had
been so sure, not only that the affair on Keppoch Moor constituted
a case of attempted murder, but that the man was Cresswell. And
the sergeant's case against Cresswell was far stronger than MacNab's
against Joliffe.

Rintoul paused in his thought for a moment to note how Toplis
cropped up in connection with each of the two suspects. Cameron
had caught him out in an attempt at lying, and MacNab believed him
to be spying on himself in the interests of Joliffe. Rintoul's mind fastened on that coincidence. Of the two, Joliffe seemed the more likely,
since he and Toplis were old friends, and, so far as was known, Toplis
had no particular interest in shielding Cresswell.

MacNab saw Rintoul suddenly straighten himself and come towards him. His decision had been made.

"By what time will you know to-morrow?" he asked.

MacNab knew he was referring to his belief that the search among
Mrs. Brent's papers had been made by someone who suspected him
to be in the house for a purpose other than was alleged.

"By sunrise," MacNab promptly replied, "say about six-eighteen,
I'll know if the attempt has been made."

"And breakfast is about eight-thirty?"

"Any time from eight to nine."

"Very well," Rintoul nodded. "The mail goes out at nine-thirty.
Sergeant Cameron will be up at the house delivering a note at eight-
fifteen. If he sees you on the terrace he will take it that you've succeeded—that you know you've been right. Then I'll hold up the letters
and see what they contain. On the other hand, if you have failed—
well—just keep out of his sight—and mine, too," he added with a grin.

But it was the odd circumstance that Charles Toplis came into
sight in the way he did that was responsible for Superintendent Rintoul's decision to hold and inspect the Arrochmore mail.

CHAPTER XXII

TROUBLE WITH THE SUPERINTENDENT

MacNab slept very badly that night. Once he allowed himself to turn over in his mind the various possibilities and chances, it was not long before he began to toss and turn over in body as well as mind. But when sunrise came he was fast enough asleep.

It was a curious intermittent knocking at his door that ultimately made him sit up and rub his eyes. He did not take morning tea, and could not imagine what the knocking portended. Slipping from his bed, he peeped out to discover Mrs. Brent bumping her wheel chair against the door. He was amazed to find her there.

"You needn't gape at me like that," she said. "I expected you to be up long ago."

He glanced at his wrist watch and discovered it was nearly eight o'clock.

Late as it was for him, it was early for Mrs. Brent. It flashed through his mind that if she was seen it would certainly surprise any-one to find a client consulting her solicitor at such a time and place. The same thought seemed to occur to her. She waved him back.

"Put on the essentials and I'll come in," she commanded. And then, slewing her chair round, passed along the corridor.

He dressed as quickly as possible, but she was back before he had finished shaving. Razor in hand, he shut the door behind her.

"I awoke so early. When my tea came I got the maid to help me dress. I wanted so much to know about that box."

"The deed-box, you mean?"

"Yes. I had a nightmare dream about it. I dreamt about that *scintilla*— What do you call it?"

"*Aspera?*" he suggested. "What about it?"

"Well, I had a horrid dream about it. I dreamt that I saw all the red spots on its wings move one by one to its head, then it made itself quite small, and after running round inside the box very fast, it crawled up to the lock and poked its head out of the keyhole."

MacNab, turning to stare at her, almost cut himself.

"Yes, it was horrid. I knew it hated me. I saw it looking at me, and except for the red hair on its head the face might have been the face of that man Joliffe."

MacNab recovered himself.

"You were thinking too much about it before you went to sleep," he said.

"Yes, I know. But I wouldn't go into the sitting-room this morning without you for a lot, curious as I am to know what's happened there."

The speed with which he completed his toilet was not due mainly to his own curiosity about what had happened in her sitting-room; he felt fairly certain about that; but Rintoul's messenger was due in fifteen minutes, and that left him a bare ten minutes in which to ascertain what had happened in the room before showing himself to the police officer on the terrace.

Fortunately Mrs. Brent's bedroom door almost faced his own, otherwise Mr. Toplis, swinging past the end of the corridor as he came downstairs, might have seen the chair emerge from MacNab's room. As it was, from the hasty glance he threw along the corridor in passing, he would only suppose she had just left her own room. MacNab joined her a moment later.

"Got the key?" she whispered.

He now believed her to have invented that nightmare.

Not much good her going to the room, since she could not open the box. He already had the key in his hand.

"Quite a common ordinary key," he said, showing it. "I dare say there are dozens like it in dressing-tables and suit-cases."

The deed-box was on the table by the window, as Mrs. Brent noted, in exactly the same position. He inserted the key in the lock.

"Now," he said, "we'll see whether my moth has developed a face and red hair in the night." He fumbled a bit in getting the box open;

so much hung on what he found inside. Mrs. Brent had plenty of time to get her chair close to the table. Her lean neck seemed tense with expectation as she craned over.

The box was empty.

He showed her the inside. He showed her the lock; there was no hole inside through which the *scintilla aspera* could have crawled, even given the nightmare capacity of reducing its size to the dimensions of a flea. MacNab, leaving the box in her hands, hurried off, afraid of missing Rintoul's officer. As he crossed the hall he saw Toplis standing by the table on which letters were left for the postman's call at eight-thirty. In his hasty passing glance he perceived that the morning's outgoing mail looked considerable. Rintoul would have to be speedy in his examination if they were not to miss a post.

He had only taken a couple of turns on the terrace before he heard the soft whirr of bicycle wheels, and then the sliding of a foot on the gravel. Turning round, he saw a police sergeant in the act of dismounting. The man looked at him curiously. With the faintest inclination of the head MacNab wheeled round and resumed his promenade. But he did not go in to breakfast until the postman arrived to deliver the incoming mail and collect the outgoing.

Mr. Toplis, stirring his coffee while reading one of his letters, looked up as MacNab entered.

"Early bird," he nodded.

MacNab laughed outright. He would not have described Toplis as a worm exactly.

"You or me?" he inquired.

Toplis looked up again.

"Well," he admitted, "I'm earlier than usual. And here's another," he said as Miss Cresswell came in with a bright good-morning nod.

"How is Phil getting on?" Toplis inquired. "Still at St. Andrews with Jerry?"

Brenda Cresswell had been reading a letter which the secretary had evidently identified.

"All right," she said without looking up. "They do two rounds a day."

"Just had one from Ronnie. He's back at work, poor beggar. Says it's out of the question for him to come back here now."

Miss Cresswell broke the seal of another letter.

"Well," she said, "Phil and Jerry say they could come up here again sometime next week."

"Oh, I hope they will. It would do Mary good, I'm sure. Urge them to come. I've failed, you see, with Ronnie."

"Well, curiously enough," the girl said, "I've just written to do that."

MacNab experienced rather a chill. He could well understand that Joliffe had no great wish to return to Arrochmore for a while to come; but now he realized that Toplis had been too quick for him. It looked as if a vital letter had gone before it could be intercepted. More than that: he had been too late even to intercept the reply to it.

Mr. Willoughby and his son came in together. Their host seemed unusually affable.

"Dick and I are going fishing to-day," he remarked. "Not burn fishing, you know," Dick explained from the sideboard, "but big fishing in the boat on Loch Linnhe." Getting back with his full plate of kedgeree, he spared time for a glance across the table at MacNab. "Like sea trout?" he inquired.

"Better than salmon," MacNab asserted stoutly.

Mr. Willoughby laughed.

"Dick," he admonished, "don't offer what you haven't got yet. How about coming with us yourself, Mr. Francis?" he suggested.

As Dick looked at his father in round-eyed amazement, Mr. Willoughby continued, "We shall be quite alone, you know."

"Oh, father, he wouldn't like that at all," Dick put in.

They all laughed.

"Come, come, Dick, we're not as bad as all that," Mr. Willoughby said. Dick flushed up.

"I didn't mean that," he said. "I meant he wouldn't like fishing."

"Why not?" Toplis asked. They were all looking at Dick.

"Well, he's a lawyer, isn't he?"

"And what has that to do with it?" Mr. Willoughby persisted.

"Well, hang it all, fishing's sport," Dick replied.

They laughed again, Mr. Willoughby loudest of all.

"Dick," he explained, "can't see the two in combination."

"Oh," said MacNab, "I used to do quite a lot of fishing when I was a boy on the Teith at Callander."

"When you were a boy," Dick pointed out in self-defense.

MacNab let it go at that, and, as Mr. Bray came in, declined the invitation to a day's fishing, on the ground that already he did too much sitting. He would go for a long walk alone.

"Ah, yes," Mr. Bray commented. "One impulse from the vernal wood, if you know what I mean, to commune with Nature."

"D'you know," Mr. Willoughby said, as he chipped his egg, "if I may say so, I'm surprised that one of such decided character as Mrs. Brent should take so long to settle up her affairs."

MacNab considered before replying.

"I had not Mrs. Brent in my mind," he said; "but as to that, my experience tells me that people of decided character need most guidance; they are so apt to do rash things."

He was glad he had toyed so long over his breakfast when it came out that Mr. Toplis and Miss Cresswell were taking Miss Willoughby for a drive in the afternoon, and that Mr. Bray, free from work with Dick, intended to devote the day to the study of Butler's *Analogy*. MacNab felt he must see Rintoul, and he now knew that a visit to the police station would have little risk attached to it—for Rintoul he had to see, to find out what luck had attended his fishing.

Till lunch he put in the time with Mrs. Brent. She agreed with him that the deed-box had been opened by someone who must have been moved by a much stronger motive than curiosity. Such trouble would only be taken by some person who had developed doubts about his being a lawyer—someone looking for documentary evidence which would allay the fear that he was not. But two things troubled Mac-Nab. One was his own fear that the interception of the letters had come just a day too late; the other was that in his haste he had put the pseudo legal document he and Mrs. Brent had concocted into his pocket. Had he put it in the box along with the moth it probably would have set the searcher's mind at rest; and MacNab just at this stage would have given much to achieve that.

That afternoon, having entered the little town he strolled about looking at the shops, then entered Fraser's, and drank coffee at an upstairs window, from which he could look along the street. Finally, after a leisurely look round the museum, with its relics of the '45, he passed quickly into the police station. His first glance at the superintendent's face told him nearly all he wanted to know.

"Yes," he said before Rintoul could speak, "I was afraid we were too late. You got nothing."

"Nothing about the case," said Rintoul; "but there was something about yourself in one of the letters."

MacNab's hope rose at a bound.

"That might be almost as good—to begin with, anyway. What was it?"

"I took a copy of it." He put down his hand to pull out one of the small side drawers of his writing-table. "It's an extract from a letter from Toplis to Joliffe."

MacNab took the sheet of paper eagerly and read:

> "You ask if we have any new people. Well, only one, a lawyer, name of Francis, who's come to fix up Mrs. B.'s affairs. Doesn't seem to be doing much; making a long job of it, of course—the law's delays, you know, pay so well. He's a strange chap, though, with a face as long as a fiddle, and sleepwalker's eyes. Yet he is most curiously inquisitive, for all that; mightily interested, you know, for all his abstracted eyes and furrowed brow."

At sight of MacNab's face Rintoul burst into sudden laughter, his ill-humor gone.

"Ourselves as ithers see us," he remarked.

"Ay," MacNab admitted, taking the allusion, "but I don't see from what blunder it will free us."

"No?" Rintoul was serious again. "Well, speaking for myself, this will save me from repeating one bad blunder, anyway."

"You mean you will not again invoke the power of the post office, I suppose?"

"You may put it like that," Rintoul agreed. "To be candid, I don't like playing Peeping Tom in this way. It would be different if we got anything, but we have not. There's nothing in the letters I have the least right to know, and a good deal I don't want to know about their private affairs. I don't want to know what Mrs. Brent considers the best cure for varicose veins, nor what Mr. Toplis thinks of Mr. Bray, nor of Miss Cresswell's experiences with Vortex Underwear. Neither do I like reading her brother's appeals to her for money, nor do I like hearing Mr. Willoughby's opinions about myself. Have a cigarette." Rintoul pushed the box across the table. MacNab sat down, ignoring the offer.

The debate that followed between the two lasted long. At times it even threatened to degenerate into a wrangle; but Rintoul remained firm. He would not again risk being made to look foolish in his own eyes, as he now seemed to himself, when he yielded to the specious arguments set forth in that same room by his own sergeant. By the greatest good luck no actual harm had come of his weakness then; but Rintoul did not like being made to look foolish to himself, and he held out against MacNab's arguments and pleadings like a rock. The other man almost despaired. There was a point, in fact, when he stretched out a hand to lift his hat from the table; but when Rintoul said nothing he changed his mind, and instead picked a cigarette from the box. Rintoul, who had long ago risen as if to terminate the discussion, now stood on the hearthrug, hands behind back, looking every inch the Superintendent of Police.

"You know," MacNab said after a puff or two, "even this extract from the letter is not without significance, when associated with the search into the deed-box." He pushed the paper across the table. Rintoul remained where he was. "For one thing, why should this man Joliffe ask Toplis about any new people at all? Surely after what had happened it was only exceptional circumstances which could bring new visitors there so soon. He could hardly have had a new house party in his mind when he put that question, since he and the others had left because of the tragedy."

"Ye-s," Rintoul nodded. "I take your point. He had knowledge of some exceptional circumstance which might bring new people to the house. But the exceptional circumstance may be something perfectly innocent about which we know nothing."

"Oh, well," MacNab conceded, "I know I've got hold of nothing big and conclusive. They are all small points—straws, if you like. But how many straws does it take, all pointing in the same direction, too, to make a police superintendent see where the wind blows?"

Rintoul picked the paper from the table. He neither frowned nor smiled at the other's jape, but his eyes narrowed as he read. Suddenly he looked up.

"'Most curiously inquisitive,'" he quoted. "He draws attention to that and to your 'abstracted eyes.' That is, he seems struck by the contrast between your appearance and your habits."

MacNab rose and came over to take the sheet from Rintoul's hand.

"You're right," he said in affected surprise. "Quite right; it is odd he should stress the difference between what I look like and what I do."

"Ah—one little straw you missed," Rintoul said complacently.

"Oh, I've no doubt I've missed many." MacNab tapped the paper. "This, of course, is the letter he wrote after getting the deed-box open and finding it empty; that's why he was able to say I didn't seem to be doing much. Well, Rintoul, it's a pity you and I can't work together. I'm not likely to do much without you." He laid down the paper and took up his hat. Rintoul hesitated.

"Look here," he said at last, "if only I could be sure this fellow, this Toplis, had been searching your room—"

He got no time for more.

"I'll prove that," MacNab cut in. "I'll prove it to demonstration this evening that Toplis suspects why I am in the house. But you alone, Rintoul, can get your hands on the essential proof."

"You mean through intercepted letters?"

"Exactly. Stop them, both ways—those that come and those that go."

For a moment the issue hung in the balance. Then Rintoul succumbed.

"All right, I agree," he said, relaxing.

After that they put their heads together to fix up their plans. Rintoul, it appeared, was keenly anxious to get on with the affair, since Mr. Willoughby had pressed him so hard for the arrest of the man who had attempted the life of one of his guests. MacNab perceived that the superintendent, being only human, would be rather more than pleased if he could show Mr. Willoughby that the attack had come from one of the guests themselves. Then, having arranged their means of communication with each other, MacNab left the office.

It was close on six before he got back to Arrochmore.

CHAPTER XXIII
THE BEDROOM DOOR

MacNab had assured Rintoul he would establish that evening the identity of the person who had twice searched the sitting-room. He did not doubt in his own mind that the man was Toplis, neither did he doubt that Toplis, having become suspicious but not certain, was acting in his friend's interests. But if he could prove that the secretary had been ransacking the room, it would not only fortify Rintoul, but also be evidence supporting whatever the intercepted letters might contain.

He had evolved a method by which he thought Toplis might be trapped. It was a trick he had used before with success, and as soon as he entered the house he began preparing it. At breakfast Mr. Willoughby had suggested they would like to see him at dinner that night if Mrs. Brent would spare him.

MacNab was already familiar with the habits of the house. He knew that it was the custom for the men, after having dressed, to take their cocktails in the billiard-room and, if sufficient time remained, they might play a hundred up. Seeing no one about, he entered the billiard-room now, and, finding it empty, went in to remove a cube of chalk from one of the table pockets. He then went to the sitting-room. Mrs. Brent seemed to have retired earlier that day. Anyway, she was not there, though a glance around revealed the work-basket which contained her various sewing materials. From the basket he pocketed a reel of white cotton. He then went to his own room and put in half an hour with a book before changing. Then he set his trap.

MacNab's argument with himself led him to the conclusion that his bedroom was the next place likely to be searched for informa-

tion as to his real identity. The sitting-room had yielded nothing conclusive, therefore the man would argue that this might mean one of
two things: either that there was no secret to hide, or that everything
vital to his real identity had been removed from the sitting-room. But
the bedroom, though much less easy of access than the sitting-room,
must contain clues which would settle the question whether Mac-
Nab was a lawyer or a detective. MacNab's idea now was to make his
bedroom much more accessible. Accordingly, having finished dressing by a quarter-past seven, he set about dressing his door. It was
a nice door, all white enamel. He broke off a length of cotton from
the reel and, after having drawn it many times across the cube of
chalk from the billiard-room, fastened each end of the thread from
one side of the door to the other, at a height of about four and a half
feet from the ground, then, stooping under the thread, he closed the
door after him. There was no one about yet. From various angles he
examined the result; the thread was quite invisible against the white
background of the door. He was aware, of course, that during dinner
his room would be entered by some housemaid; but the trap would
have sprung, if it was to work at all, before then.

On entering the billiard-room once more he found its only tenant
to be Miss Cresswell. She was already dressed and passing the time
by knocking the balls about.

"Yes," she said, "I'm down early because I've a special cocktail of
my own mixing for to-night. You must try it."

MacNab expressed his willingness and took up a cue. As he was
glancing along its length she said: "I see you play."

"Very keen on it, but I don't get many chances," he replied.

"How about a game till the others come down?" she suggested.

He had reached twenty-seven to her thirty-five when the door
opened and Toplis looked in. His eyes widened as he saw MacNab
stretching over the table to get into position for a difficult cannon
shot. He stood still until the shot had failed.

"Ah," he said, after a glance at the score board, "no chance for me
till after dinner."

Before Miss Cresswell could offer him her cue he disappeared.

The girl seemed troubled.

"Do you think he was annoyed?" she asked.

"Oh, no, I don't think that," MacNab said, sure that Mr. Toplis, having missed one chance, had gone to take another.

"They're all rather late to-night. We all got back rather late, you know."

"I'm afraid I'm playing rather badly," MacNab said as he missed another easy shot.

"Would it help you if I promised to give you your cocktail at the half-way mark?" she laughed.

"You will have run out before I reach there," he said. "Give it me now."

She won the game when his figure stood at forty-seven. Slipping her cue into the rack, she turned, hesitating:

"Afraid I must run up and see Miss Willoughby now; the others must be down in a minute."

"Five to eight," MacNab agreed, after a glance at his watch.

Miss Cresswell fluttered out. MacNab's pulses quickened. Within the next minute or two he would see that faint white mark—where would it be? He began to calculate Toplis's height—yes, somewhere near the shoulder, across the lapels, just high enough to be above the radius of his eyes. Someone would draw his attention to it, perhaps. MacNab was sure he could not escape the thread if he entered the room. Sharp as his eyes might be, he would miss the thread, even if as he paused outside the bedroom door his sharp eyes were not looking up and down the corridor to make sure he was not observed. Once inside the room, the glance he had cast on the scoring board would tell him he had no need to hurry.

MacNab was sitting with his unfinished cocktail in his hand when his keyed-up ear heard someone approach; but he was surprised when the door opened to see Mr. Toplis enter. He had been smart indeed.

"Hullo. Game finished already?" he cried.

"Too good for me," MacNab admitted, rising and putting down his glass. As he did so his eyes went to Toplis's nicely-fitting dinner-jacket.

It was as well the glass had left his hand before he looked, for there was no mark of any kind on that jacket. MacNab could not believe his eyes. He rubbed them and stared again—all over the jacket. Toplis stared at him in turn.

"Anything wrong with me?" he asked.

"Wrong?" MacNab echoed weakly.

"Well, you're looking at me as if my tie had worked up under my ears."

"Sorry," MacNab responded. "Your tie is all right. I was just thinking."

When he had finished his drink Toplis began to knock the balls about.

"Dinner's put back fifteen minutes," he said. "Mr. Willoughby got home so late."

MacNab made no comment. He had told Toplis he was just thinking. In point of fact, he was doing nothing of the kind; he had been too stupefied to think, but he began to think now. It was as well he had declined the game Toplis offered him, for he would certainly have cut the cloth. "Not Toplis," he was saying to himself, "not Toplis." Then who? His mind took a wild swing back to his suspicions of Willoughby; but he could not readjust or co-ordinate the relevant facts at that moment. He could simply go on repeating to himself that it must after all be Willoughby.

Then the door flew wide open, and Willoughby entered. At first MacNab sat too far away to perceive any chalk mark on his breast, for after a glance round, Willoughby went to the other end of the table where Toplis was practicing a cushion shot. Even when he stood talking to his secretary it was outside the radius of the shaded green lamps. But MacNab was content to wait; the moment he stooped over the table to play a shot the full light would be on his chest.

So Willoughby, after all, was the man. "Why not?" MacNab asked himself. He was the strongest character of them all, and he had the strongest motive. The complete sequence of events flashed into a coherent whole as MacNab sat there waiting. Having failed to stop his daughter's infatuation for this undesirable son of an insane father, Willoughby had, pretending to accept him, invited him to Arrochmore as the best place in which to contrive such an accident as would excite the least suspicion. His chance came when, pursuing the poacher Haggerty, with Murdoch the gamekeeper well behind, he saw where Haggerty hid his gun. He kept quiet about that gun, for he meant to use it. And use it he did, when the mountain mists came down on the evening he got back from Inverness, afterwards throwing it into the water. How easy! He need only have had the weapon in his hands for a few moments. Had any one seen him before or after those few minutes, he was the one man of them all who stood beyond the possibility of suspicion. He had shot Brent in the library while Dr. Frossard was upstairs and before Mrs. Brent had been carried down. The door was shut and locked when she came down, and the wheel chair removed, making her suppose her son had been already wheeled away by Mary. He had used a silencer on the revolver, afterwards taking that away, but leaving the weapon to suggest suicide. The shot the housekeeper heard was the shot the boy Dick had fired from the lawn to frighten his tutor. The daughter alone appeared to suspect her father, if her refusal to see him meant anything. She alone would know the strength of his hatred for Brent, since she must have heard many times over all his arguments against the match.

While this was flashing through his mind MacNab maintained a strict watch on the two men at the far corner of the table. At any moment a hand might go up to brush away the chalk mark on Willoughby's coat. He might even inadvertently touch his coat with the tip of the cue he had picked up and was now himself chalking as he talked with Toplis. MacNab had to make sure that neither of these things happened unobserved by himself. Suddenly Willoughby stepped away from Toplis and came round to the side table on which the tray of cocktail glasses stood at MacNab's elbow. He nodded pleasantly to the watcher.

"Pity you didn't come with us to-day; we had a good catch," he said. Then, before any reply could come, he bent forward to lift the glass, and in the act MacNab could see there was not the slightest trace of any chalk on his coat. There was no doubt at all. On that smooth black cloth MacNab knew that he could have seen even a grain or two of the chalk, had any been left on its surface by a hasty hand brushing; but there was nothing. His head in a whirl, he murmured some vague reply to Willoughby's remark on the day's good sport.

"Had a good walk, I hope. Sorry dinner's late, but we wanted the trout for it to-night," Willoughby said, as if he thought MacNab's silence might be that of a hungry man kept waiting.

MacNab contrived to make a more articulate response this time, and his host with a nod went back to make his first stroke. For a time there was nothing to disturb thought but the click of the billiard balls.

Where was he to look next? Who could the man be who had opened that deed-box? It certainly had been opened. There was the escaped moth to prove it. Someone beyond question had gone to the trouble to try heaven knew how many keys till one was found to fit. And it assuredly could not be a passing curiosity that lay behind all that. But if it was neither Toplis nor Willoughby, who remained? As MacNab put the question to himself the door opened a little and Mr. Bray put his head inside the room questioningly, much as if it might be an unseemly place for him to enter. Mr. Willoughby laughed, anyhow.

"Come in, Mr. Bray," he said. "There's no money on this game."

Mr. Bray, entering, sat down gingerly beside MacNab. Toplis looked across.

"You know, Bray, I'd have expected you to take up this game," he said cheerfully.

"Me?" Mr. Bray cried.

"Why, yes," the other responded, "for the same reason that you took up smoking."

"I don't quite see that," Mr. Willoughby put in.

Toplis made no reply till he had finished his shot.

"Well," he said, "he started smoking to get on friendly terms with the men of his future parish. Billiards would be a second string to his bow in that respect."

"Oh, but," Mr. Bray cried, "any skill I might acquire in this game might be taken as evidence of an ill-spent youth, if you know what I mean."

Mr. Willoughby laughed.

"That's one for you, Toplis."

Toplis ignored the good-humored gibe and nodded to Bray.

"You're not likely to become as good as all that at the game," he said.

"You're judging him from the smoking," Mr. Willoughby said.

"Well, let him try billiards; at least it wouldn't hurt him like the pipe."

While they were discussing the relative merits of smoking and billiards as aids in parish work, MacNab rose and unobtrusively left the room. He felt all at sea. There was just the one thing he could do. If no one had yet entered his room the unbroken thread would still be stretched across the door. Although he himself had left the coast clear for that entrance, something unforeseen might very well have prevented Toplis—or, yes, he must include Willoughby now—from taking the chance he had offered.

He mounted the stairs rapidly. At the far end of the corridor he saw a couple of maids idly gossiping together while they waited for the dinner gong which would set them at liberty to enter the different bedrooms. That was all right, then, they had not yet begun. He passed along towards his room, hoping to find the thread intact, since, if the thread was still unbroken, his suspects still lay open to suspicion. If, on the other hand, he found his thread broken, he must look elsewhere, for he knew that no one could enter his room under such conditions and remain unmarked by the chalk.

At sight of him the two maids had disappeared. Reaching his door, he stopped. The two ends of the broken thread hung down on each side of the door. Then from below the gong thundered.

CHAPTER XXIV
THE THREE POSTAGE STAMPS

On the afternoon of the following day MacNab took another risk and went to see Superintendent Rintoul. Rintoul betrayed no surprise on hearing of his failure to establish the identity of the person nosing about the detective's room. He had, it seemed, expected this from his own failure that morning with the letters. There had been letters from Mr. Willoughby, Miss Willoughby, Miss Cresswell, Mr. Bray and from Toplis, though none from the last named to Mr. Joliffe. In none of them was there a word that could be remotely connected with the supposed crime.

"Not even a small pen portrait of yourself," Rintoul said.

"Well," MacNab remarked, "the thread was broken, you know. Someone did enter my room and go through my things."

"Yes, there's that in it," Rintoul admitted. "It does look as if somebody in the house is mighty keen to find out something about you."

"Not for nothing," MacNab said.

"No, but not necessarily for what you think," he replied. Rintoul toyed with his pen. "You assume it's somebody who wants to find out whether you're a detective or a lawyer. But, allowing you're suspected of playing a part, what is there to show they don't suspect you of being—let's say—a burglar?"

And although MacNab felt the suggestion to be absurd, he was without any concrete data to advance against it.

"That's just nonsense," he said curtly.

Rintoul, however, reading his depression and perhaps smarting under his own failure with the letters, rubbed it in.

JOHN FERGUSON

"Nonsense?" he cried, snapping his fingers. "Why, man, it would be only natural if they were nervous and suspicious. Think of the revolver left in Duchray; nobody knows anything about that. A man shot while the house is supposed to be empty, the weapon accidentally left behind."

"Stuff and nonsense," MacNab reiterated. "There's Mrs. Brent to vouch for me."

Some devilry possessed the superintendent.

"Had she ever seen you before you came here?" he demanded. "There's such a thing as impersonation, you know."

MacNab was not slow to see that all this simply foreshadowed the superintendent's refusal to intercept the Arrochmore letters again. He spared him the trouble of refusing, and to Rintoul's astonishment took up his hat and held out his hand.

"So that's that," he said.

"I'm sorry," Rintoul replied. "I'm really sorry, you know."

"I think we're going to have a change of weather," MacNab said. "There's rain in the air."

That rather took the superintendent aback.

"You'll go back to the fishing, then?" he asked in a new tone.

"On Loch Laggan, yes. My three days are up, and Dunn is due to be back there to-morrow night."

"Look here," Rintoul said, "I'll stretch a point and have another go at the letters. After all, the authority I received is still in force, and the letters are not delayed by my examination."

This time MacNab offered his hand in quite a different spirit, and Rintoul gripped it like one who has sealed a contract.

That evening MacNab had a long consultation with Mrs. Brent over the position. As he had told Rintoul, the three days for which he had come would expire tomorrow, and it was Mrs. Brent who had informed Willoughby that her business affairs could all be settled inside that time. Somehow an extension of the time had to be contrived. At the outset it had been arranged that if necessary Mrs. Brent should have a collapse and be unable to transact any business till she recovered. That scheme had not only the disadvantage of tying her up in her room, to which she was most averse, but also would prevent

MacNab from seeing her in the interval. It was Mrs. Brent herself who finally hit on the most promising pretext.

"I know," she said, sitting up in sudden triumph. "All that's necessary is for me to send to Somerset House for my Uncle Robert's will."

"Somerset House?" he echoed.

"Yes. That's where wills are kept. You can get a copy of anybody's last will and testament from them for eighteen pence."

"Quite," he agreed, "but—"

"See," she interrupted, "I'm going to say that I can't settle my own will until I refresh my memory about how he disposed of his effects among his other nephews and nieces."

He could discern no flaw in this proposal.

"That will at least give me three extra days," he said.

"Very well, then," she said. "Let's hope you'll make more use of the last three than you've done with the first."

His own hopes were chiefly centred on what Rintoul might discover in the letters. But this time he quite appreciated the trick that had been played with his chalked thread. Somehow the thread had been seen. He could not imagine how it could have been seen against the white enameled door. But later that evening he made an experiment which revealed what could have rendered the thread not merely visible, but prominent. Almost opposite, and next to Mrs. Brent's room, was the bathroom, and he discovered that if its door were left open the light within became deflected on a section of the thread across his own door; not only that, but, provided the bathroom door were left only ajar, the light did not reach the surface of his own door, and so left the white thread very noticeable against the shadowy background. He was quite certain, therefore, that the bathroom door had been shut when he attached his thread on the previous evening. If it had not been shut he would have seen how the thread stood out so visibly.

This led to another discovery. Having experimented with the bathroom door and the resultant effect from the light when the door was set at various angles, he shut the door and switched off the light. Then, taking the chair, he stood up and looked through the fanlight above the door, to discover that it was quite possible for any one in that position to maintain a watch on his bedroom door without being himself seen.

MacNab, stepping off the chair, did not doubt there had been a watcher there the night before. Someone standing on that chair had seen his operations on his own door—someone who had been waiting for him to go down to dinner, and who, although knowing he would be unlikely to return till the end of dinner at earliest, was yet anxious to lose not even one moment of the time available. Yet dinner at Arrochmore usually lasted about an hour, and in his room there were no more personal possessions than two small suit-cases could hold. Why, then, this anxiety not to lose a moment?

He could find no answer except that the person behind the bathroom door was one who, like himself, would presently be seated at the dinner table. Abruptly as he thus tried to reconstruct the happenings of the previous evening, MacNab came on another detail. Last night the dinner had been put back a quarter of an hour. He had not known that till Willoughby told him. Had he been aware of it he would not have dressed so soon or left his room so early. But the others knew—even Bray, who had not entered the billiard-room till after the usual time was past, appeared to be aware of the change.

Well, there remained one fact he himself was aware of, which by no possibility could be within the knowledge of any one else in that house: he alone knew what was happening to their letters; and when his mind reverted to the broken thread, he drew some hope from that fact, for the man who had watched him fix the thread, who had stepped out of the bathroom, laughing no doubt to himself, need not have broken the thread at all. Seeing it there, he could easily have turned the handle of the door, stooped under the thread, entered the room, made his search and gone without touching the thread at all.

Why, then, had he deliberately broken it? Mere bravado? If there was any other answer than that, MacNab could not find it; and that self-confident bravado was all to his liking, for he judged it not unlikely to be repeated in one of the letters. Next morning he made so sure that Toplis—he had now little doubt that Toplis was his man—would be unable to keep from telling Joliffe the story of the white thread, that he had a look at the letters before the postman arrived.

He knew there would be one addressed to Joliffe. But he was wrong—there was no letter to Joliffe. But just when he had finished turning over the pile, the postman rode up with the incoming mail, while Toplis himself was in the act of coming down the stairs with a letter in his hand and a cheerful good-morning smile to MacNab on his lips. MacNab's smile in return had more than the hint of a grin in it, and may well have mystified the secretary if, as MacNab thought, Toplis had been watching for the postman's coming to hand over the letter in person.

The afternoon brought MacNab one of the greatest surprises in his career when he went to see Rintoul. He now scarcely thought of taking any precautions about entering the police station, for, after that encounter with Toplis, he considered disguise to be practically at an end between them. All the same, he had marveled over the self-confident smile which the other man had given him. Toplis, to be sure, was not himself the man actually guilty of the crime; but he could not be so ignorant as not to be aware that in shielding the other man he rendered himself *particeps criminis*, and liable to the same sentence.

But no sooner was MacNab closeted with the superintendent than it became clear why Toplis could afford to smile at MacNab: the letter had not contained a single word that could even be twisted into the most remote connection with Brent's death or MacNab's presence in the house. And MacNab had built on that letter. Following his discovery the previous night of how his own trick with the thread had been made to look foolish, he felt certain it would make a story Toplis could not resist telling Joliffe. He was aghast to find no reference to it in the copy Rintoul had made. It shook him up. He could not believe that with such a story to tell any man standing in the relation which he thought Toplis stood to Joliffe could make no reference to it, especially in a letter which he had himself taken care to hand over to the postman direct.

MacNab left the office with shaken nerves. On his way back he came on Mr. Bray seated by the loch's side close to the road. The young man was deep in a book, his whole attitude indicating intense absorption. MacNab, feeling at a loose end if ever man did, sauntered up from behind. His projected shadow caught the reader's eye and he turned swiftly. Mr. Bray greeted him cheerfully. MacNab, stooping, picked up the volume just put down.

"Hullo—Butler's *Analogy*, eh?" he said. "Pretty stiff reading, I'm told."

"Well," Bray assented, "the man who wrote it did have to have some brains, if you know what I mean."

"And the man who reads it, too, no doubt."

Mr. Bray smiled deprecatingly.

"Parts of it are quite simple," he said; "what he says about probability, for example."

MacNab knew Mr. Bray could not guess how apt his chosen example was to his hearer.

"Probability," MacNab cried. "Does such a thing exist?"

"Oh, dear me, yes," Mr. Bray assured him. "In fact, if you study Butler you'll see it does much more than exist. Probability, he says, is the guide to life, if you know what he means."

MacNab threw the book on the grass again.

"I do," he said. "He means that as we live in a world in which nobody can be certain of anything, we are forced to act on what is probable."

Mr. Bray nodded, fishing out a note-book.

"That's it, in modern speech, of course. I must make I a note of it."

"But I don't agree with him."

"Oh, really, I say," Mr. Bray protested. "You forget he was a bishop."

"The whole thing's a toss-up. You pay your money, but you get no choice," MacNab persisted. "Probability is as rare as certainty. Pick out any horse, the odds are always against you."

Mr. Bray seemed rather shocked.

"Oh, but, you know, I don't think the bishop could have had horses in his mind when he wrote about certainties, if you know what I mean," he said, as MacNab began to walk away.

The next day was equally barren of results, so far as Arrochmore was concerned. In the afternoon he went down to the station once more, and the shake of the superintendent's head was sufficient. That was on the Thursday. On the Friday Rintoul did not receive him with a shake of the head—he simply looked at him; and that look was more than enough in its silent eloquence.

He did not go to see Rintoul at all on the Saturday. Having touched the depths of despair in that connection, he began to cast about for another angle of approach. This took him once more to the scene of the shooting on Keppoch Moor, and he spent about a couple of hours going over the ground and studying the possibilities. Sergeant Cameron's plan made it easy to identify the various positions of the men, and he considered that, given the misty afternoon, Joliffe could have little trouble in slipping down the burn unseen to a point from which he could shoot Brent as he passed. But he had to admit that the attempt could as easily and more safely have been made by one coming up the slope from the big burn at the bottom of the valley to which the other was merely a tributary.

Then the clouds which had been rolling up for several days finally made up their minds to break, and presently the rain drove him to seek shelter. Taking what he reckoned would be a short cut home along the hillside, he thought it would be easy to recognize the pinewood above Arrochmore when he reached it. The going, however, was very rough, and after a couple of miles, coming on a cottage set amid a clump of trees, he went up to ask for shelter. The man who opened the door, a sturdy bearded fellow of fifty, had the gamekeeper written all over him. He appeared to know who MacNab was, and invited him to step inside in a hearty but not in the least deferential tone.

"Losh, but you're wet, sir—just fair dreepin'," he exclaimed. "Come in bye to the kitchen, where there's a fire."

Murdoch, as he slung the jacket and waistcoat over a chair to dry in front of the fire, explained that his wife was down in the town for her week-end shopping.

"You're the law gentleman from London, I'm thinking," he said. "Come to settle up after the young gentleman's death, they tell me."

This was near enough the truth for MacNab to let it pass. As Murdoch himself was smoking, he fished out his own pipe and filled it.

"Ay, a bad business, thon," Murdoch went on. "You'll no' have heerd if they've got the man yet?"

"They're not yet sure who he is," MacNab said.

The gamekeeper, in the act of setting his guest's shoes to dry on the fender, spat his contempt into the fire. "Everybody hereabouts knows fine who did it," he declared. "One o' those daum poaching road navvies."

Murdoch's venom against his natural enemies was very manifest.

"Pity you weren't there yourself," MacNab said.

Murdoch's teeth gleamed.

"Ay, I'd soon have seen the skulking scoundrel; but they did na' let me know they were going out. If they had I'd have stoppit them. No' a day for the moor, yon. Ay, but young gentlemen are a' the same. They must have what they fancy at the moment the fancy comes. So what do they do but raid the gun room, and off they go wi' the first gun they can lay their hands on and any kind of ammunition forbye."

There was one question that had occupied MacNab's mind ever since he became aware that he had entered the gamekeeper's cottage. He put it now.

"I suppose," he said, "there's no doubt it was one of those poaching navvies who fired at Mr. Brent. The size of the shot taken from his shoulder corresponded, I'm told, with the size of the shot in two cartridges found later on one of them."

Afterwards he remembered the pause that followed. He had been holding out one of his feet to the blaze, while Murdoch stood behind. When no comment came, he turned his head and saw Murdoch standing quite still, slowly pulling his black beard, but with something of a sardonic smile on his outshot lips and a gleam in his eyes.

"Ay," he said as soon as he saw MacNab's stare. "Ay, that's so. The fellow had come up to bring away Haggerty's gun, and when he'd taken his chance he threw the gun into the water."

MacNab was puzzled. Something lay behind. At a venture he said:

"Queer thing for him to do, surely—when he'd gone up there to get it."

"Ay," Murdoch agreed, "an act no' to be accounted for, unless he'd used it in the way he did on Mr. Brent and got frightened he'd be caught."

In the talk that ensued, MacNab was able to gauge the extent of a gamekeeper's hatred for poachers. He left the cottage very certain that Murdoch's evidence against any poacher would be largely discounted because of the animosity he could not conceal; but he also felt that, all the same, Murdoch had kept his mouth shut about something, and that he would have been unable to do it unless it was something that might tell in the poacher's favor. No questions, however deft, could get anything out of him, and as MacNab had only that queer sardonic smile to go on, he reached Arrochmore undecided as to whether that grin had any connection with what he himself had been saying. In any event he now knew that it was about as hopeless to try and persuade Murdoch to open his mouth if it didn't suit him as it would be to try to persuade one of his own steel rabbit traps to open.

On the Sunday night it was borne in on MacNab that the Arrochmore case was not to be one of his successes. Having gone down to see Rintoul in the hope that the four mails which must have passed through the superintendent's hands since his last visit might well have yielded some result, he was taken aback by Rintoul's announcement that they had now ceased to stop and examine the letters. From a drawer Rintoul picked out an envelope and threw it on the table.

"Look at that," he said. "See what happened on Friday."

MacNab picked up the envelope and saw that it was addressed to P. H. Cresswell, at St. Andrews.

"It's the back that matters," Rintoul snorted. "We damaged it so badly that anyone could see it had been tampered with; so Sergeant Cameron had to put the letter it contained into a new envelope after he had made a tracing of this handwriting."

Turning over the envelope, MacNab saw the tearing which had made a fresh envelope a necessity. So when it was pointed out by Rintoul that they had stopped and examined seven outward and six inward mails with no result, he could only agree that there was no use in carrying on with the inspection. For all that, he believed that somehow or another Toplis was contriving to keep Joliffe posted with news. He felt as much from the attitude of the secretary towards himself. Toplis' apparently innocent questions about the progress of the legal conferences with Mr. Brent, were often hard to answer. MacNab, in fact, felt that he had become as much of a joke to the bright young secretary as Bray himself—not quite so openly, perhaps; but it was only a matter of time till that came. And his extra days were up, with the case at a standstill. He would wire Dunn to-morrow that he was going back to Loch Laggan.

A cloud of depression overshadowed him, and under its influence he found himself ready to believe that there might be, after all, nothing in the affair beyond what everyone else supposed. As for Toplis, why shouldn't he laugh at him? He had merely seen him nosing about inquisitively to fill in the time in order to send in a big bill to a stupid old lady. Was that it? It might well be, for all he had been able to get hold of. Rintoul, too, had again become convinced there was nothing in it that wasn't open to an entirely innocent explanation. And Rintoul, having reverted to his first opinions about the affair, would now remain immovable.

Probably it was Superintendent Rintoul's blunt, categoric refusal to hold up any more letters that proved decisive. He made up his mind that night to leave early next morning. Having intimated his intention, he sat down and wrote a note to Mrs. Brent, which he left in her sitting-room on his way to bed. The Arrochmore affair was not by any means his first failure, and he did not suppose it would be his last; but all the same he felt the sting of defeat was sharp enough to keep him awake half the night.

When morning came he rose at an hour when he thought only a housemaid would be about. Somehow he felt like getting away unseen, curiously ashamed of his failure. The car was to be at the door at a quarter to eight. Struggling with a collar stud, he looked through his window and saw the overcast sky, and rain was still coming down. Well, at least the fishing on Loch Laggan would be better now. A knock came on his door. The man entered, picked up his suit-case, and went out again. MacNab followed quickly, almost on tiptoe. Descending the stairs he saw Mr. Bray standing in the hall as if waiting for someone. Seeing MacNab, he came forward, smiling.

"Early riser," MacNab greeted him.

"Yes. Didn't quite like the idea of your going like this. Wanted to speed the parting guest, if you know what I mean."

MacNab was touched.

"Really? That was kind of you, Mr. Bray."

"Oh, not at all. Haven't you a waterproof? It's raining, you know."

MacNab's waterproof was at Loch Laggan Hotel with his other things.

"Forgot to bring one," he said.

They were both standing looking through the door at the falling rain. The car had not yet come round, and the man with MacNab's traps was standing in the shelter of the porch.

"Strange how people forget their umbrellas and their waterproofs in a climate like ours," Mr. Bray remarked.

"Umbrellas, yes, but surely not waterproofs," MacNab amended.

"Oh, yes, waterproofs too," Mr. Bray asserted. "You've just said you forgot yours."

MacNab smiled.

"I'm afraid your Bishop Butler would not support you there, Mr. Bray. He'd call that a generalization from a single instance."

Mr. Bray, still with his eyes on the falling rain, nodded.

"Yes, I know; it's bad logic to do that. But I'm not really. There was Mr. Willoughby, who forgot his when he went off to Inverness. And there was Brent, too, who forgot where he'd put his that same morning. And Cresswell, who forgot he'd taken it from the cloak-room where Brent forgot he'd put it the day before, and—" He broke off suddenly as the footman pushed open the door and entered.

"Sorry to keep you waiting, sir," he said. "Green must have forgotten. I'll go and hurry him up."

MacNab let the man go without a word. He had been startled. He was uncertain whether or no Bray had been saying something he wanted to say or only blundering out something, the significance of which he did not appreciate. As he stared hard at him Bray turned to the table close to the door and began to play idly with the letters there deposited to be collected later by the postman. One of them took his eye, and with a little laugh he pushed it apart from the others.

"So she got them, after all!" he said.

MacNab saw the letter was one addressed to P. H. Cresswell, Esq., at the Regent Hotel, St. Andrews.

"Got what?" he asked.

Bray's finger went to the three green postage stamps on the letter.

"The two halfpenny ones she was looking for last night. I offered her one three-halfpenny one, but she said she had a halfpenny stamp, and just wanted two others so's to use up the one she had." Mr. Bray laughed again.

"People say women are generous in big things and spoil it all by being mean in small things that don't matter; but I don't believe it was that in her case, anyway." He turned round. "D'ye know what I think makes her always use three stamps on her letters?" he inquired.

MacNab's heart had begun to thump.

"No," he said in a voice that to himself seemed not so loud as the drumming in his ears.

"Well," Mr. Bray nodded confidentially as the car wheels sounded on the gravel outside, "I think it's pure superstition that makes her do it. Her brother does the same in his letters to her, as I've noticed. Superstition—green for luck, if you know what I mean."

MacNab was not sure he had meant all he said; but when the car reached the town he sent it on with his things to the railway station and then himself made for the police station.

Sergeant Cameron was seated at his desk as he entered.

"The superintendent in?" he asked.

"Not till nine, sir," the sergeant replied.

MacNab saw the stripes on his sleeve and guessed his identity.

"Sergeant, tell me this: When you re-addressed that letter to P. H. Cresswell, what stamps did you put on it?"

The sergeant, although taken aback by the question, answered promptly enough that he had put on the right postage.

"One of the pink three-halfpenny ones?" MacNab insisted.

"Certainly, sir," Cameron replied, rather astonished at the particularity with which the color was mentioned. MacNab waved his hand at the telephone.

"Then for God's sake get the superintendent here at once," he said.

There was that in his tone which made Cameron jump for the instrument.

CHAPTER XXV

EXPOSURE

Cameron found the receiver snatched from his hand the moment he was put through.

"That you, Rintoul?"

"Who is speaking?" Rintoul stiffly returned.

"I've got the man."

"What!"

"It's Cresswell."

MacNab did not overhear the sharp intake of breath from Cameron, who pulled up short in the act of walking away; but Rintoul's gasp came quite audibly.

"Look here," MacNab said, taking advantage of the fact that he had for the moment struck Rintoul dumb, "it's urgent that you intercept to-day's mails."

"But—are you sure?" Rintoul found his voice at last.

"Certain. This is urgent. Minutes may make us too late."

The jar of the replaced receiver came through. Rintoul had got on the move without further argument. MacNab turned to discover the petrified sergeant standing at his back.

"Cresswell—after all," he said in round-eyed amazement.

MacNab nodded. "Yes, after all, you were right, Cameron. We're just back to where you started."

The sergeant scratched his head slowly.

"Of course I had no proofs, sir, but I'd never quite given up."

"Who used to go for the Arrochmore mail to the post office?"

"Oh, the superintendent himself, sir."

"We'll have to wait, then," MacNab said, beginning restlessly to pace the floor.

The sergeant, apparently rooted to the spot, gazed at him with bewildered eyes.

"Cresswell," he murmured again.

MacNab turned to him suddenly.

"How did you usually open the letters?" he inquired.

Cameron came to himself.

"Oh, we just put a kettle on the gas-ring and steamed them open," he said.

"Then get your kettle ready now," MacNab ordered. When he had gone, MacNab's mind was busy reconstructing the evidence against Cresswell. Before he had finished, however, Rintoul entered. Reading MacNab's face, he deposited a bundle of letters on the desk.

"The outgoing and the incoming mail," he said.

MacNab's fingers slipped rapidly over the letters. He picked out two, one addressed to Cresswell, the other to Miss Cresswell. Both letters were stamped with three separate halfpenny stamps. MacNab, followed by Rintoul, entered the small room where the sergeant stood by the gas-ring. The kettle was belching steam. He handed one of the letters to Cameron, who, now familiar with this job, promptly applied the back of the letter to the kettle's spout.

"No, no," MacNab said. "The front, not the back." He held up the other letter to Rintoul, indicating the three green halfpenny stamps.

It took Rintoul a moment or two before he understood.

"My God!" he breathed.

"Yes, that's how," MacNab said.

They stood waiting in silence till the stamps were saturated with the steam. Then Cameron handed the letter to his superior. Rintoul saw it was the letter addressed to Cresswell. His thumb-nail fumbled uncertainly at the edge of the stamp. It looked as if the steam-sodden gum might become adhesive again. MacNab took the letters from him and peeled the three stamps clear. The writing underneath was quite visible.

Over his shoulder Rintoul read:

"It's Joliffe now. But it will be you to-morrow. Why haven't you gone?"

Sergeant Cameron got busy with the letter to Miss Cresswell. They were too impatient for speech, both watching. This time the letter was handed to MacNab. Affected by their impatience, the soaking had not been so thorough, and the stamps came away with difficulty, leaving an adhesion of yellow gum on the paper; but underneath this the writing, microscopic as it was, could be read clearly enough:

"Got passport. But try room again. Make sure."

"Craig Dhu!" Cameron cried. "That was clever."

"Nothing about varicose veins there," MacNab snorted, "or Vortex Underwear."

Rintoul seemed beyond speech. He was still gazing stupidly at the envelope in his hand. MacNab jogged him into activity.

"If it's not too late," he said, "you can get the St. Andrews Police to detain him on suspicion."

"Too late!" Rintoul echoed. "How too late?"

"I mean after the warning you gave him on Saturday."

"Warning!" Rintoul echoed again. "What warning did we give him?" Cameron, too, seemed incredulous.

"Look here," MacNab cried, "this is a bit too sudden for you. You haven't had time to grasp its meaning. I'm referring to the fact that on Friday last you told me you had enclosed his sister's letter in a fresh envelope on which you had put one three-halfpenny stamp. That letter would reach him on Saturday morning. For all your tracing of the address, that stamp and the absence of any message underneath would be a warning."

"You're right." Rintoul nodded, his eyes staring. "You're right there; but I've still got the envelope." He made a dash through the door for his office. Cameron replaced the kettle on the gas-ring.

"I aye had a suspicion of him," he said.

"And I," MacNab remarked, "had suspicions of almost everyone except him."

The kettle was in full blast again by the time Rintoul got back with the envelope. He held it himself into the cloud of steam and himself tore off the three stamps.

Over his shoulder MacNab read:

"No immediate danger. He's all astray. Am watchful.
But be ready."

MacNab shook his head over this message.

"Pity that didn't go," he said.

Rintoul stared.

"We wouldn't have seen it if it had," he said.

"And he wouldn't have seen your three-halfpenny stamp with nothing underneath," MacNab said.

Rintoul whistled.

"Yes, that's it," MacNab nodded. "This would have soothed his fears. What you sent—well, must have alarmed him. I'm afraid, Rintoul. This letter should have reached him on Saturday afternoon; instead, he gets your envelope with no message beneath the stamp. I wonder what he made of it!"

"He'll wait," Rintoul nodded confidently, "he'll wait for the next one at least."

"Well, I hope you're right. Look at this last message from him to his sister. He seems all on edge."

Rintoul stroked his chin thoughtfully.

"In any case," he remarked, "I haven't got enough evidence to apply for a warrant yet."

"No," MacNab admitted. "By themselves this interchange of messages proves nothing. But I believe we can get enough evidence before the day is out to hang him, only, you see, I'm afraid he won't stay to be hanged."

"Look here," Rintoul said quickly, "I can put a call through to the St. Andrews police to keep him under observation while we are obtaining the evidence you speak of."

"Good. That will do," MacNab agreed, "and the sooner you get on to them the better."

As they made for Rintoul's office MacNab saw the sergeant lingering uncertainly behind. It was obvious that Cameron wanted to hear the whole of MacNab's story about the man who was his own suspect. He beckoned him to follow.

"We'll want the sergeant," he said to Rintoul while the superintendent was looking up the number.

"Certainly," he agreed. "After all, this is Cameron's man."

They had to wait several minutes before being put through the different exchanges. Rintoul made them sit down.

"It's queer," MacNab said, "how once you know the truth all the disconnected facts seem to fall into their places and make a complete story."

Rintoul had replaced the receiver to await the call from St. Andrews.

"Begin at the beginning, then," he said.

"First of all I want to get hold of Murdoch, the gamekeeper," MacNab said. "It'll be some time before I bring him into my tale, but, as it's likely I'll reach him before he gets here, you'd better send for him at once."

Rintoul looked across at the sergeant.

"Munro has not gone on the road yet, sir," he said.

"Good." Rintoul nodded. "He can get up to the cottage and bring him in on the pillion."

Cameron hurried out as a motor-cycle engine began to throb outside.

"Well?" Rintoul said expectantly.

"Wait. I'm not going to deprive your sergeant of his share. Don't you see how eager he is? Besides, there's something else I want you to do."

The telephone at Rintoul's elbow whirred suddenly.

"Yes," he said. . . . "Yes, that's right. Superintendent Rintoul speaking. This is it: There are two men staying at the Regent Hotel, name of Cresswell and Harwood. . . . Got that? . . . Yes, Cresswell and Harwood. That's right. Well, can you keep them under observation till you hear again . . . ? Yes, it is, very serious indeed. What's that . . . ? Yes, do. Thank you."

He replaced the receiver.

"They are going to call me up when they establish contact," he said.

Cameron returned, and his entry reminded Rintoul that MacNab had spoken of something else he wanted done.

"Yes," MacNab said, "but this will be a longer job. I want you to find out at what shop the Arrochmore people buy their tennis-balls. Having got the shop, you must try to see the man who sold a dozen balls to Mr. Cresswell on—let me see . . ." A light suddenly broke on MacNab's face. "Of course," he said, "he'll remember the day; it's little likely he'll forget the day on which one of the Arrochmore house party came for the balls, since it was the same day on which another of the party was shot. Put it like that to him and it will come back fast enough," he said to Cameron. And when Cameron nodded agreement he added, "The thing I want is for him to give us as near as he can the precise time at which Mr. Cresswell called."

"That won't be difficult," Rintoul said. "I'm sure he's told his friends a dozen times over."

As Cameron once more made for the door his superintendent called to him:

"Send Grant on the job, Sergeant," he said, smiling to MacNab. And, while they waited for Cameron's return, Rintoul shoved across the box of cigarettes. Cameron, however, was back before his chief had his own cigarette lit.

"And now," he said, "that we've set the wheels running and the wires humming at your behest it's time we heard how you discovered the secret of the three halfpenny stamps."

"That's the end of the story, not the beginning. Besides," MacNab added, "you've got it wrong. I didn't discover the stamp secret, and I wasn't the first to suspect Cresswell."

Cameron glowed with pleasure.

"Then for God's sake tell it in your own way," Rintoul burst out.

MacNab had a sense of relief. He was beginning to realize it as he sat there. The shock of Mr. Bray's unconscious revelation, all the greater because it had come at a moment when he had accepted defeat, was passing. The immediate initiative had passed on to the St. Andrews police, to Munro and to Grant. Till their work was done there was nothing for him to do but wait and be as lazily reminiscent as he liked.

"They're a mighty clever family, these Cresswells," he said as he touched off the end of his cigarette into the ash-bowl. "That sister of his, now, she—what's the new phrase?—led me up the garden every time. I'd like fine, Rintoul, to have seen all the other messages she sent him under her three halfpenny stamps. But maybe it's better for my self-respect that I can't. 'It's Joliffe now,' she writes. Mark that 'now,' Rintoul. She knew I was after Willoughby before I got on to Joliffe, and it wouldn't surprise me if she even knew it was Bray before him, and Toplis also. And it was herself who put me on to Joliffe. Yes, Joliffe made a good suspect after I heard about his loss of temper on the tennis courts. She has a nerve! I wonder if she laughed at dinner that night. Everybody else knew that dinner had been postponed fifteen minutes; that I discovered afterwards. She didn't tell me about the postponement, you see. I was the only one she didn't tell, because she thought I might go back to my room, and she wanted all the time she could get in my room for herself. Rintoul, that was why I couldn't tell you who the man was who was searching my room." MacNab banged his fist on the table.

"How she must have laughed when she saw me looking for the chalk mark on Toplis, on Willoughby, and even on Bray's coat; never thought of looking at her. But it wouldn't have been there if I had. Yes, and about that shooting party; I had almost forgotten that." He looked across the table again. "Rintoul, there's another man I'd like to send for—this tutor, Bray. I fancy he knows more than I do about that white coat. When she saw me heading for the truth she said the shooting party was suggested by Joliffe. I rather fancy that was a lie, and if you would send for Bray—"

Rintoul cut in.

"Afraid I haven't another officer to spare," he said. "Till Grant comes back we might get on to Cresswell himself."

Cameron gave his silent approval to the suggestion.

"Oh, his case is simple," MacNab said. "He murdered Brent because he hated him, because he loved Mary Willoughby, and because he wanted Mary Willoughby's money."

"Well," Rintoul said, "as for the money, in his letters which we examined, he was always dunning his sister."

MacNab nodded assent.

"Yes, and he didn't hide that with any stamps," he said, "but he didn't mean to go on doing it. He meant Mary Willoughby to supply his needs."

Rintoul waved an impatient hand.

"Any one of these three motives may lead to murder," he said. "The trouble is," he went on, tapping his points on the table, "how did he do it? As far as we can see, he stands absolutely clear, as Cameron here can testify, from the attempt on the moor; and, as I myself as well as Cameron can testify, he was not near Duchray when Brent was shot."

Of course Rintoul knew that MacNab must somehow have got behind the evidence which cleared Cresswell, but he could not guess how. And now he sat forward with an expectancy equaled only by Cameron when he saw MacNab was ready to explain.

On the other side of the broad table MacNab sat forward, too, his arms resting on the leather-covered surface.

"When I first sat in this chair," he began, "and we talked this case over, I remember your saying that a murder staged—staged was the word you used, I think—a murder staged as a shooting accident looked like the perfect murder. If I didn't quite agree about that, I certainly agreed with you when you said there were only two difficulties to be overcome—to get close enough to your victim, and to make sure there was at least one spent cartridge left in his gun."

"I ought to have put a third," Rintoul interrupted: "You have to make sure, too, that the size of the shot afterwards found in the body is the same as that which the victim was using in his own gun."

From the far end of the table Sergeant Cameron glanced at MacNab to see how he could possibly overcome this difficulty.

"Yes," MacNab agreed, "that was a hard nut to crack. Brent was using No. 6's, and you found No. 5's in the body. For while it seemed to prove an attempt on his life, it averted suspicion from the other members of the party who were using the same ammunition as Brent." He looked up. "Candidly, it's a nut I haven't yet cracked; but

I've a notion that when your man brings in the gamekeeper, Murdoch, we'll open it all right."

Rintoul fidgeted in his chair, like a man with something to say who is not sure whether to say it or not.

"It's rather late in the day to speak of it," he said, after a moment, "but I may tell you that Haggerty's gun didn't fire that shot. After we recovered it from the water Haggerty was informed of the fact, and he admitted he had thrown it there on the day he was caught in the wood."

"Good!" MacNab said, "that's useful. You'll see why presently it's not at all too late in the day to be sure of that. Now, the first difficulty you spoke of needn't keep us long," he resumed with a glance at the sergeant.

"Cameron here worked that out. I don't doubt Cresswell made his approach exactly as he thought; and just as he supposed, too, Cresswell's precaution against being seen by Brent or any of the others prevented him from getting quite near enough. No trouble there. The trouble was to solve the problem presented by the gun."

Just as Cameron, hearing this, sat forward in eager expectancy, the telephone whirred abruptly. Rintoul picked up the receiver and Cameron sat back to wait.

"Oh!" they heard Rintoul say as he listened.

A lengthy silence followed, in which they saw the superintendent's face first cloud and then brighten.

"Very well," he said at last, "ring me up as soon as they return."

He replaced the receiver.

"That was the St. Andrews people. They've been round to the hotel, and find Cresswell and Harwood left on Saturday, to spend the week-end in Edinburgh. They were away last week-end, too, it appears."

"No Sunday golf at St. Andrews, perhaps," MacNab suggested.

"Don't think so," Rintoul said.

"The St. Andrews people don't think it a flight?" MacNab asked.

"Oh, no. They only took suit cases with them; said they'd be back round about six."

"There was that letter you sent with the wrong stamp on it, Rintoul."

Rintoul looked at his sergeant with a smile.

"He probably left before it got there," he said. "Spoiling the envelope made us miss the mail that time. Cameron there will tell you how annoyed with him I was."

They all laughed; then Rintoul once more became the superintendent.

"Now, about that gun, if I'm to have a warrant out against their return it's time we had the facts."

"Oh, there's time enough to explain that and much more before six," MacNab said. "As a matter of fact, his trick with the guns was more simple, and yet more subtle, than any of us supposed. It was the sergeant's theory that Cresswell, after shooting Brent, intended, in the confusion which followed, to get hold of Brent's gun and slip an empty cartridge into the breech; but when the sergeant found two unspent cartridges in the gun, he supposed that Cresswell had not found an opportunity of doing that trick."

Cameron nodded assent.

"Yes, sir," he said. "When we got there Mr. Brent was lying within six yards of where they'd put down his gun, and all the others were standing around."

"Watching the doctor?" MacNab suggested.

"Yes, when we got there, anyway."

"And you think Cresswell had no chance to do his trick with the gun?"

"He may have dropped his empty cartridge, and he could hardly then have fired off his gun to get another," Cameron said.

MacNab shook his head in a decisive negative.

"No, no," he declared. "Cresswell could have left his gun behind like the others if he had wanted. His trick was not one with a spent cartridge, but with a live one. He had to bring in his gun. He did make a change of cartridges; only it wasn't the risky one of extracting a live one and then inserting a dead one in Brent's gun, but the much more easy trick of exchanging a spent for a live cartridge in his own gun." Pausing to see a light break in on the others, MacNab saw only two foreheads furrowed with thought.

"Look here, sergeant," he resumed, "in your report you say that when you asked them to indicate the spot where Brent fell they picked up their things and you then followed them to the spot?"

"That's what happened," the sergeant said.

"Yes. You followed with the one gun that had been left, which you naturally assumed to be Brent's."

Cameron sat up with a jerk.

"You mean Cresswell deliberately took Brent's gun?"

"Of course. He had to. Brent was in no state to claim his gun, and the others wouldn't notice at such a moment, anyhow. You see why it was he had to bring in his own gun, after inserting a fresh charge? If he'd left his gun behind he couldn't pretend to have taken up Brent's gun by mistake."

Here the sergeant's growing excitement overcame him. His heavy fist came down with a bang on the table.

"*Craig Dhu!*" he cried. "That's just what he did, and then had us to prove himself at least was innocent, since it was *his* gun I got fully loaded."

"Exactly," MacNab agreed. "That's where the subtlety comes in."

Rintoul was impressed. When a knock came on the door he took no notice of it. He wanted more. This, when taken with the messages exchanged under cover of the postage stamps, made first-class circumstantial evidence. But he was impatient to know how much more they had. Not that time pressed; no action could come before six that evening, when Cresswell and Harwood got back to St. Andrews. Then it would be enough to 'phone through to the police there that a warrant had been issued.

"And how about the No. 5 shot?"

MacNab drew his attention to the knock on the door which had been repeated. Cameron rose.

"That is Munro, sir," he said.

"He's just in time," MacNab said, "if he's got the gamekeeper with him."

At a sign from Rintoul Cameron opened the door, and in a moment the gamekeeper was ushered in. Murdoch appeared hardly to have enjoyed his ride as Munro's pillion passenger. He looked rather shaken.

"Excuse me, sir," he said to the superintendent. "I'd like fine if I could sit and give my inside a chance of settling down again."

Rintoul motioned him to a seat, at the same time indicating Mac-Nab, who rose to take up a position on the hearth-rug.

"This is the gentleman who wanted to see you," Rintoul said.

Murdoch's eyes revealed recognition when he saw MacNab.

"It's about the little talk we had the other day," MacNab began.

"Ay, I mind it fine," Murdoch assented.

"It may interest you to know none of Haggerty's friends fired that shot at Mr. Brent," MacNab went on. And as Murdoch stared he added, "You see, Haggerty in prison has just admitted that he dropped his gun in the burn the day you and Mr. Willoughby caught him in Keppoch Wood."

"Do you tell me?" the gamekeeper ejaculated.

"I do," said MacNab. "You can take that as truth. There's just this that's bothering the police: We don't know how Mr. Brent came to have No. 5 shot wounds in his body."

"No?" said Murdoch, with a pleased, sly smirk. He was aware they were all watching him, and his smile was that of the proud possessor of exclusive information he did not mean to disclose.

"Look here," MacNab said sharply, "we think you know, and we're going to make you tell."

Murdoch's eyes opened wide.

"That's a nice way for you to talk to me," he cried; "me, who gave you shelter and dried your clothes the other day."

Then Rintoul took a hand. Looking very much the Superintendent of Police, he rose to stare at the man much as if he were about to order him to the cells.

"Murdoch," he said, "maybe you don't know what happens to people who withhold information from the police in a criminal case."

"You canna hang me for it, anyway," he said defiantly, a little shaken all the same by the vague threat.

"Ah," Rintoul nodded, "don't be sure of that. In a case of murder an accessory after the fact takes his stand in the dock along with the murderer."

"Murder!" Murdoch gasped. The word had shaken him up far more than his ride on Munro's pillion. Rintoul allowed him to digest the possibility in silence. The gamekeeper passed his hand across his face.

"I'll tell you all I know," he said. "Fine I ken what it is. You see," he went on, "I didna want any of the young gentlemen to be blamed for shootin' one another—that's why I kept quiet about it." He paused for breath. "Didna I say Haggerty had a gun that day? They didna believe me in the court. I knew he had—that's what sent me looking for his cartridge bag. I got it, too, in the middle of a clump of whins, and put it in the gun-room at Arrochmore. How was I to know the young gentlemen would go out shooting on a day like that? They didna take me with them. I wouldn't have gone. But when they raided the gun-room they took all they could find, Haggerty's cartridges as well."

There was silence again. MacNab looked at Rintoul.

"Thank you, Murdoch," Rintoul said in an almost kindly tone. "That clears you, anyhow. But for the life of me I can't see why you made a secret of it."

The new tone emboldened Murdoch.

"Oh," he said, "I knew you were after one of Haggerty's friends. You surely didna expect me to come forward and save one of them."

When the gamekeeper was dismissed Rintoul questioned Mac-Nab.

"Did you just guess he knew?"

"Well," MacNab admitted, "I had been looking for an explanation. It was clear there must be one—clearer than ever when you told me about Haggerty's gun. You yourself saw just now how Murdoch showed himself to have inside knowledge. He acted in the same way the other day with me. That's all."

"Not quite," Rintoul observed; "but I suppose we can't carry the case further till Grant comes back from his tour of the shops."

"I can tell you in advance what he will say," MacNab remarked, he, too, being pleased with the results obtained from Murdoch. "He'll tell you how Cresswell constructed his alibi. Rintoul, when the car passed the tennis court, Mr. Toplis and Miss Cresswell were playing and Joliffe and Harwood looking on; but where was Cresswell?"

Rintoul stroked his chin. He thought there was a catch somewhere.

"He'd come in to get the tennis balls, hadn't he?"

"Not him. If he had, the car would have passed him on the road."

"But we ourselves saw him going back."

"Yes, after he'd shot Brent. When the car passed the tennis courts Cresswell was in the wood below the drive. As soon as he saw it go he knew his chance had come. The house was empty except for the housekeeper; but notice this: When he got to the library door he found it locked; but he had another key in his pocket. He had got that somehow, for he knew his best chance of coming on Brent alone would be in that same room. Why didn't he use it now? He couldn't, because the other key was in the lock." MacNab bent forward to tap the table with a very stiff forefinger. "Rintoul, you found all the windows shut and fastened when you got there. Who shut the one Frossard left open? Who shut it? Tell me that! That's what took my eye whenever I read the precognitions. Frossard said he was sitting reading by the open window. Frossard said he was getting enough fresh air by the open window without going out in the car. Frossard went back, or tried to, because he was afraid his notes would get blown away in the draught from the open window. But you found no open window when you got on the scene."

"Well," Rintoul said, "Brent himself may have shut it."

MacNab rapped the table hard.

"Not him! He'd have escaped death if he did—that day, at least. But somebody shut it; and there was no one else to do it except Cresswell. Even supposing Brent shut the window, he had no need to fasten the catch; but Cresswell had need to fasten it, just as he must leave the revolver. A dead man with a revolver beside him, the key of the door in his pocket and all the windows fastened—clear proof of suicide! What else could it be? Indeed, I doubt if Cresswell tried that door at all. He wouldn't if he saw the open window. Anyway, he entered by it in his tennis shoes without being heard by Brent, whose back was to him while he sat at the desk writing that letter to Miss Willoughby after seeing Toplis come with her to invite him along to the tennis courts. He shot him as he sat there, slipped the key into Brent's pocket, took three strides to the window, shut it, opened the door, locked it from outside and put that key in his own pocket, and was off down—"

"One moment," Rintoul interrupted. "Don't you think all that would take time? Surely he knew the risk he ran of being seen."

"The risk was less than it looks. Once outside the library door, even if the one person in the house came quicker than he'd bargained for, he had only to pretend he'd found the door locked and was trying to get in after hearing a shot inside. But, as a matter of fact, he had actually minutes to spare, for Mrs. Murchison said she went upstairs to call the maid before going to the front part of the house to investigate."

"Quite true," Rintoul agreed, "she did say that."

"Then," MacNab resumed, "with the key in his pocket he ran down the same footpath I discovered the night I 'phoned you from the house, picked up the box of tennis balls he'd planted in readiness earlier in the day, jumped the wall, got on to the main road and started walking back towards the gates of the drive as if he'd been all the way to the town for the tennis balls and was returning with them. You'll observe," MacNab ended with a smile, "that he had police evidence to clear him both on the moor and at Duchray."

Rintoul nodded slowly, biting his lip.

"Yes, it's a good reconstruction," he said. "It could have been done like that. But if he did play that trick with the box of balls, and we can prove he did, it will be one more link in the chain of circumstantial evidence against him. Indeed," he went on, "if we can prove that trick with the tennis balls it, together with the trick with the stamps, will do the trick with the jury." He glanced at the clock. "Grant seems to be having trouble, though."

In saying this, Rintoul had voiced MacNab's own apprehension. There could not, he was sure, be many dealers in sports goods in such a small town. Finally Rintoul, now very restless, dispatched Cameron to look for the constable. The superintendent had been stung to the quick by the way in which he himself had been used as a witness for Cresswell's alibi. He did not doubt that Cresswell had hung about on the road waiting for the police to pass him but if he had gone to the town even as little as two hours earlier than the time at which they passed him—well—he would find his trick cut both ways.

Grant was apologetic when Cameron brought him in. He had found the shop, Macpherson's in Nevis Street, but the assistant who had sold the box was ill in bed at home. Rintoul cut him short.

"Did you see him?" he asked.

"Yes, sir. He remembered all about it; but he didn't sell the gentleman any tennis balls on that day."

"What?" Rintoul almost shouted.

"He stuck to it, sir. He knows the gentleman well by sight; said I could go back to the shop and see the daybook with the sale entries for myself. The which I did, sir."

"He got them somewhere else," MacNab asserted.

Rintoul was visibly perturbed.

"You are quite sure?" he said to Grant.

"Quite, sir. There was no entry against Mr. Cresswell for that day—only a dozen balls he'd got the day before." Grant's jaw dropped with amazement at the effect produced by his last words. Rintoul almost leaped to his feet; but it wasn't anger—Grant was quick enough to see that even before he spoke.

"Thank you, Grant," he said, "that will do."

"Conclusive?" MacNab suggested when the constable had gone.

"Entirely," Rintoul nodded. "I wonder how he'll explain buying the balls on Tuesday and carrying them back on Wednesday. Of course he planted them somewhere to pick up at the right moment, as you guessed."

MacNab had lunch with Rintoul. There was nothing more to be done till six o'clock. Before leaving the office, however, Rintoul got through to the Procurator-Fiscal and the Chief Constable, with the result that he was able to tell the St. Andrews police that the warrant had been issued for Cresswell's arrest on his return.

After lunch they spent a long time together in Rintoul's garden. It was a pretty garden, for the superintendent was an amateur in rose culture. But for that afternoon at least the slugs had it all their own way; indeed, had the slugs been as big rats, it is doubtful if the superintendent would have noticed them. MacNab told him the story of how he had discovered the trick with the stamps.

"The simple young man," he said, "didn't have the least notion of what he was telling me. He thought they were just using these green halfpenny stamps for luck."

Rintoul laughed. "Well," he said, "it isn't everybody would guess that the three green halfpenny stamps were being used instead of the one pink stamp because they covered a larger space on the envelope."

"That reminds me, now I think of it," MacNab said. "I think we'd better have Mr. Bray down to see you. He seems to know something about that white Burberry as well."

They were back in the office waiting for the call from St. Andrews long before the hour of Cresswell's return from Edinburgh. Rintoul was all on edge. As for MacNab, the excitement in the case was already over, and he had begun to think of the fish in Loch Laggan once more. To fill in the last slow-moving hours Rintoul dispatched Munro to invite Mr. Bray to the office. At six o'clock he called up St. Andrews for news. MacNab admired the self-restraint which had stopped the superintendent from doing this earlier. But the St. Andrews police had no news to give, except that their men were already in the hotel to arrest Cresswell the moment he returned—which, of course, Rintoul knew already. At six-thirty no call had come, but soon afterwards, as if to fill in the blankness and relieve the tension, Mr. Bray was ushered in together with the evening's mail, the interception of which Rintoul had forgotten to countermand. When Rintoul discovered among the letters one addressed to Miss Cresswell, the meek little tutor was given a seat against the wall. Rintoul silently held the letter up with its three halfpenny stamps. MacNab stared at it.

"Yes," he said; "but it's the postmark that matters now."

Rintoul twisted the envelope round to read it.

"Dundee!" he whispered.

"Posted nine forty-five, Saturday night." MacNab nodded. "You might look into the shipping intelligence in the *Scotsman*."

"It's a boat, is it?" Rintoul said.

"Looks like it. Remember he said he'd got his passport."

As they stared doubtfully at each other the voice of Mr. Bray sounded over in his obscure corner.

"There might be something under the stamps."

They had both forgotten the tutor's presence. While Rintoul accepted the reminder without surprise, while MacNab stared over at the tutor, Cameron was sent off to operate on the stamps and Rintoul started searching for the *Scotsman*. With the paper spread on the table, MacNab joined in the hunt for the shipping intelligence column. Rintoul's thumb, however, got to the item first.

"There," he said. The entry read:

Saturday. S. S. Fenella. Riga and Baltic ports.

"He means Russia," Rintoul cried. "He'll be safe there."

Again the voice came almost plaintively from the other side of the room.

"Riga isn't in Russia now. I was instructing Richard about that yesterday," Mr. Bray said.

Rintoul looked over at him as he leant above the Scotsman on the table.

"Quite sure?" he inquired almost deferentially.

"Oh, yes!" Mr. Bray reassured him; "and it comes before Russia, if you know what I mean. This boat, that is, would get there first."

Rintoul's big fist thumped the table.

"Then, by God, we'll have him yet!" he cried.

"Oh, really!" Mr. Bray protested as Cameron entered with the stripped envelope in his hand.

Its message merely confirmed the conclusion already arrived at:

Suspect tampered letter. Don't like it. Clearing out.

Rintoul laughed scornfully.

"This will only make it a more noteworthy case," he said. "We'll get an extradition order and have him taken off the boat at Riga."

"The correct pronunciation is 'Reega,'" Mr. Bray amended softly. "Richard made the same mistake yesterday."

Rintoul glared across at the young man.

"Look here," he said, "you seem to be full of useful information. Perhaps you'll tell us how you knew about the three halfpenny stamps?"

Mr. Bray bent forward on his chair.

"Oh, that's quite simple," he said. "You see, it's all my idea, if you know what I mean."

Rintoul, after a momentary stare, planted himself in front of Mr. Bray.

"We don't in the least know what you mean," he said, looking down at him. "A man with all your information should be capable of putting it more plainly."

"Oh, I have plenty of practice at that with Richard," the tutor agreed amiably.

"Try it on me, then!" Rintoul growled, his color deepening.

"Well, you see, noticing your concern with that letter just now, and remembering this other gentleman's curious behavior this morning when I was telling him how Mr. Cresswell forgot he'd taken Brent's coat away and then gave him Mr. Willoughby's, and his yet more curious behavior when I drew his attention to Miss Cresswell's letter, I put two and two together, if you know what I mean."

"Not yet," Rintoul said.

"Well, it's all quite simple, really." He waved his hand encouragingly at Rintoul. "You see, remembering all that, it came back to me. I once told Miss Cresswell I had just lost one of my most valued possessions—a threepenny piece with the Lord's Prayer engraved on one side of it—complete, if you know what I mean."

Rintoul gaped for a moment as if he were about to say something. Then a light broke in upon him.

"So you think that gave her the idea for the stamp trick?"

"Naturally," Mr. Bray nodded. "Wouldn't you?"

Rintoul did not reply to the question.

"Well," he said, "I'll say this for you: you're not half so big a fool as you look. You'll make quite an exceptional parson."

"Oh, I don't know," Mr. Bray said. "People will still go on thinking about us as they do. It's that play, *The Private Secretary*, if you know what I mean."

John Alexander Ferguson (1871-1952)

Ferguson was a Scottish clergyman and writer who spent most of his ministry as chaplain at schools in Kent and Culross. He wrote at least ten mysteries and thrillers, six of them featuring his series detective Francis MacNab.

COACHWHIP PUBLICATIONS
COACHWHIPBOOKS.COM

THE

RUMBLE

MURDERS

Henry Ware Eliot, Jr.

COACHWHIP PUBLICATIONS
COACHWHIPBOOKS.COM

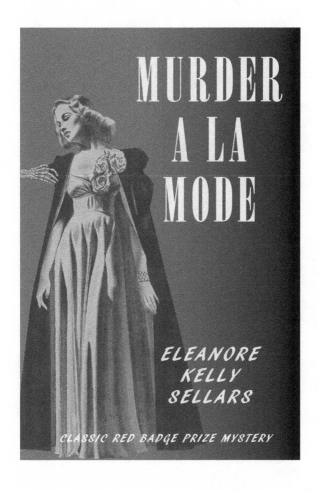

MURDER
A LA
MODE

ELEANORE
KELLY
SELLARS

CLASSIC RED BADGE PRIZE MYSTERY

COACHWHIP PUBLICATIONS
COACHWHIPBOOKS.COM

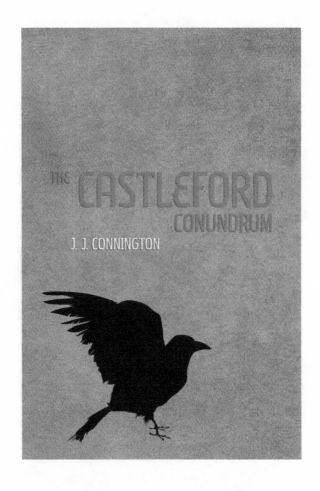

COACHWHIP PUBLICATIONS

COACHWHIPBOOKS.COM

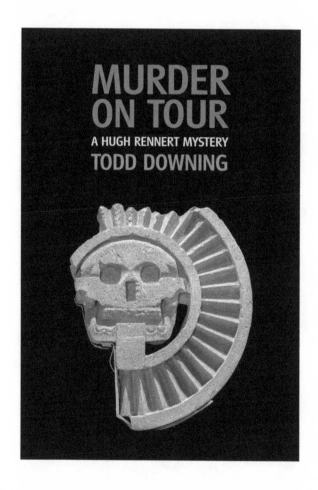

MURDER
ON TOUR
A HUGH RENNERT MYSTERY
TODD DOWNING

COACHWHIP PUBLICATIONS
COACHWHIPBOOKS.COM

THE
DEATH
OF A
CELEBRITY

HULBERT
FOOTNER

AN AMOS LEE MAPPIN MYSTERY

COACHWHIP PUBLICATIONS
COACHWHIPBOOKS.COM

THE QUINNY HITE
MYSTERIES
CHINESE RED · HERE LIES THE BODY

RICHARD BURKE